"Not only does *The Carpenter's Notebook* give great rules for doing different jobs, but Mark ties them with life lessons as well. It is really interesting and enlightening. A very sweet and loving story. Well told."

Brent Hull, author of Historic Millwork
and founder of Hull Historical in Fort Worth, Texas

"*The Carpenter's Notebook* hooked me after the first few pages with a simple, engaging and heartwarming story that reveals that the craft of building holds the keys to life's lessons."

Mike Guertin, contributing editor to Fine Homebuilding magazine
and author of Precision Framing and Roofing with Asphalt Shingles

---

"Reading *The Carpenter's Notebook* was like having a depth-charge set off in the deepest recess of my mind—shaking me out of the routine of my life, waking me back to the beauty, love, and things of value that surround me. It was a reminder of who I am, who I could yet become, why I made the choices I have, and how I might learn from my trade to make better ones. My father died 19 years ago tomorrow and I have used his tools (the ones I keep in a toolbox, and the ones I keep in my heart) to build a home and a life for my family.

As a young builder, I read Tracy Kidder's *House*. Kidder put into words what I only felt about building, and after reading that book, I knew what I was going to be doing for the rest of my life. Almost twenty years later, after reading Clement's *The Carpenter's Notebook*, I now know why.

Part of the value of a story well-told is that it throws us back upon ourselves while securing for us the truth of our shared humanity. This book does that."

Dave Crosby, custom builder and writer in Santa Fe, New Mexico

---

"This story put me in touch with my own life in a new way. But it also shows that when you fulfill a promise, the whole world opens up to you.

Anybody who builds should read this book and see the legacy and memories they will leave behind for their children."

Rick Schwolsky, Editor-in-Chief of Tools of the Trade
and El Nuevo Constructor magazines

"As a fourth generation builder who grew up hearing family tales and musings of a heritage steeped in the proud but perpetually struggling trade of shelter, this story rings as true to life for me as plumb and square is true to a structure. A great lesson of home spun philosophy for those who have lived it, and even greater for those who haven't."

Don Dunkley, coordinator of JLCLive!, the construction
industry's only live demonstration trade exposition

"Clement's simple story tweaks many old job-related aches but also finds redemption in the personal victories delivered by plans well-made and followed to their end. Anyone who works for a living, but especially those enactors of allegory who build and remodel homes and whose line between work and personal time is often blurred, are sure to connect with this affirming tale—I polished it off in one satisfying sitting."

Dave Holbrook, former builder and current editor
at The Journal of Light Construction magazine

THE CARPENTER'S NOTEBOOK
MARK CLEMENT

CenterLine™ Media

THE CARPENTER'S NOTEBOOK
MARK CLEMENT

Publisher: Theresa Coleman
Editor: Jessica Poppe
Cover Designer/Typesetter: Evan Potler

ISBN 0-9754212-4-7 (hardcover)
ISBN 0-9754212-3-9 (paperback)
© 2005 by Mark Clement

Library of Congress Control Number: 2004109372

Disclaimer
This publication is designed to provide accurate and authoritative information in regard to the subject matter covered. It is sold with the understanding that the publisher is not engaged in rendering legal, accounting, or other professional service. If legal advice or other expert assistance is required the services of a competent professional person should be sought.

—From a Declaration of Principles jointly adopted by a Committee of the American Bar Association and Committee of Publishers and Associations.

Cover photo © DavidSharpe.com

For more information, please contact:
CenterLine Publishing
1021 Arlington Blvd., Suite 1206
Arlington, VA 22209
www.centerlinemedia.com

For Alexis, with every ounce in my heart.

CONTENTS

ACKNOWLEDGMENTS

I could never list nor thank all of the people who have made this book possible in any kind of reasonable order, because each thought, idea, and conversation works together, one building off the other. Besides, after nine years of thinking, writing, re-writing, then re-re-writing, I may have forgotten some of you. But, I know where to start:

Janice Clement, my heroic mother. Without your love and intelligence mixed with passion for finding the unequivocal truth in life's mysteries— then expressing them beautifully— this book could not exist. You are my teacher, my hero. Kevin "Mad Dog" Morrison. Thank you for the title, your friendship, and unbridled enthusiasm for living a happy life. My friend Mike Walsh for your reverent and detailed stories about the carpenter who raised you, and for your kind and insightful assistance designing and refining the projects in this book. "We do good work." Dunk, Rick Schwolsky, and Steve Veroncau. At *Tools of the Trade* you guys have not only become my great friends, but you've mentored me through both home improvement and life projects with a kindness, concern, and interest few can match. I can neither repay nor thank you enough for your care and guidance. Old Gideon couldn't have existed without each of you. Michael Bollo for years of encouragement and contacts. Without your support, the chain of events that led to anybody reading this would still only be one link long— thank you. Lara Asher, the literary agent who saw something in this book when there wasn't much to see. Brett Witter, Lara's successor, who gave me the single piece of advice that I needed to take this book to the next level—"Don't say Johnny runs fast. Show Johnny running!"—Brett changed the pages that follow from an idea into a story. Pete Taft, thank you for years of interest and help. When I didn't know who to turn to, I could always turn to Pete. Kevin Smith, I must thank you not only for your friendship, but also for the long conversations we had on a cross-country trip and endless runs in the woods that developed the core of many essential themes in this book. Thanks to John Dempsey, whose insightful questions about his life and living it well many years ago inspired my answer: "Well John, it's like carpentry...." To Dave Juliano, who does what is right, not what is easy—and loves seeing the difference between the two. Mark Gauthier, the PR pro and new friend, who hired himself to work on this project. All of a sudden, he took a stake in the story's success and changed what it could be. Thanking him enough is futile, but I will try. Evan Potler, the talented designer who "saw" this book and turned its cover and pages into a visual theme that tells its story. David Sharpe, the photographer and friend who captured the cover image and whose opinions improved its power. Nick Stajka, the real-deal carpenter/builder whose eyes burn on the cover. Jessica Poppe for insightful story advice and detailed editing. Good stuff. And, to Theresa Coleman at CenterLine Media: my publisher, my friend. Without her limitless energy and enormous skill, without her hunger and care, this book would not breathe life—there is not a good enough way to share my gratitude or admiration.

PREFACE

This book is more than just a story to me.

The projects, tools, and life lessons you'll read about are real. I learned the lessons first hand on my own jobsites while I was a home improvement carpenter working for clients, and then in my spare time while renovating homes I've lived in. Walking top plates, digging holes, and hanging crown molding is how I've earned a living for my family and how I improved where I live. It was doing this work and practicing the craft of it that I was tested by the mental and physical challenges carpenters face every day. It was there on my jobsites that I learned true things about how a building works. And how life works.

At its heart, though, this is not a book about carpentry. It's about love, family, and a search for meaning. You can find meaning anywhere—anywhere you look for the underlying truths of existence that I believe tie us together. It is the looking that matters. And the faith that those truths are there to be discovered.

Building its physical struggle and mental challenges—is half of what brought these truths alive for me. Instead of limiting these truths to the jobsite where I discovered them, however, I brought them into first my business, then my life. I used what I discovered while digging a hole or hanging crown or working with a client as best I could to understand my world and manage my destiny. I also learned we all have a destiny we can manage, if we make that choice and don't question it, but instead get busy with the work and dedication of getting it done.

People I admire, revere, and love are the other half of this book coming to life. My mother, my daughter Alexis, friends old and new, and even clients along the way, helping me grow my small home improvement company, showed me that life truly is a team sport. I gleaned from each of them insights and inspirations to improve my own existence. Whether I see them once a year or every day, those people live lives full of possibility, growth, and greatness, and I admire them more than they know. Without them, their perspectives, and their willingness to share their lives with me, I would be a poor man. And this would be a different story.

In the following pages you will read notebook entries written by the character Gideon, a home improvement carpenter. Like many of my own notes for this book during the past nine years, Gideon's notebook entries were written over time. Sometimes the memory of an event inspires Gideon to write, often many years after the actual event occurred. Other times, he stops what he's doing to get his thoughts down on paper before they escape him so he can concentrate on more important things—like not falling off the roof. For Gideon, when the entries were written is not as important as what's written in them.

It is also important to note that each notebook entry is broken out into three sections: an Introduction, blow-by-blow How-to, and Gideon's Comments. While the How-to includes detailed descriptions and drawings of some of the techniques and site-built tools I used to help improve homes, it is really the Intro and Comments that are essential to understanding the story. The How-to is extra material; it's detailed information and drawings for those interested in building.

The point of this story for me is not to teach anyone how to build a toolbox or sawhorses or to impart carpentry experience. It is to help find meaning and understanding, much like the journey I've taken writing this book has helped me find greater understanding in my own life. I believe that living a full, meaningful, and enlightened life is possible and it is a way to activate what's best in all of us. And I believe that to live an enlightened life you must find and examine what is true and stable and real, then apply it to day-to-day existence.

Go with the grain.

mC

THE CARPENTER'S NOTEBOOK
MARK CLEMENT

INTRODUCTION

My father was a carpenter.

From sill plates to semi-gloss paint over a checkered career of boom and almost-bust cycles, he built, remodeled, and repaired houses in every reach of our small town. He did it with a fever and skill few could match, and in the end, he mastered his craft.

Working this way—loading 8x8 creosote-soaked timbers and 2-inch trap rock in a muddy retaining wall ditch one week, detailing a three-piece crown molding in a custom home the next, he learned what he called "true things." He used these true things to conquer the physical and mental challenges carpenters face; they also helped him marshal the strength, will, and endurance to build a business at the same time.

Later in his career when I was nearly grown and out of the house, he discovered he could apply these true things outside his work life. As a husband, father, and man, he built two things from this carpenter's curriculum: the homes and renovation projects that made him money and protected our family, and a well-crafted life.

CHAPTER 1 |

THE CRITICAL PATH

*The Critical Path is a carpenter's attempt to
make sense of the future, to quantify
and qualify what can be planned for, and to
make room for what everyone traveling a
critical path knows is coming:
the unknown.*

Snow wandered through the depth of the night sky, like it was lost in the dark. I stood looking out the window at the reflection of the lamp and Persian rug, and mountains of Christmas wrapping paper that awaited me to clean up. I thought that the way to really enjoy this weather, to sense the true vigor of Christmas day, would be to go outside for a while and feel the cold on my face. Standing there, I also thought a cup of cocoa might be nice, and I avoided thinking both about the wrapping paper mountains on my Honey-Do list or the fight my wife, Rachael, and I just had. I also avoided thinking about the anxiety that had taken over the life Rachael and I once had, a happiness and unity that I spent a lot of time missing. Outside, the world seemed so peaceful.

Inside, our daughters Laura and Kelly were down in the cellar watching the movies that their grandmother had just given them. It was a newly finished room with recessed lights, bright white wallboard, and spongy carpet that was fun to walk on in stocking feet. Upstairs, Rachael was doing something behind a locked door. I could hear muffled sounds coming from both directions, smell the lingering aromas of a holiday meal, and sense that the party was over.

I looked away from the window and turned my head up our wide stairs with the Persian carpet runner and brass bars on the risers to the solid white door that Rachael was behind. I noticed the fancy door hardware we had so much fun selecting when we had the upstairs remodeled three years ago: egg knobs with detailed Victorian escutcheons. They even had skeleton keys, which the girls loved. So I put all the keys on the biggest ring I could find at the hardware store and they used them to play "castle." At the time, we both thought the entry hardware added a measure of age-old integrity to an otherwise modern house. Life was better then. Business was booming and I felt like I knew my wife.

Somewhere between looking up the stairs, staring out the window, and slowly moving toward the pile of wrapping paper I had avoided all day, I heard Kelly's voice from downstairs, "Pop, Grammy's on the phone."

My 63-year-old mother, Kay, loved to be capable, to be active and able to do things. She lived an hour's drive from us in the small town where she and my father raised me—about 60 miles farther from the city than we lived. She stubbornly refused to let me truck the kids out to her place for Christmas day, knowing that we would spend the 26th with Rachael's parents, who lived three hours in the opposite direction. "Besides," she had told me, "I live alone now, and I like to get out of the house." Naturally, I worried about her as she made her way home with flakes meandering from the sky, but of course she beat them back.

I couldn't help but worry because I loved her and it was snowing. And I knew she could feel the tension radiating from Rachael and me during dinner when I caught the tail end of a concerned look from my mom across the table. After Kelly joked around somewhat inappropriately with her food, I laughed and was about to ask her not to do it again. But my reaction wasn't quite right for Rachael, whose face tensed up in a silent but serious call for our youngest daughter to pay more careful attention to her manners. My mom's easygoing talkative nature turned still and you could almost see the tension fill the dining room.

But even with the uncomfortable strain between me and my wife, my mom still moved about our modern family room with the girls, like a woman years younger than she actually was. I suddenly noticed that my mother's skin had changed, become more elderly than middle-aged, and I could hear a crackle in her springtime voice as she moved closer to the winter of her life. She walked differently now than she had as recently as last fall when I saw her tending her garden one Indian summer day. But the thing I loved so much about her is that she kept moving, kept busy, kept going. Nothing kept her from living. I imagined her gamboling along on her daily walk along the sidewalks and side streets of her little town through searing summer heat or knee-deep winter snow—nothing kept her away from it or other things she valued. A painter by avocation, an art teacher by vocation, she loved to see. She loved to see the houses change, the flowers grow, the leaves fall. And she loved to meet and be with the people populating her life and her world. She wasn't out selling herself, trying to be liked. As she strode around the block wearing a blue windbreaker that was too big for her and dark sunglasses that dated back to the last time she really cared much about style, perhaps caring enough about her town to stop and pick up stray paper from the sidewalk and slip it into her pocket as she moved, she was real and genuine. She was involved.

My mother is a great observer. I didn't think Rachael and I were hiding anything from her as we feigned being nicer to each other than we really wanted to be, acted like we cared more than we really did, and smiled more broadly than we should have as the kids' eyes lit up with every new gift under the 14-foot tree that was sheltered beneath the family room's sky-high white cathedral ceiling. I think my mom could tell—with eyes that saw things but didn't always communicate what they really knew—that sometime over the last year Rachael and I had stopped looking at each other when we spoke. Yet, like she always had, my mom gave me room to move, to figure things out, to grow, before I came to her for help.

"I'm home," she said, staring out her kitchen window. "And the snow got me thinking."

My father had been gone for two years, and since that time I couldn't recall gravity like that in her voice. My heart sunk like a stone for fear she was going to tell me she was sick.

"I had time on the drive and I've been thinking about something your father said the last time he and I visited your house together. Do you remember?"

"We talked about a lot of things, Mom," I said, pretty sure I knew exactly what she was going to say—but I didn't "know" it, not in my head. Somewhere, something in my skin or my belly or my hair pricked up as if a vestigial instinct was trying to come back to life.

"We sat around your kitchen island one evening after Laura and Kelly had gone to bed." I remembered clearly the ladies sipping tea from small, gentle looking cups and the guys drinking beers from thick-walled brown bottles. Somebody joked about being old and we all laughed. "Your father said, 'You know, my poor bride here is like the cobbler's kid—the cobbler fixes everybody else's shoes, but hasn't got time to fix his own kid's. When I kick the can,' he said, (I recalled him pulling a swallow from the beer in front of him) 'Kay needs to promise me that she'll use up some of that huuuuge life insurance policy I have and finally build that art studio she's always wanted.'"

I recall laughing nervously at that, my back to the group as I put some dishes in the sink and snow flecked the sky like salt on black paper, past the flowery curtains outside my kitchen window. And I remember feeling my father's eyes on me, just for a second. I remember noticing an almost imperceptible pause in the action before Rachael smilingly chimed in, "Not that we want you gone, Gid, but think about how nice it would be...." The dishes were stacked, soaking in the sink, and I went on with the night like the moment didn't mean anything, like my father would be around for a hundred more years. It stayed with me, lived inside me. He was vibrant and strong and there was no way I was ready to think about life without him.

"He was serious, you know," Mom said.

"I know."

Mom went on to tell me that he made her promise to convert his old workshop (a one-car garage in their backyard) into a high-ceilinged art studio full of big windows, bright sunlight, and solid maple boards. She knew he kept the plans he'd drawn up in his shop, but she told me she hadn't been able to bring herself to turn the key in the padlock and search through his things.

But something changed for her that day.

"I'm ready to build it," she said. The reverence in my stunned silence was overwhelming. I dismissed the feeling that was growing inside me, as if it were an invisible sapling not yet sprouted above the blanket of needles and leaves on the forest floor I walked through. Yet, an old feeling I couldn't identify started rebuilding itself and I heard my voice reply: "I'll take a look at the plans, Mom. Maybe maybe I can even take on the job myself," I weakly suggested. And then I remembered in a white-hot flash the intensity with which my father approached his work that always started with his building plan. He called this building plan—a project schedule that attempted to manage materials deliveries, construction phases, subcontractors, pay schedules, and completion dates—the Critical Path. He used it to make sense of the chaos, he would say a jobsite can quickly turn into when there was nothing to guide it. Then I remembered when I was his helper so many summers before, witnessing him walk that critical path, on a mission to see it through, to follow it to its end. I recalled that I was there, but just along for the ride.

Then, like now, I was coasting, wandering, not really engaged in what I was doing—a witness more than a participant. I floated through my life like the aimless snow on Christmas day and had become lost. And embarrassed. I envied my father's energy, his will, his focus and daydreamed for a passing moment that I could be more like him, even for a little while.

My father didn't know how to quit and he always moved forward. I don't know where he got it. He was not close with his own father, an uninspiring man. He didn't get it in the military because he was colorblind and they wouldn't take him, even though he registered for the draft and saw many friends leave home, never to come back. No one could accuse him of being the world's best businessman—it took him a long time to work up the courage and skill to go from home improvement projects to homebuilding. And yet, there was always time for my mom and me.

We almost never went out to dinner, but he took us to the beach every year for a week. He worked so many Saturdays I grew up thinking the "work week" had six days. But he was always there on the sidelines of a home game. He was there after parent–teacher conferences to set me straight. Holidays were a true celebration and although our family was small, there was no place I'd rather be. And nobody I'd rather be with.

My father was good at living. The moment of wishing I could be more like him was pure and beautiful. But it passed too quickly and the fuel inside me now—a low-grade anxiety mixed with low-octane desire—returned, stranding me somewhere along the side of the road.

"Good," she said with serious brevity that contrasted with her usual warm-eyed charm.

"I'll check with Rachael and come down to look for the plans soon," I said. "I love you, Mom."

"I love you, too, Bren."

Before I set the cordless phone back in its cradle, I felt desire—rising like groundwater—to take the summer off from a business that wasn't what it used to be, and instead converting the white clapboard garage into a studio for Mom to paint, and dream, and wonder in. I thought about fulfilling their dream—building the place she had always wanted but could never have—and I could hear a note of my father's voice in my own head when I thought in total and dismissive silence, "I can even build it the way Dad would have, from the foundation to the finish nails."

* * *

I sat for the few cold days between Christmas and New Year's with my secret notion of spending the summer's mercifully bright and long days at my mother's house, building. It would almost be like the way I spent summers working with my father in my youth, and it made me feel younger than I was.

For the first time in a long time, I anticipated feeling something other than happiness for my kids' achievements or dread from Rachael's uninspired reactions to something I did—or failed to do. I anticipated something other than loneliness while Rachael populated her life with an increasing number of projects and duties, keeping her and me separate. And I anticipated something other than the sickening sense of failure as my once top-drawer home sales declined and my colleagues vied for my top spot. What I anticipated was achievement and activity.

I had become just another worker in a long line that had fallen victim to getting ahead, and I lost sight of everything else. While I wanted to be the best, I recognized that I could not do so at the expense of everything my family, my wife, my very well-being. I think my father would have said that "best" has a very broad definition. My effort at being the best had made me a top producer for several hot years in our market. Even though my sales had started to fall off, I was sure the managing partner at my firm would allow me a leave-of-absence as he had for others with family emergencies or enough money saved up to take extended vacations.

As it turned out, although business had been just downright bad for me all of December—and I was running out of gas for going on my umpteenth weekend in a row of open houses and cheerfully carting prospective clients around the metro area in my Volvo station wagon—I had listings to show between Christmas and New Year's. This, mercifully, got me out of the house. And buyers shopping at this time of year are usually serious, so I was at least hopeful for a nice hit. Once out of the house, I had time to think and to frame exactly how I would present my idea to Rachael, who was never a big fan of change.

On New Year's Day with a not-so-late night behind us, I waited until Laura and Kelly went to go hang out with their friends next door before approaching Rachael. She was in the kitchen, busy cleaning the solid-surface counter with anti-bacterial something-or-other spray, and cleaning up after the kids' lunches.

"You know, Rache, we really haven't decided about sending the girls to summer camp," I said, trying to sound cheery. When I'm nervous or trying really hard to say something that is awkward, I have a tendency to be indirect. Maybe it's the salesman in me, but it's how I handle stress.

She kept wiping, her eyes fixed determinedly, not on me but her work, as I sat down at our kitchen island on a backless stool.

"Can we talk about this later?" she asked seemingly in a rush to get on to the next thing in her compulsion to get the house back in order.

"Well, I was really hoping we could chisel out some time now. I have calls all week and the girls are gone now. Can we please talk about it?"

"Fine," she said blandly but with a chill, as she agreed to pay attention to this important detail of our life. Treating it like a surprise chore, like spilt milk or muddy boot prints that needed immediate cleaning, she finally turned to talk about it. I could see that her mind was pouring into what she had to do next rather than really listening to me, and for a moment all I could think about was that it wasn't always like this. Something important had gotten so very far away from what we thought we wanted out of our marriage, when we first started our journey together.

I knew she would offer almost nothing to the conversation other than evaluation of my ideas, but God, I loved the way she looked. Even after two kids, she took care of her body, and as she bent to drop some fragment in the trash, her Levi's tightened around her backside and I looked at her with the same desire that I always had. Even now, as she turned with her arms crossed under her full breasts, with tension creasing her face, I could still see the beauty in her that I had always seen, and recalled the photo of her I used to carry in my wallet before we got married. Her friend had snapped the picture with her Instamatic camera sometime during the day Rachael and I met. Rachael stood with her feet in the water and a look of youth and freedom, and possibilities for the future shone through her ocean-green eyes. That look, mixed with the gentle lines on her face and a genuinely kind smile, created the portrait of someone I wished would come back. Instead, the Rachael before me knitted her brow momentarily before her expression simply went blank.

"I think camp is a good idea for them," I said. "Our marriage counseling has been moving along slowly and I think a break from the tension would be good for them. Plus, I don't really think that it's good for the girls to see us fight—or walk on eggshells every-day—while we figure this out."

"I don't know if they should be so far from home, Brendan. Not for that long."

"But don't you think at 7 and 9 they're old enough to spend a few weeks learning new things and meeting new people in a safe and really fun place? After all, we found out about this camp from your sister who sent her kids. It's only two hours away. And every-body else we've talked to raves about it. Besides, we have to sign the papers by the end of the month or we risk losing the deposit and the spot we reserved back in the fall when we agreed this was a smart idea."

"This is the same argument we keep having, Brendan. I'm sick of going in circles with you about this," she said sharply without raising her voice an octave. I had to practically chew my tongue off to keep from replying, to keep from fighting back against the void of what was once there. Of course it was the same argument. It's always the same argument, because nothing with her ever fucking changes! And, this argument "we always have" has almost nothing to do with camp. The real problem at work here, at the core of our marriage, is another baby.

When Rachael and I married, we loved the idea of a big family.

But, two kids into it, changes in how we related to one another began altering those desires, at least for me. Before Laura was born, Rachael and I went out on at least one "date" every month. Nothing fancy, but we made time to connect with each other. She'd hold my hand at the movies or I'd steal a kiss when I came back from the bathroom at a restaurant. We even tried to pick something new to do together like picking apples on a fall day or going to a wine tasting festival. After Laura was born, we put our dates on hold until she was about one. Then, we brought her along and it was great.

But when it came to just the two of us, Rachael no longer seemed interested. She said she was uncomfortable hiring a babysitter. Her mom watched Laura a few times, but she made it out to be a major undertaking, so our dates slowly went away. Then, in an instant, another year was gone and Kelly was born. The chance or desire for a babysitter and an easy-going Friday between the two of us—time for us to connect—disappeared. My requests to go out turned into her lists of things that needed to be done.

By the time Laura was 5 and Kelly was 3, life had become an endless errand for Rachael, and playgroups, T-ball, school, and every pre-schooler's birthday party in the school district took on monumental importance for Rachael. While she is a dedicated and heroic mother, her interest in our marriage—and me—seemed to fall by the side of the road. I got caught up, too. Like her, I loved Laura and Kelly and would walk through fire for them. But, I got busy—then got busier—selling houses. I was the lead dog in my firm for four consecutive years and I made a big pile of money doing it. But I still made it to every holiday and birthday party and fed them breakfast nine days a week. Sure, our marriage was put on hold when they were babies, but when I tried to woo Rachael back to the us that existed before—just sometimes—to have fun again, even to be sexual, her heart clearly wasn't in it, not like it had been.

So, after another year of everything being more important than our marriage and contending with the mounting rejections from

Rachael, I announced that there would not be a third baby. Not from me. And that's when we really started pulling away from each other, and the unstated mission in our lives became "staying together for the kids." It was only years later in counseling that either one of us even articulated this thought.

"Well, another reason I was thinking about it was," my heart hammered with explosions of blood and energy in my chest as I calmly said, "that my mother needs my help. It would get me out of the house, too." I looked out the window in defeat. "She wants me to help build something my father started before he died."

She asked, after a long, almost invisible breath passed between her full lips, lips that had not kissed me in too long, "When would this happen?"

I stared down at the ceramic tile floor, noticing the grout lines for the first time.

"I'd leave right after the kids got out of school."

* * *

By the time Laura and Kelly were back in school after the Christmas recess, Rachael and I had become quite good at avoiding each other in our big house. Although we always landed in the king-sized bed at night, our home was big enough that we could pretty much avoid each other most of the day until dinnertime, and then we'd talk only with the kids and not each other. I came and went to business meetings, worked in my home office, which Rachael did the same thing in her office upstairs. On good nights, we made small talk while we brushed our teeth and she washed her face. On good nights I longed for the passion we used to have. On great nights I would even try to kiss her before I fell into a restless sleep.

After our third weekly counseling session of the New Year, Rachael finally agreed with my plan for the summer. The girls would be away at camp for six weeks and the time alone for each of us, we thought, would help. At least it might ease the crushing sorrow that stalked both of us from the emotional shadows of our daily routines.

In February, when winter days are short, the nights are deep, and our heating bills are at their highest, I rummaged through the garage for the tan leather toolbelt my father had given me 25 years ago. I found it hanging on a 16 penny nail on the far side of the minivan, behind towers of clear, plastic storage boxes, beside a tiny workbench in back where I kept a smattering of tools. I threw the tool pouch in the back of my car with a duffel bag full of old clothes and my workboots. I thought I'd go to my mom's for a couple of days to check out what needed to be done, and if I could really do it. The rest of the tools I'd need were already there.

I knew that I would have to empty his shop and move the tools, boards, and boxes to another spot. And no matter if I did the work myself or someone else did—nobody was going through his things, his history, but me.

I drove through the white walls of plowed snow on either side of our curved street down the snow-packed blacktop and headed to my mother's house. This drive was practically automatic for me after all these years of driving out to see them, but since Dad died the drive felt different. And that day it felt different for another reason. This time, I was taking the first step away from my family as the ghost of divorce hung like a thunderhead on the horizon. I didn't dare think about it for fear that it might become real and my world would change irrevocably and for the worse, but the cloud hung there still, just hung there. My car radio was quietly playing the Great Big Sea shanty "Gideon Brown," but I could hear nothing other than the crunch of snow under my tires and the voluminous silence of the voices I would not hear when I woke up in the morning. I wished my little girls were with me, even for these few short days. And I wished I felt guilty for being relieved that Rachael and I would be taking even this small break, but I didn't. Instead, cutting the tension and giving the invisible 10-ton elephant walking around our house a few days off seemed like a welcome respite.

It was an easy drive through the cold, dark winter afternoon but when I got there, I was tired. Tired from holding the secret of my marriage from my mother; tired from the meaningless daily battles with Rachael; tired from the emotional fallout of a marriage I more and more saw crumbling into ruin, like an old building with a leak in the roof that allowed too much water down to the foundation with every passing storm. I remember the energy Rachael used to put into being together. She was the girl who liked to rub my shoulders and neck without being asked, after she learned I had a particularly hard day. While we often traded dinner duty, Rachael used to like making a surprise candlelight meal if she knew I'd be back late from showing a house. It used to make her happy—and me too!—to care about being together. She used to like turning an hour on a Tuesday evening in the middle of the year into a little carnival, for no other reason than it was fun to share the beauty inside her. I missed that beauty and saw the leak in our marriage more clearly every time she looked at me without a single emotion visible in her eyes.

Mom and I made small talk and we caught up on the details of our lives. She was working on a new concept for a painting she called "Snow by the Sea" that she hoped she could do in oil, and I told her that I had just sold a house and had another high-priced property on deck, but that I was really losing zeal for my work and that I thought it was affecting my job.

Then she asked if Rachael wanted to spend the summer with us, too—if that would make coming out here to tackle this project any easier, and that, for her, having another friendly face in the house would be great. I nearly fell out of my chair.

There was no way I could look my mom in the eyes for more than two seconds, with the secret trying so hard to push its way out, as I responded that Rache and I had already discussed it. She had some travel she wanted to take advantage of for her consulting business, and with the girls at summer camp it would be the perfect time to hop on a plane and go drum up some new clients.

My mom has no problems chatting. She's garrulous and friendly and likes to know about people, so we talked for a while longer. My anxiety subsided as I asked questions about old Mrs. Macropolis and the Washingtons down the road, and then about how her plans were coming along for the trip she takes annually to Florida with old friends of hers and Dad's. I began to feel good again and checked her fridge for a beer.

"Bren, I'm so glad you're thinking about doing this job, you know. It would make Dad happy, I think, to see you out there." This remark found its way inside me and stoked an ember I hoped would burn the minute I unrolled the plans—if I could find them.

"I don't know that I can even handle it yet, Mom," I said, trying to hold off committing to the project. "I don't know that I can build this or get the time away from work. You know how it is." And even at that moment, sagging in the middle of the rope-and-plank bridge over the rushing river beneath, hanging between a lie and the truth, I felt a roiling desire to go out and look for the plans, to answer the question, to see if I could do it. I heard myself saying, "Well, now's as good a time as any to find out." I stood up, walked over to the door, put my hand on the loose old lockset, and began my journey down the back walk and into my past. Excuses for not accepting this challenge reformed themselves into the desire to see what it would be like if I could do it.

CHAPTER 2

BUILDING PEACE
OF MIND

*There's more to living than just doing
your duty. Living well is a mission,
and missions require plans.*

I had never really appreciated my father's love of blueprints, of forethought, but it was the search for the project's plans in his old shop that turned this renovation project into an unexpected lesson in living a good life, and changed my perspective about plans and planning. And about everything else.

The expedition from the house to his shop is short. Just outside the back door from the kitchen and down a fissured concrete path leading to the edge of the driveway is the side door of his shop. The building's flaking paint gathered like dandruff on the tread-worn red oak threshold, and the tools, boards, and secrets resting inside had sat untouched since I clicked the lock 24 months before. The single-pane windows in the door were clouded from a lifetime of sawdust cyclones, but they seemed even cloudier now with the dust of stillness. My hand nearly trembled with a sense of awe and respect as I raised the little bronze-colored key to the galvanized lock. I was exploring for the first time a piece of my history, and, I'd soon discover, glimpsing hope for my family's future.

I took one reverent first step inside and sunk into a pallet swirled with familiar old colors. The smells and sounds I anticipated, almost expected, had been replaced by silence and comatose air. Some visceral part of me anticipated a powerful smell, because his last day started here. And while my memory echoed the sounds of action I knew this place to be full of, I couldn't even hear my own breathing. The saw motors, lumber on the move, and furious tinker's dams that defined this space rung freely in my memory. But those sounds never left my mind to ripple the air, like a rock falling in still water, to create a live noise. As real as they sounded in my mind, there was only silence to greet me.

I silently brushed my finger through the powdery dust on the cast iron table saw deck as if it were a fossil I shouldn't touch yet couldn't resist, and I saw mostly shades of gray: the super smooth decks of the band saw, table saw, and jointer were darkest gray; the concrete slab floor, the soldier-courses of shelved wooden and metal toolboxes were a bit lighter. Even the lumber scraps and saw-dust, once maple yellows and oak reds, now lying on the floor or on racks, had grayed like cedar clapboards held too long to salty weather. There were other colors, though, whose hibernating ebullience was undiminished amidst all that foggy gray. The carbide teeth on the miter and table saw blades leapt from the rusty blade plates. The bundle of perfectly coiled yellow and orange extension cords and nail gun hoses hung brightly from a homemade wooden hook by the door, still charged to go. And hanging from a framing spike was the red-hooded sweatshirt my father wore in cold weather. The white silkscreen peeled like paint, but it was still easy to make out the company name, logo, and slogan my mother had designed for him before I could even read. A sketch of a heart-shaped plumb bob with a perfect point descended from a string and next to it read, "Herlihy Improvements, Building Peace of Mind."

I stood in the center of the shop and pondered. Where among these ceiling-mounted lumber racks overflowing with planks, floor-to-ceiling shelves strong enough to park a dump truck on, and library of tools would Gideon Herlihy store the plans for his wife's studio? My eyes followed the fading sunlight from the window above the wooden workbench around the room and I thought of my father working out here nights under the articulating arm of an old govern-ment-gray desk lamp and bare-bulb ceramic light fixtures. Looking for it now, I saw that the lamp was screwed to an exposed wall stud and plugged into an outlet a few feet away. The cord arched like the cable of a suspension bridge between the power source and the 100-watt bulb. The spring-tensioned articulating lamp arm was folded compactly, stretching the springs, as was the chair he used to sit on to write, as if his workbench were a proper writing desk. Underneath the pocked, chipped, saw-kerfed, and pencil-hieroglyphed bench top something caught my eye. It was the only new looking thing in the entire shop and I knew I was on the line.

There under the dust of stasis was the last thing my father ever built—a toy box-sized container made with his favorite material, #2 common pine. He had dovetailed the corners and glued up wide pieces into panels to make the lid, which was beautifully imperfect and full of knots. There was something my father had always loved about pine. From the lumberyard, pine is soft and easy to work but far less perfect than a piece of hardwood like alder, oak, maple, or cherry might be. But pine can be caressed and worked into shape to make nice things. Also, the stuff is a workhorse and eclipses the common capabilities of other kinds of lumber for really important things—like shelter. My father liked that it could be beautiful and functional in the same breath. Even some framing stock is cut from pine trees, and anyone who's driven nails into new, sappy 2x4s knows they go in easy and hold tight. And anyone who's ever tried to nail into an old stud, rafter, or joist in a remodeling project will tell you, as new pine dries and stabilizes in a building, it grows oak-hard. The wood is a lot like him in many ways, I thought, as I raised the lid. Inside was a tray segmented into squares and rectangles, which I recognized as a place for nails, screws, and hand tools as if this were an old-fashioned cabinet-makers' tool chest. I lifted the tray off the cleats that kept it from sliding to the floor of the box and, as I expected, lying lengthwise along the front of the rectangular box, were the rolled up plans for my mom's studio.

I don't know how long I stood there, but the cold of the night finally shook me loose and I remembered that my mom was waiting. I took the plans from their spot beneath the bench to my mom so we could look at them together. She was sketching in the living room, her studio for the last 45 years, and looking peacefully out the bay window, almost as if she were expecting the future to round the corner of our short road in a delivery truck. She had used this space to quietly craft her humble creations from paint, ink, and charcoal throughout my life; the masterpieces that no one had ever paid admission to see and that had hung not in museum halls and salons, but on nails and hollow-wall-anchors in the front hall, bed-rooms, and bathrooms of our family's home. She competed with noise from my father and me, my boyhood friends, and TV. Or maybe these were the fuel that inspired her to create those beauti-ful things.

I called my mom into the kitchen and then unrolled the plans on the table, casting my own shadow over them as I leaned under the dim overhead light. My mom came in and sat down. Adjusting her glasses, she leaned in to see what he had drawn.

He called for the studio to be a mirror image of his garage, built perpendicular and attached to his existing shop. In his trade parl-ance, he would've called this a reverse-gable addition, which essen-tially turns a simple rectangular building into a "T" whose rooflines intersect like the leg intersects the head of the letter T. Assuming the existing garage was in adequate condition, I would only have to do interior work to it and then build and tie the new structure into it. In the plans, he also carefully laid out where the windows, doors, and skylights should go and what sizes they should be.

* * *

Over the next few days my mother and I enjoyed some unhurried time together. We went out for lunch and I took care of some things around the house, spent an hour following up on my prospective sale, and even managed to reconnect one night with my old college buddy Kevin, who lived just two towns away. I called Laura and Kelly each evening, too. We talked and I told them I loved them. "I love you, too, Daddy," each one said with a smile I could hear from the other side of the phone.

When I left my mom, I took the plans back home to read them and awaited winter's end, which I hoped would come quickly. While scouring every word of the plans as I'd seen my father do so many times before, I tried to embrace his vision of the project and the new, finished space. I began preparations for the critical path: foundation

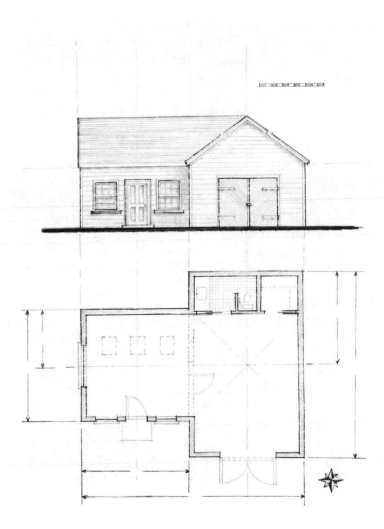

work first, then demo, framing, fenestration, shingles, etc.

But I was also buried with work and home life—trying to spend extra time with the girls, communicate and survive with my wife, and finalize the business arrangements that would have to be in place so I could leave for 12 weeks.

In the meantime, while Rachael took leave of loving me romantically, she augured herself into life as a mother, professional, and homemaker. It seemed there was always something to get done, which I usually considered less intergalactically important than she did. My Honey-Do list seemed endless, and through it all she found a way to make me feel as though I worked for her, that I owed her something. I tried not to get mad or confront her, because fighting with her had exhausted my spirit and I was beaten. I also knew that how she treated me, treated our marriage, was a result of how her parents acted. It was her model as a child. I also backed off because I knew it would be over soon, too.

Her father very much kowtowed to her very powerful mother. When Rachael and I met, I read her as fiercely independent and single-minded—and I liked it! I respected it. I wanted more of it. There is no doubt that she reminded me of my mother, and as I've learned in a year of counseling, people have a tendency to marry their parents, for good or ill. That independence mixed with her genuine affection for me early on, but I grew to find that something else was taking its place and that she was following directly in her parents' footsteps—without even making any new marks in the fresh fallen snow of our lives. And, it seemed, in some back room of her soul, she made the assumption that I would follow suit and be just like her father after we married. It was in her chemistry that I should follow without question.

Even as she told me that she'd rather I not go to my mother's— that we face this head on—she behaved like she wanted me the hell out of there by giving me the "here's your hat, what's your hurry" treatment and made our once warm home an unfriendly place to live. She refused to talk about us outside the counselor's office. She locked down any information about herself that could help us solve the problem, and conversations turned lifeless. We could share meals and talk with spirit and energy with the girls. She was even syrupy and courteous with me in front of them, but when the bedroom door shut behind us at night, it was like all that remained was her antiseptic stare and hands-off anger. And truth be told, what she really didn't want was for Laura and Kelly to leave her for those six weeks. Her fear of life without these two growing girls she wanted to stay as babies became the wellhead of her intensity.

Rachael increasingly coddled the girls—overly sympathetic to a skinned knee, hypersensitive to the importance of their activities and schedule, easily giving in to a tantrum at the grocery checkout for a candy bar, and even allowed them to sleep in our bed with her when I was out of town. But at times she was sharp with them, especially when it came to manners in front of family. At those times it was almost as if she expected them to be angels—her angels. And as I sat, propped up on king-sized pillows in bed under the wash of my bedside table light with my father's unrolled plans in my hand and a pencil between my teeth, Rachael asked curtly, "Brendan, you haven't built anything in 20 years. Why don't you just hire someone to do it?"

I bit down on the pencil nearly hard enough to crush it into three pieces. I needed to read those plans—carefully—many, many times. I needed to understand them. But on the other hand, she was right: it had been a long time since I built anything and even then it was my dad who built while I just helped. He was the one who walked the Critical Path. I just tagged along for the ride.

But still, as important as it was for me to read the plans carefully, I put most of it off until I got to my mother's house in the spring, because it was comments like that that had me up at night, too tired to focus, but too tortured to sleep.

Spring thankfully came quickly, and I prepared to leave a place

I once knew to be full of love, happiness, unity, and genuine kindness. Wanting to keep our girls safe and sheltered from what was really going on with their mom and dad, Rachael and I decided to tell the girls that I was doing business with a client near their grandmother's house and that while I may come and go while they were off at camp, I'd spend most of the summer at their Grandmother Herlihy's house.

Saying good-bye was so hard that I found myself blank inside, in a self-imposed emotional anaphylactic shock, yet I said an affectionate good-bye to Rachael anyway, hugging her right there in front of the girls whom she would take to camp that very next weekend. I tried hard to care about her—to show her I cared with just a hug, a look straight into her eyes, but with no words to confuse things. I tried to give her as basic a signal as I could that I wanted to be there for her, that I wanted this trouble to go away, that I wanted us back. But all I felt from her was the cold courtesy of a pat on the back, like a hug from your friend's mom.

My girls were a different story, and my soul toggled through the range of emotions from trying so hard with Rachael to feelings that effortlessly gushed out of me as I held each one close, trying to radiate all the hope in my broken heart through my skin, arms, and eyes.

Then I left to rebuild my father's temple.

CHAPTER 3

ONE HALF SETUP, ONE HALF CLEANUP

Often just getting ready—nevermind the work—is as hard as the work itself.

The alarm cut through my dreamless sleep like a circ saw screaming through a hangover and I recalled just how early 5 a.m. really feels. Even though sunrise wasn't officially for another 18 minutes, a gray half-light filled the shadeless windows of my old bedroom. I flailed sleepily for the snooze bar on my digital travel alarm clock before pulling the covers over my head for just eight more minutes of rest.

Instead of silence, though, my head filled with the sounds and feelings of the people I would not hear that day. I tried to close my eyes a little harder, hoping I could just drift off to sleep for a little while longer. Despite my efforts, my body tensed up and I knew that trying to sleep peacefully again would be futile. No matter how far Rachael and I had grown apart, I loved her once, and wanted her body by my side—and not the pillow that had become a surrogate for her, which I now clutched to my chest. As my mind filled with the anxious thoughts of her, and what had withered before us, it was clear that I would be out of bed in a few minutes, not able to withstand lying there in the dim light with only these thoughts to fill an opaque consciousness. I swung my legs out from under the covers and put my feet on the braided oval rug that lay across the red oak-strip floor.

At this moment Laura and Kelly were behind doors upstairs in a house I wasn't in anymore, themselves nearing the end of their night's rest. I recalled that when they were younger I would get up before them and let Rachael rest, and spend the minutes before the girls rose enjoying the quiet and calm of a house that I felt I belonged in, that felt like home. As the sun's light brightened just a little in the windows, the thought of beginning my first day of living without them, away from home, weighed me down, as though my soul had gained 100 pounds overnight, growing fat and thick and slow. I missed them already, and it was only going to get worse.

Nine years ago our first daughter, Laura, was born— healthy, vibrant, beautiful, and totally defenseless. I was there at the deliv-

31

ery doing what I could to coach my wife through her heroic marathon of pushing and pain. Nine years ago our lives were drawn inexorably together by the gentle, yet unmistakably powerful, force of that little girl lying helpless and beautiful under a heat lamp, swaddled in a pink and white striped cotton blanket.

Two years later, our second glorious daughter, Kelly, was born in the same hospital, in the same healthy way. Her incandescent eyes looked blindly into a world whose colors she would not even see for weeks to come.

But the baby that seemed to matter most in our marriage was the one who was not here, the one who was not coming because our love had taken a backseat to something else.

I guess I did sit there on the edge of the bed for another four minutes, motionless, with only my thoughts racing. The second alarm kerfed through the silence of dawn, cutting through the noises in my head, and my eyes felt heavier than my heart. I so deeply wanted to continue sleeping. Instead, those sounds and conversations I wouldn't hear today tugged at me and I skulked to the bathroom to brush my teeth. This was the first time I could remember choosing not to be with my girls, the first time I ever elected not to hear their sounds, the noises that express the girls they are and the women they'll become. I heard, too, the silence of my wife's absence. Staring into the bathroom mirror at the whiskers on my chin, the sunken look in my eyes, and the paunch around my gut, I couldn't describe how sad I felt. I suddenly found myself wishing I hadn't gotten so out of shape in a life I lived too passively. Behind my desk, at the wheel of my car, and in front of my big TV, my body had grown weaker and more internal than it was designed for. I hadn't walked outside, run, or smelled flowers in far too long. Instead, I just wore the ruts in my life deeper each day, not realizing that being alive has so much more to offer than commuting, client meetings, cable television, and being an involved but passive spectator to my children's youth.

I also felt, for the first time in too many years, the buoyancy of freedom and autonomy. Today was the first day in years that I wouldn't be greeted by an emotionless look, or feel someone shrink away from a just-'cause-I-love-you hug. Realizing this, wakefulness and alertness darted to my brain like the punch of strong coffee and I sucked in dark air to bellows the fire I needed to start this project that smoldered inside me.

I dressed in jeans, boots, and an old T-shirt, and headed for the kitchen. I left the plans unrolled on the desk beneath the window where I grew up doing my homework, and I took with me only memories of my father and a mental list of preparations he'd made for this project.

* * *

When I visited my mother back in February, I had planned to take a closer look at the footings and short foundation walls my father had already built for the addition from poured concrete and concrete blocks (called a stemwall or pony-wall), but they were buried in snow. While I was reading the plans over the winter I realized that all the plywood and 2-by stock, which was neatly stacked and kept dry under tan oil-skin tarps behind the shop, was for the gang boxes I'd need to store all my father's gear in while I did the demo work. The schematic for the gang boxes in the plan appendix was as clear as the rest of his pencil drawings. But there was one thing in the plan appendix that seemed a bit out of place, yet still pertinent to the project.

Rolled into the desk calendar-sized blueprint pages was a simple piece of paper, torn from an old ledger. On it was a note from my father, written with a thick pencil. However, his block letters were so rough, it appeared as though he was trembling as he wrote: "You're going to need one of these…." Below the note was an old photo and a clear sketch—as if it had been drawn previously—of a site-made hand-carry toolbox, the likes of which rode in the back of his pickup truck for all the years I knew him. It was a workman-like pine box filled with hand tools, razor-sharp chisels carefully rolled in a leather pouch, and any other carpentry implements he required.

Upon closer examination, it was clear that the drawing was intended to do more than show what the project was, because the sketch was really an exploded drawing, a drawing showing all of the pieces individually and their relationship to one another. It was intended to illustrate how the toolbox went together.

Cryptically, at the top of the page was another note, almost a code to himself for organization. It said: Job Name: Pelletier, Project: Toolbox.

I did get a better look at the foundation when I came back a second weekend in March to build the gang boxes—and the toolbox— that would store the contents of my father's shop until his tools could find a new home. I cringed at the thought of having a yard sale. To me that was like taking the Rosetta Stone to a consignment shop, but they had to go somewhere.

Today, at the end of June, I steeled myself to empty out a place that had represented so much of who my father was—to put it all into giant coffin-like boxes, and begin creating something new, something gleaming, in which my mother could find happiness, inspiration, and some peace.

YOU'RE GOING TO NEED
ONE OF THESE:

JOB NAME:
  PELLETIER
PROJECT:
  TOOLBOX

STEPS:
1. CUT PIECES TO LENGTH

2. PRE-DRILL AND COUNTERSINK
SCREW HOLES

3. ASSEMBLE PIECES

CUT PIECES.
  - CUT ALL PIECES TO LENGTH. FOR THE
ANGLED PIECES (SEE DRAWING) I CUT
EACH ONE TO LENGTH THEN CLAMP
THEM TOGETHER WITH THE BOTTOMS
FLUSH. I THEN CLAMP THE BOARDS
SECURELY TO MY CUT BENCH AND TRIM
THE ANGLE WITH A CIRCULAR SAW. THIS
ENSURES THAT BOTH PIECES ARE
EXACTLY THE SAME.

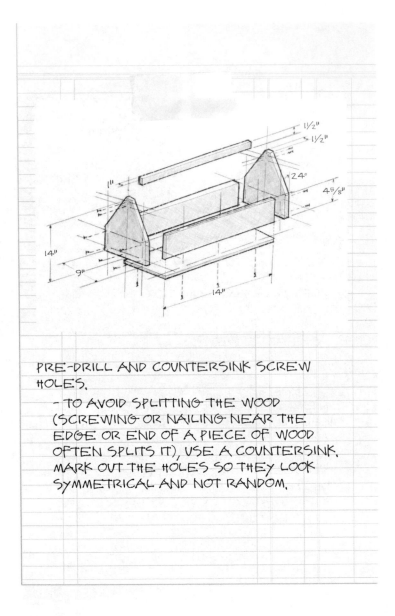

PRE-DRILL AND COUNTERSINK SCREW
HOLES.
  - TO AVOID SPLITTING THE WOOD
(SCREWING OR NAILING NEAR THE
EDGE OR END OF A PIECE OF WOOD
OFTEN SPLITS IT), USE A COUNTERSINK.
MARK OUT THE HOLES SO THEY LOOK
SYMMETRICAL AND NOT RANDOM.

ASSEMBLE PIECES.

- WORKING ON A FLAT SURFACE, FASTEN THE BOTTOM PANEL TO THE SIDES.

- FASTEN THE END PANELS TO THE BOTTOM PANEL AND SIDE PANELS.

- FASTEN THE HANDLE TO THE END PANELS. USE 2 SCREWS ON EACH SIDE.

- WIPE DOWN ALL BOX SURFACES WITH SEVERAL APPLICATIONS OF BOILED LINSEED OIL AND LET DRY. LINSEED OIL HELPS REPEL MOISTURE AND BRINGS OUT THE LUSTER IN THE WOOD.

Down in the kitchen, I toggled the coffee-maker's on button, illuminating the switch's red bar in the dark of the kitchen. I hit a wrong light switch by the back door, and lit the cellar stair instead of the kitchen. It was enough to see by, so I sat at the kitchen table in half-light reviewing my day-one bible—my checklist for what I needed done by sunset this evening.

How many times must my father have done this routine? I looked at the thermometer in the window and wondered if I'd need his red sweatshirt. It read 48 degrees—cold for June. I felt like the winter would never let go, and decided to pull the sweatshirt over my uncombed hair. I stared out the kitchen window, picturing the studio I was here to build in my mind's eye, suddenly happy I had torn myself from sleep, happy to be on the move so early—and thrilled for strong coffee.

In the silence of the pre-dawn kitchen, its pine plank sub-floor squeaking beneath my boots as I moved to warm up my mug of coffee from the pot, I got my first head start on a cold spring morning leading into a summer full of long days. My father loved head starts and would do whatever he could to get one. He used to get up so early to read plans, load the truck, or meet a delivery that I remember stumbling in on him one morning after getting home from a night of carousing while on a college break. Most of the world slept without him. I remember thinking then that getting up that early was a sacrifice more than a mission. I also hoped that he wouldn't say anything about the gallon of beer on my breath. Then, I think some part of me, which I find decreasingly admirable, vowed to be different and for my life to be easier and more free, though I had no concept of what a free life really was.

That morning, I saw my father not as captain of his ship, not as someone striving to be better than he was, but as a slave in the hold. I saw him as in thrall to a business that did not earn him the fortunes it appeared my friends with larger homes and nicer cars had. I saw him as indentured to his life, deeply altered because of me, and then I vowed not to be like him.

But now, as I sat there in his chair doing what he did while steam curled from the cup before the sun rose, many years before, it started to become clear to me what the energy was that drove him. I was ashamed because after only a glimpse of how hard—yet how vibrant and real—his life was, I could not say I had achieved my goal of being free. I saw him as trapped then, but now, here, in his footsteps, it is me who was the slave—to a dying marriage, to a soft body, to a featureless career.

I realized all of this, buried it somewhere inside me to deal with later, then walked toward the door. My life had been lived and that river water had passed. I felt ashamed, yes. But there was work to do, work he wanted done.

I began lugging items out of his shop slowly at first, almost half-heartedly, but something lit a fire under me and my pace quickened. My embarrassment at my own life and lifestyle made me feel ashamed and I walked faster between the gang boxes and the storage shelves in the garage, a slow stroll turned into a purposeful stride. I was really moving. Or, as Dad would've said, "walk like you're going somewhere!"

My body moved and found a rhythm in the lifting and strain, and I made better progress than I anticipated. I had planned two days to empty this building out, scheduling breaks and down time, but the building's inventory was quickly finding its way to its new home: one day, done deal.

I jogged between the gang of boxes and the garage when my arms were empty. And when they were full, I still walked faster than during any relaxed house tour I had done in 16 years of selling real estate. I had long ago dumped my father's sweatshirt on a plastic patio chair and was now sweating through my T-shirt. I remembered something my father used to say when we built his first house together—"It's one half setup, one half cleanup. The rest is work."

Only now, as a middle-aged man laboring to get to the starting point of a journey I might not even be able to finish, did I begin to see what my father's life was like. When I was younger, building had been a game, an hourly wage and a way to fill time and make beer money. There was no pressure; no need to be anywhere. But now, with an expiration date on how long I could stay away from my work and family, the pressure of adult reality changed things for me. I caught a glimpse of what his life was really like, and I wished I had known him better. I even wished that I could live a life and have a marriage he would be proud of. Yet, while I was honest with myself about this thought, I ran past any break time I had scheduled because there was no time for self-pity. This was the simple, but all-encompassing, world of hard work. There was a job to do.

He's gone, but today—this day—we were on a mission. We were together.

* * *

The last thing to come out of the shop was the last thing my father ever built: the fresh looking pine carpenter's box I had found the plans in four months earlier. His aluminum contractor's clipboard also had been in there. I hoisted the box to my belt line and decided to put it down on the corner of the studio's foundation between the garage and the gang boxes. I felt sad momentarily as I exhumed the last thing from deep in the heart of my father's shop, the last thing from the last place he was. The last place he was truly him.

This box was part of him—because anything built with love for the thing itself and care for the craft of building it well becomes part of the one who built it. This was a fine thing, something that required the shelter and care of indoor living, and I immediately thought of giving it to my daughters. Perhaps if he were still alive, my father would have given this to Laura and Kelly himself. Instead of handing each one a birthday card with a

$50 U.S. savings bond—his usual gift. He might have given them the box, their cards and bonds inside. I carefully rested it on the corner of the concrete block pony-wall and lifted the lid. His clipboard was still in there, glinting dully as it reflected dim light, and I reached for it.

It was a weary aluminum contractor's clipboard, scratched and bent. Looking at it here, in this place, with sweat pouring down my back and beading on my forehead, my hands still trembling from activity. Seeing his handwriting on paper had snapped the bands of memory, which now spilled loose in my mind.

If he were a missionary, this boxy metal clipboard would have been my father's bible. It sat next to him on the seat of his truck every day of his life, and he took it with a tape measure and schoolboy pencil to every estimate he ever gave. He carried that muted silver box with him and wrote notes on the voluminous pages that were tucked under the lid for as long as I can remember. It makes me think twice about my laptop and cell phone and wonder how he ran his business, much less ran it well.

There were papers on top, creased and curled both by the tension of the clip and the pressure of the pencil in his hand. Inside it, there were more papers and a cloth-bound bookkeeper's tablet that looked even older than him, had he been alive. At first glance there were lots of seemingly insignificant notes, and a few sketches, but they looked familiar. As I looked closer though, I got the feeling that this wasn't his typically bad filing system of old estimates and invoices. It was something more.

A carpenter's notebook is usually a hunk of wood or old packing material—anything you can find to write on, really—that carpenters take jobsite notes on. You usually find things like drawings or materials lists, a to-do list, or even a change order form from a customer.

My father's notebook contained all the typical site drawings you'd find scrawled on a piece of 2x6 or scrap of $1/2$-inch plywood—a gate layout, framing diagrams with headers and king studs, drawings for fence post layouts, etc. It was my dad's take on "tricks of the trade."

He structured the handwritten entries similarly to other jobsite notes I'd seen him take while working summers with him. I could tell from the job name that he wrote most of this book during the summer after my senior year in high school, when we worked together building his first house. Stashed inside the clipboard in no particular order, each of the entries was built the same:

```
JOB NAME:
PROJECT:
HOW-TO:
COMMENTS:
```

It became clear to me where I had seen this before. The schematic for the toolbox that I built along with the storage trunks over the winter must have come from here, must have been torn out of the notebook—almost like he knew I'd take this project on. But as I investigated further, I saw that the notes on these entries were different. They were more detailed. The Project entries read like a rough draft for a home improvement manual you'd find spread open on a garage workbench. Each entry started with a detailed how-to and a photograph of the finished project.

Deciphering his penmanship on the precipice of that short foundation wall dropped every other thought from my mind. I had to see what he had written, to find out what it was, but the day had run out of sunlight, making the pages harder to see. I was already lost in my father's metered block letters recalling notes he used to leave on scrap pieces of pine or drywall for himself or us around the house so he wouldn't forget. I leafed through the crinkled paper long ago stamped with the seal of a graphite carpenter's pencil and went inside to read. I thought of sitting on that wall but found that I had already started moving up the back walk, reading and lifting old pages for a peek ahead as I went. I opened the door to the house without really looking up from the clipboard, and went inside to find out more.

CHAPTER 4

RISE AND RUN

*It is in naming your goal—a specific goal—
that you draw yourself to the event
horizon of success and meaning.*

JOB NAME:
 PELLETIER
PROJECT:
 DECK STAIRS

FIGURING—AND FAILING TO CORRECTLY
FIGURE—STAIR STRINGERS SHOWS ME
SOMETHING ABOUT HOW THE WORLD
WORKS.

IT SHOWS ME MY PLACE IN IT. IT SHOWS
ME THAT AS A CARPENTER AND A MAN, I
AM FLAWED. IT ALSO SHOWS ME THAT I
CAN OVERCOME THOSE FLAWS. WHILE I
CAN DO MUCH OF MY JOB WITHOUT
THINKING UNTIL MY BRAIN HURTS, LAYING
OUT STAIR STRINGERS ISN'T ONE OF
THOSE EASIER THINGS. IT'S A HURDLE.
YET, WHILE I STRUGGLE WITH THEM, I
HEAR AN OLD BOSS'S VOICE: "IT'S NOT
DONE UNTIL IT'S DONE RIGHT, GIDEON.
THAT GOES DOUBLE FOR STAIRS. DO IT
AGAIN. THIS TIME, FIGURE OUT HOW TO DO
IT RIGHT."

HOW-TO:

IF YOU'RE A BETTER MATHEMATICIAN THAN I AM (AND EVERYONE IS), THEN CALCULATING STAIR STRINGERS MIGHT SEEM EASY. YOU CAN PLUG THE TOTAL RISE AND THE TOTAL RUN INTO THE EQUATION, CONVERT THE RESULTING DECIMALS TO INCHES, DOUBLE CHECK ALL THE VARIABLES (LIKE FINISHED FLOOR THICKNESSES), AND BE DONE WITH IT. ME? I'VE STRUGGLED WITH CALCULATING GOOD STRINGERS SINCE I STARTED BUILDING.

IT SEEMS LIKE NO MATTER HOW CAREFUL I AM OR HOW MANY TIMES I CHECK MY MATH AND ALL THE OTHER VARIABLES, SOMETHING GOES WRONG. AND SINCE I CUT STAIRS INFREQUENTLY AND FOR ODD RISES, I DON'T GET MUCH PRACTICE. FOR THOSE REASONS, I'VE BUILT IN HOMEGROWN FAIL-SAFES THAT SAVE WASTED TIME, MONEY, AND A TANTRUM I CAN USE SOMEWHERE ELSE. IT TAKES EXTRA EFFORT ON THE FRONT-

END, BUT SAVES TRIPLE THAT EFFORT—
AND TIME AT THE END OF THE DAY.

PERFECT STAIR STRINGERS ARE
IMPORTANT BECAUSE YOUR FOOT CAN
DETECT A 1/8" DIFFERENCE BETWEEN
STAIR TREADS. HAS YOUR FOOT EVER
CAUGHT ON THE FLOOR, ALMOST TRIPPING
YOU, AS YOU WALK ACROSS A SHOPPING
MALL OR DOWN AN AIRPORT CONCOURSE?
IT CATCHES ON A SLIGHT IMPERFECTION
IN THE FLOOR THAT YOUR EYES CAN'T
SEE—BUT YOUR FOOT CAN.

IN OTHER WORDS, AFTER CLIMBING OR
DESCENDING A FEW STAIRS, YOUR FOOT
EXPECTS THE REST OF THEM TO BE THE
SAME AS THE FIRST FEW. WHEN THEY'RE
NOT, THAT'S A "TRIP-STEP."

IN MY CARPENTRY BOOKS, LAYING OUT A
SUN-DECK STAIR STRINGER LOOKS SIMPLE:
THE STRINGER NEEDS TO CARRY THE
STAIRS UP X-INCHES (SAY, FROM THE
LAWN TO THE TOP OF THE DECK BOARDS)
AND THE STRINGER NEEDS TO PROJECT Y-

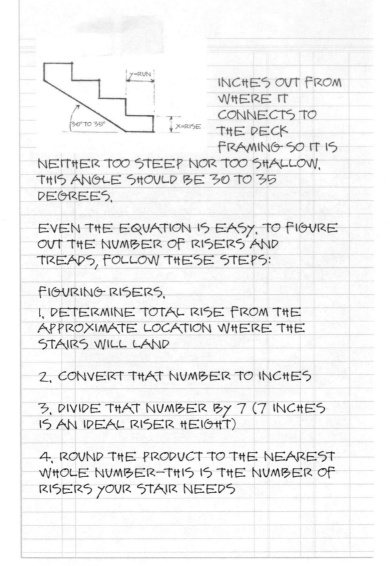

INCHES OUT FROM WHERE IT CONNECTS TO THE DECK FRAMING SO IT IS NEITHER TOO STEEP NOR TOO SHALLOW. THIS ANGLE SHOULD BE 30 TO 35 DEGREES.

EVEN THE EQUATION IS EASY. TO FIGURE OUT THE NUMBER OF RISERS AND TREADS, FOLLOW THESE STEPS:

FIGURING RISERS.

1. DETERMINE TOTAL RISE FROM THE APPROXIMATE LOCATION WHERE THE STAIRS WILL LAND

2. CONVERT THAT NUMBER TO INCHES

3. DIVIDE THAT NUMBER BY 7 (7 INCHES IS AN IDEAL RISER HEIGHT)

4. ROUND THE PRODUCT TO THE NEAREST WHOLE NUMBER—THIS IS THE NUMBER OF RISERS YOUR STAIR NEEDS

EASY ENDS THERE FOR ME. UNLESS YOUR DECK HEIGHT MEETS THE CRITERIA ON A STAIR TABLE (SIMILAR TO THE SQUARE ROOT TABLES IN THE BACK OF AN 8TH-GRADE MATH BOOK), YOU'VE GOT SOME ADJUSTING TO DO TO MAKE SURE THE STAIRS FIT AND THE TREADS SIT LEVEL, WITHOUT SO MUCH AS 1/8" DIFFERENCE BETWEEN THEM, SO ALL OF THIS ABOVE IS AN ESTIMATE, NOT THE FINAL LAYOUT.

USE 7"—BUT NO MORE THAN 8"—AS A BASELINE FOR THE RISER HEIGHT. IT'S JUST A BASELINE NUMBER, HOWEVER, BECAUSE YOU WILL HAVE TO TWEAK THE RISER HEIGHT AFTER YOU KNOW HOW MANY THERE ARE. IN OTHER WORDS, 7" RISERS ARE PROBABLY NOT GOING TO FIT EXACTLY INTO YOUR DECK HEIGHT—OR TOTAL RISE. THEREFORE, YOU HAVE TO DIVIDE WHAT'S LEFT OVER INTO EACH RISER. HERE'S A VERY BASIC EXAMPLE TO ILLUSTRATE THE TECHNIQUE:

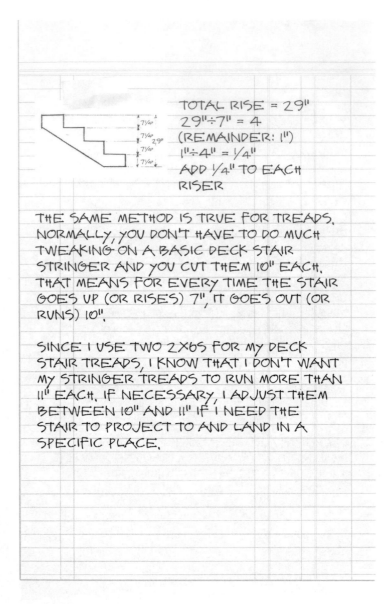

TOTAL RISE = 29"

29" ÷ 7" = 4

(REMAINDER: 1")

1" ÷ 4" = 1/4"

ADD 1/4" TO EACH

RISER

THE SAME METHOD IS TRUE FOR TREADS.
NORMALLY, YOU DON'T HAVE TO DO MUCH
TWEAKING ON A BASIC DECK STAIR
STRINGER AND YOU CUT THEM 10" EACH.
THAT MEANS FOR EVERY TIME THE STAIR
GOES UP (OR RISES) 7", IT GOES OUT (OR
RUNS) 10".

SINCE I USE TWO 2X6S FOR MY DECK
STAIR TREADS, I KNOW THAT I DON'T WANT
MY STRINGER TREADS TO RUN MORE THAN
11" EACH. IF NECESSARY, I ADJUST THEM
BETWEEN 10" AND 11" IF I NEED THE
STAIR TO PROJECT TO AND LAND IN A
SPECIFIC PLACE.

REMINDERS

- RE-ESTIMATE WHERE A STAIR WILL
LAND ON THE GROUND AFTER YOU'VE
ESTIMATED HOW MANY RISERS AND
TREADS YOU'LL NEED. RE-MEASURE
YOUR TOTAL RISE FROM THAT POINT. IF
THE GRASS OR YARD PITCHES AWAY,
EVEN A FEW INCHES, YOUR STAIR WILL
BE A MILE OFF BECAUSE YOU'LL HAVE
THE WRONG TOTAL RISE.

- CUT YOUR TREAD THICKNESS OFF THE
BOTTOM OF THE FIRST RISER ONLY. IN
OTHER WORDS, KNOCK OFF 1 1/2" FOR 2-
BY, AND 1" FOR 5/4 DECKING.

- A GOOD RULE OF THUMB IS THAT THE
SUM OF YOUR RISER AND YOUR TREAD
SHOULD EQUAL 17" TO 18", NOT
EXCEEDING 18".

- USE 2X12 FOR YOUR STRINGER STOCK.
IT'S BEEFY AND WON'T BOUNCE WHEN
YOU RUN UP THEM WITH AN ARMLOAD OF
GROCERIES.

- THE FINISHED STAIR SHOULD BE NO LESS THAN 3-FEET WIDE. ANYTHING LESS AND TWO PEOPLE CAN'T SHARE IT, YOU CAN'T CARRY LARGE ITEMS UP IT TO THE DECK (LIKE A LARGE GRILL OR FURNITURE), AND IT FEELS LIKE YOU'RE ON A LADDER. PLUS, IT'S BUILDING CODE IN MANY PLACES.

- USE 3 STRINGERS—LEFT, RIGHT, AND CENTER. LOTS OF TOWNS LET YOU LEAVE OUT THE CENTER STRINGER, BUT WALKING A 3-STRINGER STAIR IS THE DIFFERENCE BETWEEN FUNCTION AND PERFORMANCE. IN OTHER WORDS, 2-STRINGER STAIRS WORK, BUT THEY FEEL HOLLOW AND BOUNCY. BUILD IT BETTER FIRST. IT'S ALWAYS EASIER.

- USE A TEST PIECE (I'VE HEARD THESE CALLED "BETA" PIECES) BEFORE CUTTING YOUR STOCK. I USE A PIECE OF 1X12 #2 COMMON PINE OR

EVEN LEFTOVER PLYWOOD AS A BETA
BEFORE I CUT INTO MORE EXPENSIVE
2-BY STOCK. ALSO, THE 1-BY IS LIGHT
AND EASY TO MOVE AROUND AND
ADJUST. USING A TEST PIECE WILL
ALSO PHYSICALLY ILLUSTRATE HOW FAR
I'M INEVITABLY OFF.

I DO MY BEST ON THE CALCULATIONS, THEN
USE MY FRAMING SQUARE TO LAY OUT MY
LINES. I USE MY CIRCULAR SAW TO MAKE
THE PLUMB AND LEVEL CUTS ONLY ON THE
TEST PIECE. I HOLD IT UP WHERE IT SHOULD
GO AND IT USUALLY SHOWS ME HOW FAR
OFF I AM—WHICH I CAN THEN MEASURE
PHYSICALLY, ELIMINATING AS MUCH MATH
AS POSSIBLE. IF IT'S 1 1/2" HIGH, I KNOW I
NEED TO ELIMINATE A TOTAL OF 1 1/2"
DIVIDED EQUALLY AMONG EACH RISER. IT'S
THE SAME IF I'M SHORT, EXCEPT THAT I
ADD EQUALLY TO EACH RISER (WHICH
MIGHT ALSO MEAN ADDING A TREAD).

ALSO, ON THE TEST PIECE, I CUT IT ONE
RISER HIGH (WHICH MAKES IT THE SAME
HEIGHT AS THE DECK FRAMING, INSTEAD

OF ONE RISER LOWER, AS IT SHOULD BE).
THIS WAY I CAN STILL SEE IF MY PLUMB
AND LEVEL CUTS ARE ON OR NOT. IF THEY
MISS, I CAN SOMETIMES USE THE BETA
AGAIN BEFORE I HAVE TO THROW IT OUT.

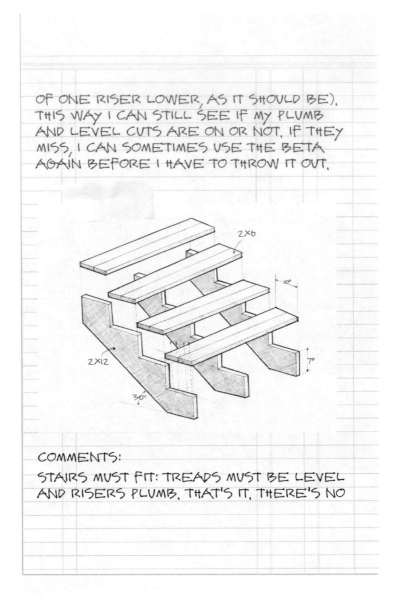

COMMENTS:

STAIRS MUST FIT: TREADS MUST BE LEVEL
AND RISERS PLUMB. THAT'S IT. THERE'S NO

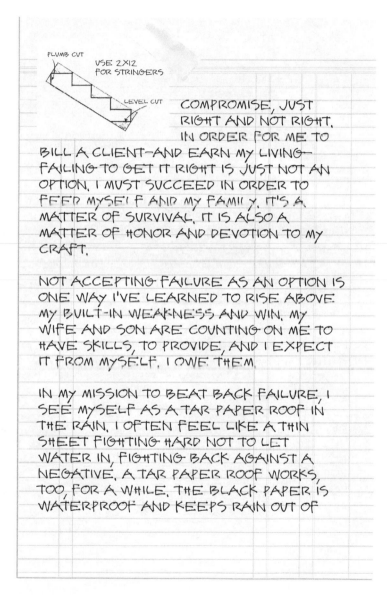

COMPROMISE, JUST
RIGHT AND NOT RIGHT.
IN ORDER FOR ME TO
BILL A CLIENT—AND EARN MY LIVING—
FAILING TO GET IT RIGHT IS JUST NOT AN
OPTION. I MUST SUCCEED IN ORDER TO
FEED MYSELF AND MY FAMILY. IT'S A
MATTER OF SURVIVAL. IT IS ALSO A
MATTER OF HONOR AND DEVOTION TO MY
CRAFT.

NOT ACCEPTING FAILURE AS AN OPTION IS
ONE WAY I'VE LEARNED TO RISE ABOVE
MY BUILT-IN WEAKNESS AND WIN. MY
WIFE AND SON ARE COUNTING ON ME TO
HAVE SKILLS, TO PROVIDE, AND I EXPECT
IT FROM MYSELF. I OWE THEM.

IN MY MISSION TO BEAT BACK FAILURE, I
SEE MYSELF AS A TAR PAPER ROOF IN
THE RAIN. I OFTEN FEEL LIKE A THIN
SHEET FIGHTING HARD NOT TO LET
WATER IN, FIGHTING BACK AGAINST A
NEGATIVE. A TAR PAPER ROOF WORKS,
TOO, FOR A WHILE. THE BLACK PAPER IS
WATERPROOF AND KEEPS RAIN OUT OF

THE BUILDING, AS LONG AS IT DOESN'T
RAIN OR BLOW TOO HARD. BUT, THE THIN
PAPER DRIES OUT AND EVENTUALLY
FAILS. MY BEAUTIFUL WIFE, WHO TREATS
ME LIKE A HERO, WOULD DISAGREE
ABOUT THE WAY I FEEL ABOUT MYSELF.
WHY SHE LOVES ME SO MUCH IS ONE OF
THE HAPPY MYSTERIES OF MY LIFE. SHE
MAKES ME FEEL WHOLE AND DRY AND
WARM WHEN WATER IS POURING IN. SHE
HAS TAUGHT ME THAT NOT ACCEPTING
FAILURE (AS MUCH WITH THE CONFIDENT,
COURAGEOUS SUNRISE IN HER EYES
WHEN THE NIGHT IS DARKEST AS WITH
HER WORDS), IS ONLY THE HALF OF IT.
FIGHTING AGAINST A NEGATIVE IS A
START SHE SAYS, AND A GOOD START.
RISING ABOVE AND GOING BEYOND YOUR
LIMITS REQUIRES MORE THAN THAT,
THOUGH. THE REAL WAY TO RISE ABOVE
IS TO CHASE A POSITIVE.

HISTORY'S GREAT EXPLORERS DIDN'T JUST
HOP ON THEIR SHIPS AND HOPE TO FIND
SOMETHING BY ACCIDENT. THEY STOOD OUT
INTO NEW WATER WITH A PLAN. THEY HAD

A SPECIFIC GOAL THAT GAVE MEANING TO
THEIR MISSIONS, TO THEMSELVES, AND TO
THEIR CREWS, BUILDING A PERFECT STAIR,
PLANNING A CAREER, OR MAKING THE
HONOR ROLL AREN'T EXACTLY SAILING
AROUND CAPE HORN OR HIKING ACROSS
ANTARCTICA, BUT THEY ARE GOALS WITH A
FIXED FOCUS. IT'S IN NAMING AND
FOCUSING ON YOUR SPECIFIC GOAL—I WANT
TO MEET THAT GIRL, I WANT TO GO TO
COLLEGE, I WANT THAT GATE DEAD ON
SQUARE—THAT YOU DRAW YOURSELF
BEYOND MERELY "NOT FAILING" TO THE
EVENT-HORIZON OF SUCCESS AND
MEANING. MAYBE THE WHOLE DREAM
DOESN'T COME TRUE, BUT STRIVING TO
ATTAIN IT WITH SINGLE-MINDED FOCUS
BRINGS YOU CLOSER THAN YOU EVER
WOULD HAVE COME OTHERWISE. IT MAKES
YOUR LIFE BETTER.

LIVING TO AVOID A NEGATIVE—I DON'T
WANT TO FAIL, I DON'T WANT TO LOSE MY
JOB, I DON'T WANT TO GET HURT—IS
SAILING THE SHIP OF YOUR LIFE UPWIND.
YOU CAN DO IT, BUT IT'S AN INDIRECT,

HARD-TO-HOLD HEADING, PURSUING A
DEFINED POSITIVE-PERFECT PLUMB AND
LEVEL CUTS IN MY TINY CASE-IS A RUN
WITH THE WIND AND THE STRAIGHTEST
LINE BETWEEN TWO POINTS.

I'VE TACKED INTO THE WIND, GOING MORE
PORT AND STARBOARD THAN AHEAD OVER
MY LIFE. IT'S TIME TO CHANGE. IT'S TIME
TO FILL MY BOY'S SAILS AND HELP HIM
CHART HIS OWN COURSE.

"Skin it back to the bones," Dad would say, and I could hear his voice in my mind as I began the first day of real work, getting the ladder set up so I could climb to the roof and begin the tear-off. I finished lugging tools the day before and locked the lids on the gang boxes, and now I could start reading my father's notebook. Immediately, seeing his handwriting on a page reached inside me to a place I had forgotten about, a place of youth and hope and optimism, even during troubling times. He always looked forward, always looked to make ground, and did his best to enjoy the ground he was on while he grew. Skinning it back to the bones was his way of saying tear out all the old stuff that would make it difficult or impossible to tie the old structure in with new work. The decayed shingles, rotten siding, chewed-up exterior trim, even damaged framing—it all had to go. This would get me back to the frame, the building's skeleton. At that point, I would be able to square-up the existing structure, if necessary, and progress from dependable control points.

With a few pages of his words resting in my mind and finding a home in my heart, I did what I could to start thinking like him, then approached the job the way I figured he would have. Buildings go in from the sill plates to the shingle caps, so I would take this one down in reverse and start stripping the roof.

This was it. I had built the toolboxes and set up the jobsite. I had gone over my plans as best I could—and as many times as I could—and I thought I knew what I was in for. But that was just prep work, all theory and thinking. This was the real deal. This was action. This work didn't require a pencil; it required muscles and ladders, calluses and steel demolition tools. This structure was the last thing standing of what was truly his, the last physical daily reminder that he was here. Tearing this building apart truly relegated all that he had ever been to the distance of our memories, to black and white photographs in old albums, and to the love in our hearts. This building that had sheltered so much of his world for so many years was coming down. My mind was packed with images of what was gone, what was disappearing, and what new thing we would grow in its place. This moment was so pure and incorruptible that I thought even Rachael, who really loved my father and enjoyed laughing with him, could see beyond the prison walls of her emotional comfort zone and feel this, see that an important yesterday was ending not with the flip of a calendar page, but with the strike of steel on wood. This was essential. It was so very real. My heart was packed with love for my father. I missed him in this moment for so many reasons.

I admired him when he was alive and sought his counsel in dark times, but I never really knew him, never really understood how intensely he worked to live an enlightened, ethical, and ultimately happy life. I never had a sense of how courageously he rose to meet challenge after challenge in a difficult and arduous life. And, I never knew how living this way made him the man I knew and ultimately revered.

When he died two years ago, the changes already under way in my life quickened. It seemed like Laura and Kelly began growing faster and more independent than I ever thought possible. I entered the last half of my life, and while that happened, the growing distance between Rachael and me spanned a gap so wide that we needed to live apart from each other now. It occurred to me that in my heart of hearts I had taken on this project to escape my life. I had to be honest about that. And that clear, honest thought had coalesced out of the frenzy of lugging boxes and boards out of my father's shop and interring them in the plywood boxes that flanked the rear property line of the half-acre yard. I was here to escape.

* * *

I swung the leather toolbelt around my waist, metal tools shifting in unison with each other inside the bags, and cinched the silver roller buckle tight over the hard hip bones hiding under my soft belly. I could feel the mass of leather and steel pulling at my skin as I leaned the orange fiberglass extension ladder against the age-stained gutter.

Next, I grabbed the shingle shovel (sort of a square-edged garden spade with jagged teeth for a leading edge and a fulcrum on the back for prying up shingles and nails) and headed up to the ridge, or roof peak.

On the first step up the roof, my left leg pushed hard enough that if I were on the ground, I would've jumped two feet in the air. Instead, my body moved weakly up the roof. Another big huff, another step, and I gained momentum, the tools in my bags rattling alongside like loose car parts as I strained up to the peak. I could feel my Achilles' tendons stretching much more than I thought they should as just the toes of my boots clung onto the crumbling shingle tabs.

Once at the ridge, I propped one foot on top to hook myself there. I walked pigeon-toed to the back end of the building, one foot on each side of the ridge, and raised the shingle stripper, its teeth poised to take the first, almost ceremonial, bite out of the building. As my weight shifted, I could feel the little ball bearings of asphalt move under my boot, and I slipped. My foot didn't react as much as my heart—and my skin! Every pore in my body felt like it doubled in size and every hair grew half again its height before it ramrodded on end, stiff as a Greek column. My muscles convulsed cable-tight and I could feel my groin and hamstrings squeeze my feet to either side of the roof ridge like pliers on a bolt head, but it wasn't enough. My left leg kicked out from below me and my body fell. Inside a second, my chest hit the peak. The steep roof speared air from my lungs. I finally clutched the rocky grit of the shingles to my chest and stopped my fall.

This was big mistake number one: the 8-in-12 roof was flat enough to walk *up,* but too steep to walk *down* standing up. Eight-in-twelve means that for every foot the roof travels toward the center of the building, it goes up 8 inches. In other words, I was standing on a 35-degree angle about 20 feet in the air. That's not so bad if you're skiing, but walking on a million tiny ball bearings to the edge of a drop—that's another story.

The roof was too steep to walk, so in order to get down, I sat on my ass. I pried up and grabbed the ends of those withering shingle tabs with my fingertips. I hoped holding the shingles would stop me if I started sliding. Then I scooted down on my butt like a toddler descends stairs before she can really walk. If I started sliding there'd be no way to stop and I'd have a front row seat to watch the ground rush up at me with unstoppable force. I was so scared I could feel my teeth sweat.

Raising the shingle tabs and sliding the fingers of my sweat soaked hands beneath them cut my knuckles open each time. I held those tabs so tightly I felt I would crush them in my grip as my feet and ass threatened to skid down the roof and over the gutter. Scoot and grab, scoot and grab. I reached the ladder with my toes, then my entire foot. Now if I could just get around it without kicking it down. I pulled myself around the ladder and all but hugged it while my heart slowed its stampede in my chest.

"Holy shit. I made it," I muttered.

I could hear my tough-as-nails father in my head chiding me already, "Rookieeeee."

Before I could check to see if anybody had seen my terrified descent, I heard the "Beep! Beep! Beep!" of a truck backing up. The truck driver's face appeared in his vertical truck mirror as he expertly backed the enormous lumber truck up the narrow driveway. He was six hours early with the framing materials, and I hoped like a teenager who realizes his fly is down at the prom, that he didn't see my embarrassing display.

The load looked a lot different in real life than it did on my paper list. Heavier, for one. Before I could collect myself and walk over to the truck, the driver had loosened the straps that held the load down and threw them over to the other side of the vehicle. He met me at the back of the truck, stuffing a yellow paper in my hand. I looked at the two-page carbon copy materials list like I was reading it. But it was far too long to compare to my original order while he waited, so I swallowed and hoped they got it right. I swallowed a second time, too, because I hoped *I* got it right. It looked like way more 2x4s than I'd ever need. My winter's night daydream of perfectly laying out every stud and window opening and quickly popping them into place already looked harder to achieve than I had thought—even after thinking about it for four months.

"I hope I can do this," I half-whispered to myself.

No sooner had I signed the paper and handed it back than the driver was at the side of the truck, pulling levers. As the steel flatbed rose like a dump truck body on stainless steel hydraulic rams and the enormous cube of steel-banded planks slid off with a 2-ton thud, the bottom of my stomach fell out.

The driver came back around the truck with more papers in hand. "This is Gid Herlihy's old place, isn't it?"

"Yes," I replied, embarrassed to admit that the son of Gideon Herlihy would ever scuttle ridiculously down a roof. "This is Gideon Herlihy's old place."

"Good man," the driver said and I handed him back his signed copy of the delivery form. Before walking to the cab of his truck, he reached into a steel box on the side, beneath the bed, and came out with two fistfuls of pencils. "These aren't free anymore like they used to be. Things have changed. But they're still free for old Gid." He dropped a handful of carpenter and schoolboy pencils on the lumber pile, then hopped back in the truck and dieseled down the driveway.

The simple answer to my problem of walking the roof was to use roof brackets and walk boards. I dug the brackets out of storage, nailed them through the shingles to the roof deck, and spread 2x10 stock across them. Now I could stand with my feet level, peel the shingles, and let the debris slide below me to the waiting dump trailer I had staged to collect the falling junk.

With the appropriate safety precautions in place, I could finally get to work. I could finally take the first ceremonial bite out of the old shed and start a new chapter, but I was so pissed off at myself that there wasn't much of a ceremony anymore. I looked down from my 20-foot-high perch at the 4,000 pounds of framing lumber in my mother's driveway, felt the weight of the shovel in my hands, and sensed the size of the project before me—really—for the first time. Even though unloading the shop had gone well, it wasn't even lunchtime on the first real day and I was already three hours behind where I wanted to be. Who was I kidding? Rachael was right. It had been more than 20 years since I'd been on a roof, and even then my father was there, coaching me and telling me it'd be OK.

At that moment, my coffee wore off and the gas gauge on my flabby body ticked past "E" without warning. I didn't usually drink coffee by the gallon, and I usually ate a whole lot more before doing nothing to burn those calories. In just a few short days, my pattern of living had shifted 180 degrees, and I was burning energy like a man on fire without re-supplying. I hit the wall like a crash test car in a 20-mile-per-hour-test and had to sit down and get my bearings or risk falling again. I took a long pull from the water bottle I kept at the far end of the staging-plank, and looked out over the boxes, foundation, and yard to the fence and trees beyond. Slowly, the fog of exhaustion lifted. At first, I thought about nothing, and in the haze of my physical wipe out, that moment of a truly empty mind was a relief. I coasted through those seconds until my brain allowed itself to think again. The thoughts that came at first weren't gentle; I was suddenly seized by the problems that tortured me. I thought about Rachael, and wished that my life were different and not so tiresome to carry around.

My marriage, and by extension my role as the father I once dreamed I'd be, was failing. Nothing made sense. My wife had pulled away from me and although we lived under the same roof, we moved around like roommates who were waiting for their lease to be up so they could move out on each other. We were not the lovers we once were, not the passionate people who created two beautiful daughters to love and hold and let go of as they grew. We were no longer two people growing old together. We were simply growing old, and the wasted time of a marriage being ignored to death coursed under the bridge and burned my insides with a fire that even a river couldn't extinguish.

I got up. This wasn't coffee, this wasn't a nice snack. Fuckin' gallons of adrenaline shot me to my feet this time. Fear—a fear that can go straight to hell—had held me down long enough.

Now, I didn't just want to tear the shingles off systematically, I wanted to kill them. I positioned myself for the first strike, and as I raised the shingle shovel to take its first bite, I was suddenly conscious of something about my father when he was raising stair stringers into place in Arthur Pelletier's house. In that split second I remembered an entry from his journal that I had read the night before. Just like my father, my hero, who battled with those complicated stairs in the complicated house built not by two carpenters skilled and engaged in their craft and driven by profit, but by one man and his boy, I would battle this roof until I won. And "won" didn't mean until the shingles were in the trailer. "Won" meant that they were in the landfill. My father taught me something at Arthur's house, not with words, but with deeds.

He taught me that something isn't done until it's done and there's nothing left to do. When there's nothing left to do, then you're done. I never once heard my father say, "I'm finished, except...." He was a closer, and I came to revere him for that in this hour-long second. He got it done.

I knew how to close a sale and knock down a deal on a $2 million condo with a skyline view, but that was different. You can't fall off carpet, you can't shoot a 3-inch-long ring-shank nail into your arm with a cell phone. Here, on the roof and way above the ground, being brave matters. Here you surpass a point of paper and calculation. You're totally involved in this because you need to bring both body and soul to it. One can't do without the other. This was real and by real, I mean really real.

Another thought occurred to me in that moment: I had grown a lot that summer in Arthur Pelletier's house. And I felt that my father was still down there cutting those stairs, still battling. He was gone, but I knew this: he didn't leave me.

* * *

The spring sun beamed down on me like it was proud for having created such a perfect piece of weather, and an eleven-mile-per-hour northeasterly cooled what would otherwise have been a sticky summer-like day. The air was dry and perfect, and I found an agitated rhythm hacking at the roof and pulling up swaths of three-tab shingle, woven together like the folded-down cardboard bottle dividers you'd find in a case of longnecks. I pried the shingles free and lifted them off the roof with both my shingle shovel and my hands, and whipped them down into the trailer. Finally, somewhat accustomed to being on a roof again, my mind was able to wander a little and I found it back in Arthur's house again.

My dad had me nailing off the second floor deck sheathing in the warm sun while he figured the stair stringers below on the first floor. Periodically, he'd call me over to hold the end of his tape measure before he'd go back to his cut station and scratch out something he had already written. I went back to nailing (and working on my tan), losing myself in the repetitious simplicity of hand-driving fistfuls of 8 penny nails through 3/4-inch plywood into Douglas-fir joists.

By the time he called me over to the stairwell opening again I had driven about 5 pounds of nails. Sweat was pouring out of my young body, and the veins in my right arm were pulsing blood to my lithe muscles; he had left me alone nailing for a long time. This time when he called me over, instead of holding the tape for him, he had cut a piece of 1x12 with plumb and level cuts on each end, the test piece his diary talks about. "How's that plumb cut look along the header?" he asked from below, looking up with blazing eyes through the stair opening and into the blue summer sky that soaked our second floor deck with light. "It looks OK," I said not quite definitively. He wrestled the board another inch to get it right on the mark he had made on the first floor plywood, having held it off the mark on purpose to test what I'd say. "Does it look perfect?" he asked impatiently once he readjusted the board.

I laid on my belly on the second floor deck and reached down into the opening to hold the test. While I looked at the meeting between the test and the framing, he sprung up into the opening on a step ladder so fast I thought he flew up. "There!" he said, twisting the board a little and locking eyes with me, "You see how that plumb-cut aligns perfectly with the header? Come on!" I saw it and understood the lightning look in his eyes as much with my heart as in my head. Then he dialed down his intensity and smiled at me, explaining carefully and gently what he had wanted me to see—and why he wanted me to see it....

Twenty-five years later standing on his roof, I heard him again. I could feel that fire in his eyes from inside me somewhere. I could feel his unstoppable will to get a job done properly, as if it were part of my cell structure. I know now that while I worked up on that sunny deck he was wrestling with the math for those stringers. He had built two floors of that house dead-on accurate, but this seemingly simple thing cost him half a day of time and effort. I also know he screwed it up, because I can remember hearing vignettes of profanity between nail head strikes with my big framing hammer. Then I heard nothing, then the circ saw, then nothing. Finally he called me over to the dark hole, requiring my eyes to readjust.

Today, I stand in the center of my springy walk board, still afraid that it will break and I'll slide 10 feet down the asphalt roof before free-falling another 10 feet to the ground. I stood just down from the peak. It took me a minute to realize that until this moment in my life, I'd been climbing those stairs my father built in Arthur Pelletier's house 25 years before. I'd been walking all this time on his perfect layout built with passion and care and every ounce of his sweat and energy. And I'd been walking without a single trip-step.

But now, here I was alone, somehow bridged between the end and the beginning, starting at the end to go backward before I could start again. I felt the hickory handle of the shingle shovel in my soft hands and knew I'd have friction blisters before the calluses showed up. I felt my fear and my rage come into balance while neither subsided.

The teeth of the shovel bit in under the asphalt shingle tabs. I pressed down on the handle, the shovel's fulcrum crushed shingles beneath it and the nails squealed painfully out of the 1x8 sheathing. The loose bundle of cracked and torn asphalt slid between my flexing walk board and the roof down into the waiting trailer. With each successive strike and nail pop was one more moment I stood on that roof. It was one more second I didn't fall. It was one more minute to feel comfortable in an uncomfortable place, and it was one more moment to strip away the fear that consumed me.

CHAPTER 5

CONTROL POINTS

*Completing this project properly
is about finding answers,
real answers.*

JOB NAME: PELLETIER
PROJECT: TILE FLOOR LAYOUT

MY SON GREW UP RIGHT IN FRONT OF ME
TODAY AT PELLETIER'S PLACE. HE TOOK
HIS FIRST LONE STEPS INTO ADULTHOOD.
TODAY MY SON BECAME A MAN.

BRENDAN CAME TO ME AND TOOK THE
HOOK-END OF THE CHALK LINE IN HIS
RIGHT HAND. HE WALKED WITH THE BLUE
COTTON STRING HELD LOOSELY IN HIS
FINGERS ACROSS THE 16-FOOT-WIDE ROOM
TO THE PENCIL MARK HE HAD MADE ON
THE PLYWOOD SUB-FLOOR. I HAD MADE A
CORRESPONDING MARK ON MY SIDE OF THE
ROOM AND WE CROUCHED TO PULL THE
LINE TAUT BETWEEN US. AS HE BENT
DOWN TO PLACE THE STRING AND WE
TIGHTENED IT, I LOOKED DOWN AT MY MARK,
THEN SLOWLY DOWN THE LINE TO HIM.

I KNEW HIS END OF THE STRING WAS ON
THE MARK BY THE WAY HIS EYES ROSE
FROM HIS WORK TO MEET MINE. HE
REACHED FOR THE STRING, PREPARING

TO PLUCK IT, AND IN THAT MOMENT I SAW THAT HE HAD GROWN UP SO GODDAM FAST. HIS EYES HELD MINE, NO LONGER A BOY'S, NO LONGER A CHILD'S. MY SON THE MAN EXAMINED MY EYES FOR THE READY SIGNAL I HAD GIVEN HIM A THOUSAND TIMES BEFORE. BUT INSTEAD, I HELD HIM THERE, IN THIS LAST MOMENT OF HIS BOYHOOD. I WANTED SO MUCH FOR JUST ONE MORE SECOND TO BE HIS POP, HIS DADDY BEFORE HE LEFT HIS MOM AND ME AND WENT AWAY ON HIS LIFE'S JOURNEY, BEFORE I TRULY BECAME HIS OLD MAN.

HE HELD THE LINE OFF THE FLOOR, CREATING A STRING ARCH—ONE OF THE STRONGEST, MOST ANCIENT SHAPES IN ARCHITECTURE. WHAT HE READ AS THE SIGNAL IN MY EYES TO SNAP THE LINE WAS REALLY MY SOUL DAMMING BACK A FLOOD OF TEARS. THE STRING LEFT HIS FINGERS AND LEFT A LINEAR MAKER'S MARK ON THE FLOOR. IT SNAPPED TO THE PLYWOOD, WHICH SOUNDED MORE LIKE A POWER LINE-SNAPPING THUNDERBOLT TO ME THAN THE DRY PLUCK OF COTTON

STRING HITTING BOOT-BLACKENED
THREE-QUARTER PLY, INSTANTLY HE HAD
HIS TAPE OUT AND MOVED TO PULL THE
NEXT MEASUREMENT, HE QUIETLY WENT
AT THE WORK THAT HAD BECOME PART OF
HIM NOW WHILE I SLOWLY REELED THE
STRING BACK INTO MY CHALK BOX.

I CROUCHED THERE, SO PROUD I COULD
BARELY HOLD IT IN, I WIPED MY EYES
WHEN HE WASN'T LOOKING, SO HAPPY TO
WITNESS THIS MOMENT. I WAS REVERENT
TO WHATEVER FORCE GRANTED ME THE
GIFT OF BEING HERE FOR IT, I WATCHED
THE BOY MARCH ACROSS THE FLOOR WE
HAD BUILT INTO THE MANHOOD OF HIS LIFE.
HE WALKED INTO A WORLD WHERE HIS OLD
POP—AND HIS MOM—WAS NO LONGER THERE
FOR HIM AT THE END OF HIS DAY, BUT NOW
A PHONE CALL OR A LETTER AWAY.
HE'D BE AT COLLEGE IN A MONTH,
ALREADY ONE-UP ON ME, AND I'M
REMINDED OF ALL THE MISTAKES I'VE
MADE, BECAUSE I DIDN'T KNOW THAT I
COULD PLAN MY LIFE.

HOW-TO:

THE TRICK TO LAYING A NICE TILE FLOOR IS TO CENTER IT IN THE SPACE OR SPACES THAT GET TILE. SINCE YOU CAN'T DO THAT WITH THE ACTUAL TILES, YOU HAVE TO DO IT WITH A TAPE MEASURE, CHALK LINE, AND PENCIL.

1. FIND THE CENTER OF THE ROOM TO BE TILED ON BOTH A NORTH/SOUTH AND EAST/WEST AXIS BY MEASURING THE ROOM DIMENSION IN THREE PLACES ALONG EACH AXIS: LEFT, MIDDLE, RIGHT. ASSUMING THE ROOM IS SQUARE, SNAP CHALK LINES BETWEEN THE CENTERLINE MARKS OF THE FACING WALLS IN EACH AXIS, CREATING A CROSSHAIRS THROUGH THE CENTER OF THE ROOM. THIS IS WHERE YOU START SETTING TILES. IDEALLY, ONE TILE WILL FIT INTO EACH CORNER OF THE CROSSHAIRS AND THE PATTERN WILL RADIATE OUT FROM THAT POINT.

2. DETERMINE THE LENGTH OF A RUN OF FOUR TILES, INCLUDING SPACERS.

3. MEASURE FROM THE CENTER OF YOUR CROSSHAIRS TO ALL FOUR WALLS. DETERMINE HOW MANY UNITS OF FOUR TILES WILL FIT IN THAT MEASUREMENT. INCLUDE THE FRACTIONAL TILE THAT'S LEFT OVER. THE TILES USUALLY DON'T FIT EXACTLY. IF THE RESULT IS THAT YOU CAN FIT 12 TILES EACH WAY, WITH ABOUT 1/2 A TILE LEFT ON THE BORDER, THAT'S GOOD. 1/2 TILES ON THE BORDER LOOK OK.

4. IF YOU END UP WITH "SLIVERS"—TINY STRIPS OF TILES—THAT LOOKS BAD AND MUST BE FIXED.

- SOLUTION: ADJUST YOUR STARTING POINT BY MOVING A SINGLE TILE OVER THE CROSSHAIRS, AS IF THE CROSSHAIRS WOULD DIVIDE THE TILE INTO EQUAL QUADRANTS. RE-PULL THE MEASUREMENTS TO THE WALLS. OR SHIFT YOUR QUAD OF TILES SO THAT ONE AXIS IS DIVIDED IN HALF BY THE CROSSHAIRS.

- THE KEY HERE IS TO ALTER THE
CENTER; REDEFINE WHAT "CENTER"
MEANS, SO ULTIMATELY IT CAN BE
DEFINED BEAUTIFULLY (AND INVISIBLY)
BY THE BORDERS.

5. MAKE CERTAIN YOU END UP WITH
SIZEABLE TILES ON THE BORDERS IN
BOTH AXES, ADJUSTING NORTH/SOUTH AND
EAST/WEST TO AVOID SLIVERS AND GET
EQUAL SIZED TILES ON THE ROOM'S
EDGES. (NOTE: THE NORTH/SOUTH
BORDER TILES DON'T HAVE TO BE THE
SAME DIMENSION AS THE EAST/WEST
BORDER TILES, AND PROBABLY WON'T BE.
AS LONG AS N/S BORDER TILES ARE
EQUAL TO EACH OTHER AND E/W
BORDER TILES ARE EQUAL TO EACH
OTHER, THE JOB WILL LOOK RIGHT.

COMMENTS:

I WITNESSED MY SON'S JOURNEY INTO MANHOOD. MY LOVE FOR HIM FLOODED EVERY CELL IN MY BODY AND IT BROUGHT ME TO A DIFFERENT UNDERSTANDING OF WHAT A GOOD LAYOUT IS. JUST AS WE SNAPPED LINES FOR THE FUTURE LOCATIONS OF ARTHUR PELLETIER'S KITCHEN TILES, TILES THAT WOULD SPILL INTO OTHER ROOMS—ROOMS WHERE ALL OUR CONTROL POINTS CHANGED IN AN INSTANT—I HOPED THAT SOMEHOW THIS THIN BLUE COTTON LINE WOULD TETHER BRENDAN TO CONTROL POINTS, CONTROL POINTS THAT I HOPED WOULD GIVE HIS LIFE CONTEXT, MEANING, AND SENSE. I HOPED THAT, AS HE MOVED THROUGH THE NEW ROOMS OF HIS EXISTENCE, MAYBE ROOMS WHERE NOTHING ADDED UP, I HOPED HIS PAST—THAT THIS SUMMER—WOULD HELP HIM SOMEHOW. I HOPED HE WOULD LIVE HIS LIFE KNOWING THAT I WOULD WALK THROUGH FIRE FOR HIM.

NO MATTER HOW PROUD I AM OF MY BOY I AM LOSING HIM. I AM GROWING OLD.

SOMEWHERE BETWEEN SELF-PITY AND INCREDIBLE ANTICIPATION FOR BRENDAN'S VOYAGE, I HOPED THE CHALK LINE STRETCHED NOT JUST ACROSS THE FLOOR, BUT ACROSS A GENERATION AND OVER THE HORIZON OF HIS FUTURE. I HOPED WITH EVERYTHING INSIDE THAT IT WOULD STRETCH TO ME, TO A HAPPY TIME, AND TO PEACE IN HIS LIFE...A PEACE THAT I'M STRUGGLING HARD TO FIND.

I REGRET THAT I DID NOT HAVE THE WORDS TO TELL HIM ALL THIS EARLIER TODAY. MY BODY WAS BLASTED WITH EMOTION AND I KNEW IF I OPENED MY MOUTH I WOULD CRY. I CHOKED BACK THE FEELINGS AND THE TEARS. IT WAS ALL I COULD DO TO JUST TAKE IN EVERY SECOND, EVERY DETAIL OF THIS MOMENT.

THE LAYOUT FOR MY OWN LIFE HASN'T BEEN GREAT. I AM NOT THE MAN I THOUGHT I'D BE. FOR TOO MANY YEARS, I DID JUST ENOUGH TO GET BY—BUT NOT ENOUGH TO BE GOOD.

I REACTED—INSTEAD OF PRO-ACTED—TO
SITUATIONS IN MY CHAOTIC LIFE AND I WAS
UNAWARE THAT I HAD THE POWER TO
MANAGE HOW I LIVED. THE RESULT: I RAN
INTO THE SAME FAILURES OVER AND
OVER AGAIN. EVERY NEW STUPID MISTAKE
LEFT ME SURPRISED, ANGRY, AND WITH A
PROBLEM I HAD TO WORK MUCH HARDER AT
THAN NECESSARY TO UNDO.

FAILURE AND MY BEAUTIFUL WIFE KAY
WERE MY TWO GREAT TEACHERS: THE
TASKMASTER AND THE GENTLE SAGE,
WHO SHOWED ME HOW TO CHANGE AND
WHO TAUGHT ME THAT SO MANY OF LIFE'S
HURDLES DON'T NEED TO BE SO HIGH—IF
YOU MEASURE YOUR WORK SPACE
CAREFULLY BEFORE YOU START
INSTALLING TILES. THEY TAUGHT ME THAT
THESE MEASUREMENTS RAISE
QUESTIONS AND WILL FORCE ME TO LOOK
AHEAD AT THEIR IMPLICATIONS. WHILE I
CAN'T USE A TAPE MEASURE TO PREDICT
THE FUTURE OF MY LIFE LIKE I CAN
PREDICT WHERE TILES WILL LAND, THE
LOGIC WORKS. HERE'S WHAT I MEAN:

MEASURING YOUR LIFE MEANS ASKING—
THEN ANSWERING—HARD QUESTIONS. AM I
TRULY HAPPY? AM I CONSTANTLY
FRUSTRATED? IS THERE SOMETHING
WRONG HERE? IF I LAY THESE KITCHEN
TILES LIKE THIS, WILL THEY FLOW INTO
THE HALLWAY AND PANTRY LIKE THEY
GREW THERE? ANOTHER WAY OF SAYING
IT IS, HOW DO I FEEL NOW AND WILL I
FEEL DIFFERENTLY TOMORROW? SHOULD I
CONTINUE ON THIS PATH, WHATEVER IT IS?
OR, SHOULD I CHANGE DIRECTION? HAVING
A GOOD LAYOUT HELPS ANSWER THESE
QUESTIONS. IT GIVES THE ANSWERS
CONTEXT. I'VE ALSO FOUND THAT IT
TAKES COURAGE TO FACE THE REALITY
OF THESE MEASUREMENTS.

TOO MANY TIMES I HOOKED MY TAPE ON
SOMETHING—MEASURED IT—BUT DIDN'T
HAVE THE GUTS TO FACE WHAT THE
MEASUREMENTS MEANT. SO, I STEAMED
STRAIGHT INTO STORMS THAT WERE
AVOIDABLE. I LITERALLY ALMOST TILED
MYSELF INTO A CORNER. YEARS LATER, I
BUILT UP COURAGE. I BUILT UP

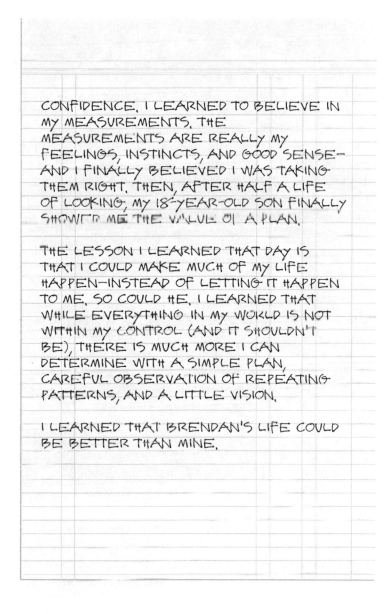

CONFIDENCE. I LEARNED TO BELIEVE IN MY MEASUREMENTS. THE MEASUREMENTS ARE REALLY MY FEELINGS, INSTINCTS, AND GOOD SENSE— AND I FINALLY BELIEVED I WAS TAKING THEM RIGHT. THEN, AFTER HALF A LIFE OF LOOKING, MY 18-YEAR-OLD SON FINALLY SHOWED ME THE VALUE OF A PLAN.

THE LESSON I LEARNED THAT DAY IS THAT I COULD MAKE MUCH OF MY LIFE HAPPEN—INSTEAD OF LETTING IT HAPPEN TO ME. SO COULD HE. I LEARNED THAT WHILE EVERYTHING IN MY WORLD IS NOT WITHIN MY CONTROL (AND IT SHOULDN'T BE), THERE IS MUCH MORE I CAN DETERMINE WITH A SIMPLE PLAN, CAREFUL OBSERVATION OF REPEATING PATTERNS, AND A LITTLE VISION.

I LEARNED THAT BRENDAN'S LIFE COULD BE BETTER THAN MINE.

Ripping the roof off and pulling all the siding down in thousands of small nail-popping eruptions spoke to my inner animal. Sweat gushed off my forehead, soaked my shirt, and dripped off the end of my nose like water from a downspout after a good rain.

The building stood with its ancient, age-blackened and bronzed skin: solid 1x6 and 1x8 pine planks nailed perpendicularly across the studs and rafters. For the first time since the 84-year-old house had been built—long before my father ever picked up a hammer and nails—the building's insides stood naked, exposed to the weather. Between the pine boards that had touched edge-to-edge and end-to-end in their sappy youth, I could now easily see through the gaps as the moisture evacuated the xylem and phloem of their desiccated vascular systems, shrinking the boards. You could put your eyeball to one of the gaps like a little kid peering through the slats of a stockade fence and see through the building.

Until plywood's mass availability in the 1950s, buildings were skinned or sheathed with one-by material. That skin, even when my father started building, let alone today, would be both wildly expensive, slow to install, and not as effective as many modern sheathing materials such as ½-inch plywood or $7/16$ Oriented Strand Board (OSB—a lot of homeowners call this stuff "particle board"). Whatever you use, its purpose is to give the frame rigidity and provide a nailing base. The skin, like a person's skin over muscles and skeleton, keeps everything in place. This skin on my father's shop had labored over the course of its 8.4 decade career, straining to hold up the overloaded shelves on the inside while flexing back against the live load of snow, rain, and gravity outside. Over the years, it had lost some grip and moved.

I was excited to start laying out the foundation, once the last of the roofing and siding were in a tire-squishing pile in the dump trailer; I thought that I was way past ready to turn the corner from tear-down to build-up. I knew what I was going to do and where I was going to start, having already focused a ton of mental energy and anticipation getting ready for framing. The primary reason I was excited, though, is because framing is a fun mix of skill and hammer-pounding adrenaline—something else that speaks to my inner animal. And because framing is so athletic, it's also fun to go fast.

My heart pumped gallons of blood through my veins. I reached for my tape more like a gunslinger going for his six-shooter rather than a timid (albeit middle-aged) apprentice afraid to do the wrong thing. I snapped it free from its formed leather pouch at my left hip, hooked it on the end of the concrete block foundation wall, and walked to the other end about a dozen times faster and more purposefully than I had ever moved on a weekend round of gut-growing golf with my buddies. I snatched my white hexagonal pencil with my free hand, ready to record the measurement before I stopped walking. Finally—finally—after all this tear off, after half a year of thinking and planning the art studio, while barely surviving the interminable and ineffective counseling sessions Rache and I attended trying to resurrect our marriage, I could start. I was ready to rebuild.

Looking down the top course of my father's perfectly straight run of blocks, to make sure the tape hadn't slipped from where I hooked its silver L-shaped nose, I held it firmly in my left hand while my right hand wrote the measurement on the block for the pressure-treated 2x6 sill plate or mud sill that would be bolted on top of these blocks. There was something wrong, though—which I characteristically and immediately ignored—right at the point where the straight run of blocks met the existing wood frame. I made my mark, then pulled my tape along the second side of the three-sided, rectangular foundation wall, scribbling my second sill plate dimension on the side of the block. Inside me, somewhere between my guts and my head, the forces of "stop and check" waged a little war against "keep going, this is fun."

The indulgent "keep going, this is fun" brigade drove me down the third side of the foundation wall, and I raced to hook my tape and get the last measurement so I could start cutting, start the dance of framing, and start showing my mother, who was outside kindly clearing our lunch dishes from the patio table, that I was actually making progress. "Stop and check," whose forces are weaker, but more prudent, launched a final, well-strategized sortie and I looked up at the problem I really would rather have ignored because I lacked the will to face it head on. "Trust yourself," I heard my father's voice say from somewhere in my youth, something he'd told me so many precious times. "Listen to your guts."

My body in motion wanted to stay in motion and my energized muscles kept sending vibrating communiqués to my legs and limbs to keep marching. But a calm from inside me outranked them and I decided to face the problem head on rather than hope it wasn't there. I decided to stop and check. I picked up my father's decades-old, 4-foot level, and the green antifreeze liquid and thin black lines on the vials showed me the way.

My father's 4-foot level looked older than I did. It was sawn and milled from old-growth mahogany, then bound in brass corners to keep it true. This "whiskey stick" (so-called because the vials on old levels have alcohol in them to keep the liquid from freezing in winter) was heavy, too, like dense exotic hardwoods usually are. I felt my muscles strain against its mass as I held it to the rear corner post of the gap-toothed brown frame. I noticed the sun's light being broken up by the full green leaves of the 80-foot white oak tree next door, then seamlessly reforming, like water parted by river rocks. The light passed through the green antifreeze vial of the level and into my eye, where I was hoping to see the transparent air bubble floating in that inch-long space between the thin black lines that divide the arc-shaped glass vial into thirds. Unfortunately, the bubble floated way to the left. I held the bottom of the level against the building with my boot, then tilted it away from the building until it read plumb. In just 4 feet, the building had racked 1 inch. Over 10 feet, the length of the wall studs, it was even greater. I put the level down and stood back, absorbing the impact of a second, unforeseen, major delay. No matter how much I wanted to start framing and building, I had to start fixing.

Facing this conclusion elicited a brief, but concise, commentary on the matter, consisting of a single, universally understood syllable: "Shit."

* * *

On the way to the coffee shop, as much to avoid solving my problem as to buy a jolt of buzz so I could get at it, I sat on the ripped vinyl of the steel spring benchseat of my father's blue Ford F-250 pickup. The stiff suspension was good for hauling lumber and tools—and really good for plowing snow—but it telegraphed every bump in the roadway right through the vehicle, and my butt bounced up and down like I was hanging from a playground swing made of bungee cords. The Solid State radio was off and the damp spring air filled the cab as I drove slowly through my hometown, not necessarily looking for anything, but hoping I would find something good to juice my spirits.

My father and I had shared countless breakfasts at Lavallee's Diner. Even though our town had gotten its Starbucks and fast food chains since, the competition has both helped and hurt local businesses. And, even though I left this town, this place, these people, this town never left me. The path my mother walks, the people she talks to and sees and loves, the roads my father drove, and the houses he fixed are all here. This is where I came from and I can feel it inside me—no new coffee blend or breakfast deal could match the history and laughs we had here in the town's oldest greasy spoon, run by a family with whom I grew up. It is also the place my mother worked until I was 12-years-old, slinging plates, refilling coffees, marrying ketchups, and making friends that would last her to this day while she saved money to go to the college she had planned to attend—a piece of her life postponed because I was a surprise.

But as great as Lavallee's was to me, the damn place could use a face-lift and a hyperlink to imagination.com. Back when it was the only game in town, people had no choice, so the Lavallee family could've served coal on sheet metal and the town folk happily would've come there to eat it. But it's different now. People have more choices than they used to. There's more competition for people's desires, and there are more empty booths and counter seats than I recall from my youth.

"Large, please. Black. To go," I said without looking at the woman tapping keys at the register. I was trying to take in and analyze what I remember Lavallee's to have been and match that up to what it had become. I was captivated by one waitress, who I believed to be one of the owners. Even at about 60-years-old, she passed out plates of eggs, bacon, and pancakes with the habitual deftness of a nimble-fingered card dealer in a Las Vegas poker room, smiling and talking to her friends and the dollar tippers about their grandkids, and opining about local news.

"$1.50, please." I thought I heard something...Don't I have a wall to fix...look at her whip those plates out...my dad and I used to sit over there a lot...my marriage has unraveled...did I just get more sad....

"$1.50, please." I looked up from my thoughts into a pair of gently smiling brown eyes that yanked a breath through my solar plexus. Every detail of her face was instantly mimeographed in my mind as if I was looking at her through a memory. Her teeth were just a little crooked, but that imperfection made her look pure, genuine, and so cute. Her neck was outlined by a black choker necklace under the collar of her white oxford shirt, and the subtle outline of her collarbones suggested a lean, well-tuned body. The cotton shirt was buttoned just enough to be appropriate, but unbuttoned enough to suggest the succulent promise below. I could tell she sensed I was lost in my thoughts.

I put a twenty on the counter, although I would rather have placed it in her hand, risking a feathery but thrilling touch. I knew that in two more sentences we'd like each other, and that in three more sentences... I shouldn't talk to her—I'm a married man, I thought to myself, even as I felt a fire starting to burn.

"Sorry," I said, "brain cramp." She laughed kindly and took the money while her eyes stayed on me a second too long, flickering a primitive, beautiful message of interest and pique. She handed me my change, coins rattling out of her hand into mine, before she pressed the bills on top of them. Then she turned and walked on to her next customer seated at a cracked vinyl booth. I left a dollar tip on the scratched glass counter case as I watched her walk until the counter obscured what the caveman in me was pleased to see. Rachael and I—despite the fact that I still longed for her, for her touch, for her full, gentle lips to be on mine—hadn't been naked together in the same room for nearly a year. "Stop and check" didn't have a prayer against "keep going, this is fun."

Maybe it was the supercharge of being noticed that fueled me, or having someone beautiful laugh warmly at a silly joke, or perhaps it was the shutter-speed moment of magnetism that brought it all together. Maybe it was the creaky old floors, memories, and ceaselessness of Lavallee's that coaxed some creativity and willpower into my mind. Or, maybe I knew the answer the whole while, and just needed a little help and time realizing it. The coffee didn't hurt, though. So, I did what my father would have done to fix the wall.

I did not do a seat-of-the-pants sales pitch to solve this problem. I couldn't. Unlike presentations I had given to a thousand high-end customers that came to our real estate firm looking for primo homes with spectacular views or prestigious frontage. I couldn't talk my way out of this one. What I was doing with my father's shop was not about being liked, nor about showcasing the details of someone else's work that I would highlight as I glided through a house for the first time, trying to make my customers believe that I knew everything about it. No, that wouldn't work here. Framing wouldn't care if you have a friendly smile, and gravity could give a shit if you like the neighborhood. Completing this project properly was about finding answers. Real answers.

In my father's notebook, he is careful to lay everything out before he talks about how to put the pieces together. He was careful to have a base before he built. He was passionate that there is order and logic in what he does so that later—when he had to improvise anyway—he was not undoing problems he could've avoided in the first place. I knew from just a few pages of his notebook that he thought he failed at this, but I also know that from the view of a boy, who revered his dad, he succeeded heroically.

Fixing this problem was just the beginning for me, and the beginning must be right for the end to work out in a building. And for the first time in too many years, I was confident; I knew what to do. I decided to face the problem head on, and make a plan. As I decided what to do about this small detail, in this small building, in this small town, I began to see something important: if I could decide what to do here, maybe I could decide what to do about other aspects of my life.

I made a plan.

* * *

With the sheathing still nailed across the studs, there'd be zero chance to rack the shop walls back into plumb. The physical forces I'd have to exert in several directions at once would be far too much for me working alone, so I decided to keep tearing the building down and pull off the sheathing.

From inside the garage, I swung an 8-pound sledgehammer like a battering ram into the sheathing, starting at the bottom course near the door on the west wall of the building. The front wall faced south, like a church. The addition—which at this pace I might actually finish someday—was on the west side. The impact from the steel hammer head shook the building and vibrated through me as the 1x8 board and rusty 8 penny bright basics tried like hell to stay where they were, holding on now as much by habit as by design. I separated the board from three studs and moved over to the fourth, swinging this time the drop-forged head like a monstrous sand wedge, increasing the force of the blow, while decreasing the steel surface area at the point of impact. This time the sheathing board, instead of squealing loose from the studs, shattered both along the grain and in half. I noticed, along the wood's jagged breaks, that underneath its tarnished skin, the pine was blonde and new looking It even smelled like a new pine board and I was overwhelmed with the notion that I had destroyed something precious and irreplaceable.

This time I stopped.

While I didn't know what I would ever do with these boards, I knew destroying them wasn't the answer. Eighty years ago they were second-rate material and hidden behind siding or under shingles. But they had survived too long now to still be second rate. I dropped the sledgehammer ("Sluggo," my father called it) and dug a nail pick out of the box of hand tools. Instead of the full-scale physical onslaught I had readied myself for, one that would be hard but mindless and fun, I chose tenderness and time for these pine antiques that had stood sentry for so long. I started at the bottom, and pried every nail loose, then removed each board carefully. I set up a tarp and some "stickers" and stacked the boards carefully, making sure to keep them straight.

Stripping and stacking the sheathing took two pound-shedding, dust-eating days. I dug and pried out every nail I could find on the wall and roof sheathing. Once each board was stacked as though it awaited investigation in a museum laboratory, the building was, as my father would have said, "back to the bones." The spindly studs were flimsy now and I could rack the walls where they needed to go. I duct-taped the level to the northeast corner post and then nailed an 8-foot-long 2x4 kicker brace, leaving the nail head proud so I could get it out later. Next, I nailed a 2x4 block to the floor parallel to the kicker brace. I then moved the wall until the level's bubble was between the lines. Moving and adjusting, moving and adjusting. There would be areas down the line where I could be less critical of how the work played out, but not here. This needed to be right on.

Finally, I got it. I sunk sharp-headed 16 penny spikes into the block on the floor and another one into the corner post, then added another brace. With one wall in line, I could fix the others without the whole building flopping around out of control. I braced the other four walls during the next hour and took a breath, letting out the tension that had built up while solving this problem. The sky had turned gray, the air humid but still cool, and I was covered with dust and dirt. My muscles ached—the muscles in my hands I had previously only exercised by typing were on fire—but I made it the long way around, back to the beginning, again.

I took a break before cutting the sill plates and went inside for a drink. My mother had put beer in the fridge for me; my watch read 6:30 p.m. She was out, busy as usual. I sat alone at the kitchen table, opened the sweaty brown bottle, and found myself wondering if I looked like my dad, who did the same thing in this chair about a trillion times. I sponged sweat from my forehead with the crook of my right arm then hung my head with my elbows on my knees. All I could see was our old floor. My next thought was of Arthur Pelletier's kitchen floor tiles. The burnt red of terra cotta 8x8s poured into my mind like water spilling flawlessly over the rounded edge of a marble park fountain. The memory further coalesced and the tile gave way to tape measures, a chalk box, and my father, all appearing in the synapse of ether between my mind and our exhausted linoleum.

The Pelletier kitchen really had three parts: a pantry, the kitchen itself, and a mudroom off the back door. "The problem with these chopped-up rooms is that you have to find the one best layout line for your tile, so it flows into each room without leaving slivers or looking like the whole pattern is set off-center. Then, you have to figure out how that layout can carry into the other spaces and still look like it grew there," Dad had said.

We measured and he thought through the implications of his measurements. We snapped lines and laid dry tiles to see how they'd run out and meet other rooms. "You can't always see the problems or rewards ahead, Brendan," he said looking at our lives with his carpenter's eye, "but you sure can look for them when you start."

Back then I thought he was just talking about avoiding slivers and shoddy work; his real message wasn't obvious to me. He was being my father the best way he knew how.

"I've come to learn that the best carpenters aren't always the fastest or the ones who build the biggest houses," he used to tell me. "They're the ones who have learned to see three moves ahead of what they're doing. Everything in a building, much like a family, depends on everything else. If you can understand the principles— the greater truths—and how the parts go together, you can understand the building, putting you in a better position to adjust to mistakes and unforeseeable events."

The Budweiser bottle felt cold and wet in my hand. The half-flat, cola-esque fizz of the beer on my tongue and the light taste temporarily quenched my thirst. I pulled my elbows off my knees and drew my mind back from memory into the present, satisfied at this time not to look three steps ahead, but to enjoy this moment and let myself believe my dead father was still alive, somewhere, deep inside me.

CHAPTER 6

KING STUD

*The way to true understanding
is to identify the simplest
component parts of a project,
to figure out which parts really matter.
And let go of the parts that don't.*

"**H**ow's work?" I asked, tentatively cradling the yellow bell phone between my shoulder and ear—the same phone I used to nervously ask Theresa Texeira for my first date more than 30 years ago. I was nervous now as I hoped against what I already knew to be true that Rachael would want to talk, to communicate on a level other than reporting the most basic and necessary facts that we must share.

"Laura's camp counselor called...today," Rachael said referring to our 9-year-old. "She had a 48-hour stomach...uh thing...they think she swallowed too much lake water in her swimming class...She was throwing up...."

I could tell from her words' well-worn path that she was doing something else while we talked. I had to try hard not to drum my fingers on the countertop while she was clearly distracted and did not give me—give us—a brief amount of her full attention.

"She's feeling much better now. Kelly's having..." her fingers found their way through the last few keystrokes and to the final mouse click of the e-mail she was composing "...a blast...She really loves the camp we picked for them. They're making tons of friends."

I wandered over to the kitchen window, and looked past the beige curtains to check, again, on the progress I had made that day. Despite my mother's flare on canvas, the inside of her home was muted. Painting indulged her need for color, life, and possibility. Spending limited money on curtains and decoration was always something that could wait. And something that always did, which made the inside of our home—with the exception of her explosions of paint on tautly stretched canvas—seem like it was stuck in a time gone by.

"The job is going well," I said, stingingly aware that Rachael no longer cared. "Lots of demo so far," I declared, forcing a conversation about us instead of the kids. I was tired of not existing in her mind's eye, of being an invisible paycheck that helped to support the household. I wanted to believe that for a second we'd have something other to discuss than our kids, realizing of course, that without them, we had run out of things to say.

"Good," she chirped with a syrupy but featureless courtesy that asked no questions, sending the clear signal that politeness without detail or real interest covered her, that it made her sound like she gave my comment more than passing concern, even though what I said had already passed out of her mind.

"I'm beginning to feel very isolated from you and the girls," I said. "After all, the camp calls you, not me. The letters that come home are addressed to you and have to be forwarded to me. I'm feeling alone out here."

"*You* decided to go out there," and with a few words she dismissed me, dismissed the value of any feeling I might have. Dismissed it as if my decision to take the project on meant that I therefore stopped feeling any connection to the life I had once dreamed of with my beautiful Rachael and my angelic girls.

"Have you thought any more about what we talked about?" Before I left for the summer, our counselor had recommended that Rachael and I think about the big steps we needed to take to save our marriage.

My wife Rachael is a successful and dedicated, but busy, professional consultant. And as good as she is at her occupation, she's doubly dedicated to being a heroic mother, something for which I will eternally respect and support her. But, when it comes to paying attention to the continuums in her life, she is lost; it doesn't seem like she thinks about them and it doesn't seem like she ever tries to understand them. Instead, she focuses on the details of everything, without trying to relate them to anything, without trying to make sense of them. She had long since stopped trying to understand us, and we had ceased to evolve.

"I don't know, Bren.... This time apart." She paused, and in that moment of silence I knew I had lost her, that she wasn't interested in the conversation and that it was over. Yet, she continued to speak while I retreated to a new thought that I knew would abandon me. "In some ways, I guess I feel guilty saying this, but, it feels good. I mean...the way we are...I don't know anymore."

My mind moved to the project outside the kitchen window. Bracketed in the rails, stiles, and mullions of the brown-stained kitchen window over my mother's stainless steel drop-in sink, I envisioned the super-strong engineered lumber I-joists spanning the open foundation wall outside and I imagined tipping up the walls under a sweat-soaked, but glorious strain. I had lost Rache in the severity and purpose of this conversation. As usual, what was important to her was somewhere else, something other than me, other than us.

"The girls miss you." I could hear emotion in her voice for the first time.

"The cards they made in their arts and crafts barn came last week," I replied at last. "I keep them next to my bed." My heart actually ached in my chest cavity because I missed them back that much. Then something clicked inside me, something important. I felt powerful and confident for the first time in a hundred years, for the first time since the beginning with Rachael when I knew damn well it was her I wanted, and my voice dropped an octave. "There's only so much time this separation is going to last, Rache. Understand that. Hate me, ignore me, whatever, I can't control that, but I know this: if we don't act, the result of this separation is the end of us."

With those words out of my mouth, I at once felt more free, and more imprisoned: I felt free because I had staked my claim and done something definitive, something that could be the basis of the next step. I felt confined because now, for the first time in too many years, I stood for something and I meant it. The pain in my heart— for my wife, for my girls, for my own loneliness—was even more poignant now. Now, I truly sensed the specter of divorce hovering like a night fog over a road slickened with black ice, and envisioned watching my girls grow up (and me grow old) in some shit-hole fucking apartment where I lived alone and didn't make my bed unless they were coming to visit. I felt alone, desperately alone. I had wandered into the living room, with the long yellow cord stretching behind me, and sunk into a chair. What I couldn't know, was that as I prepared my next question, something clicked inside Rachael, too, and a tear slowly formed in the corner of her green eye, built until gravity took it down the curve of her cheek before it dissipated and stopped like a stream that has run out of water.

"I need to understand what happened to us," I pleaded. I needed desperately to hear that she wanted a tomorrow for us, that there was something there somewhere that we once had, something that I could help re-build.

"Let's take it day by day," she suggested.

"Taking it day by day is the goddam problem, Rache! We've lost our vision for the future. We used to be headed in the same direction, living together with a purpose. Now, we just exist." There was silence and I could not sense the quickening in the air. I didn't know Rachael was really as unhappy as she was. I didn't realize I had lost her, that whatever cord of emotion and connection that creates a continuum between people was almost completely severed.

"I called a lawyer," she said.

JOB NAME: PELLETIER
PROJECT: FRAMING

THE FRAME IS THE GUTS OF
THE THING. YOU HAVE TO
UNDERSTAND THE GUTS OF
THE THING BEFORE YOU CAN TAKE
IT APART. IF YOU DON'T KNOW WHAT YOU'RE
DOING, CHANCES ARE PRETTY GOOD
WHATEVER YOU'RE TRYING TO DO WILL GO
WRONG.

A HOME IMPROVEMENT CARPENTER
DOESN'T NEED TO KNOW HOW TO SPEED-
FRAME A TRACT HOUSE, BUT HE NEEDS
TO KNOW THE PARTS—AND UNDERSTAND
HOW THEY WORK. THE REASON: AT SOME
POINT HE'S GOING TO HAVE TO TAKE A
HOUSE APART—TO REPAIR A STUD-ROTTING
LEAK, FOR INSTANCE. AND ONCE THE
SIDING IS OFF AND THE SECTION IS
STRIPPED YOU HAVE TO UNDERSTAND
WHAT YOU CAN TAKE OUT. ONLY THEN CAN
YOU PUT IT BACK TOGETHER SO THE
HOUSE STANDS AS IT SHOULD.

ALL THE PARTS TO A FRAMED WALL HAVE
NAMES. WHEN YOU LAY THEM OUT FOR A
NEW BUILDING, OR TEAR INTO EXISTING
WALLS FOR REPAIRS, YOU KNOW WHAT'S
WHAT: COMMONS, JACKS, AND KINGS.
COMMON STUDS ARE THE STANDARD 16"

ON-CENTER WALL STUDS YOU LOOK FOR
WHEN HANGING A PICTURE OR A KITCHEN
CABINET. JACK AND KING STUDS SUPPORT
HEADERS AT DOOR AND WINDOW
OPENINGS.

THE KING STUDS ARE THE PIECES THAT
HOLD A WINDOW OR DOOR OPENING
TOGETHER, THAT MAKE AN OPENING IN
THE BUILDING POSSIBLE.

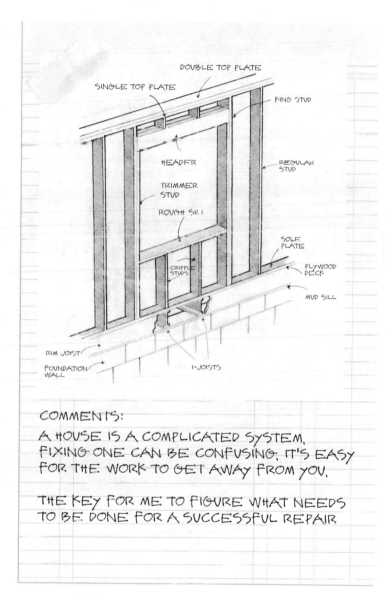

COMMENTS:

A HOUSE IS A COMPLICATED SYSTEM, FIXING ONE CAN BE CONFUSING; IT'S EASY FOR THE WORK TO GET AWAY FROM YOU.

THE KEY FOR ME TO FIGURE WHAT NEEDS TO BE DONE FOR A SUCCESSFUL REPAIR

IS TO BREAK THINGS DOWN INTO THEIR
SIMPLEST COMPONENT PARTS. I DO THAT
BEFORE I MOVE AHEAD WITH ANY WORK.
IT REQUIRES UNDERSTANDING OF HOW
THE PARTS WORK, FIRST INDIVIDUALLY,
THEN TOGETHER AS A SYSTEM.

HERE'S THE THING: THE IDEA THAT YOU
HAVE TO UNDERSTAND THE PARTS IS
OBVIOUS. EVEN I COULD FIGURE THAT OUT.
IT'S UNDERSTANDING THAT'S THE TOUGH
PART.

THE WAY TO BEGIN UNDERSTANDING IS TO
IDENTIFY THE SIMPLEST COMPONENT
PARTS OF A PROJECT—TO FIGURE OUT
WHICH PARTS REALLY MATTER. THEN LET
GO OF THE PARTS THAT DON'T.

I LEARNED THIS BY FRAMING. PUTTING
THE THOUSANDS OF PARTS OF A BUILDING
TOGETHER SMALL PIECE BY SMALL
PIECE, SOMETHING BECAME CLEAR TO
ME. IN MANY WAYS, LIVES ARE PUT
TOGETHER LIKE THIS, TOO. LITTLE THINGS
STACK UP. THEY THEN BUILD OFF OF ALL

THE OTHER LITTLE THINGS THAT MAKE US UP AS PEOPLE. LIFE, LIKE A BUILDING, HAPPENS INCREMENTALLY.

IF SOMETHING GOES WRONG, A TINY MISTAKE GETS MAGNIFIED AS PARTS GET ADDED. AFTER THAT, IT CAN SEEM LIKE NONE OF THE PARTS ARE DOING WHAT THEY'RE SUPPOSED TO, THAT THEY'RE ALL SCREWED UP. THEN YOU STAND THERE SCRATCHING YOUR HEAD ASKING, WHEN DID THAT HAPPEN? I'M LYING IF I DON'T SAY THAT BEING A TEENAGE FATHER DIDN'T MAKE ME THIS WAY.

BRENDAN, WHO I LOVE MORE THAN ANYTHING, WAS NOT PLANNED. HE CAME ALONG AND KAY AND I CHANGED OUR LIVES TO ACCEPT HIM. THERE ARE DAYS, MANY DAYS, WHERE I WISH I COULD'VE TRAVELED TO EUROPE OR MONTANA WITH MY FRIENDS, OR GONE TO HAPPY HOUR OR OUT ON A BOAT.

I ALMOST ALWAYS SKIPPED THOSE THINGS BECAUSE KAY WAS AT HOME LOVING

BRENDAN, SHE CARED FOR HIM AND
WAITED FOR ME.

I'M LYING IF I DIDN'T SAY THAT I WANTED
ANOTHER LIFE MANY TIMES. I'M ALSO
LYING IF I DIDN'T SAY THAT I LOVED THEM
BOTH, WITH EVERYTHING I HAVE. I MEAN
THAT.

AT ALL COSTS, FIND A WAY TO
UNDERSTAND THE GUTS OF THE THING.
FIND WHAT MATTERS, WHAT WORKS, AND
WHAT DOESN'T. BUILD FROM THERE. IT'S
THE ONLY WAY.

I was sad when I called Rachael. That's why I called her. So sad I wished I could just cry enough or rage hard enough against something to relieve it. But, with the silent phone hanging in my hand, yellow like a flower, like the 1970s, like something you'd pay extra for today in a retro boutique, I became even sadder. My spirit drained, and more than ever I felt farther away from a life I understood. Then I realized that we were only at the beginning of this thing. Nothing made sense. And the end might never come. I hadn't told my mother yet that Rachael and I were separated, but I know she sensed it by what she didn't do. She didn't ask me any questions about Rachael that were anything other than innocuous. My mother loves to know things and "how's the weather" chitchat doesn't really interest her. Yet, that's all she asked when she inquired about Rachael. I know from being her son that she was caring in silence, and giving me room to move and think and experience before really needing her. And when I did need her, I could always—always—count on her being there, being ready for me, and for loving me. Now that I knew there was a lawyer and that lawyers draw up papers that formally end marriages, there was something I needed to tell myself.

While the surface of my soul cried for the world to be normal again, to be the way I remember it, there was a corner, deep inside, way down in the dark, that lit the candle of relief, and pointed to a new life. And somehow, a new life could be OK.

I didn't know this until I read his journal, but my father would dedicate at least two solid days of planning for a big framing job. The night before he would snap the bands on a framing package and calculate and choreograph every move he would have to make the next day. He'd cram, too, studying rough openings for windows and doors like he was preparing for the final exams he never took in the college he never attended because I came along too early in his life.

On the Pelletier job, I remember that there was never a second of down time during the initial framing. On a mercilessly hot May

Saturday right before I graduated from high school, he had me break down the lumber delivery into parts—floor joists, wall studs, headers, floor decking, and wall and roof sheathing. I moved the entire house in one day from one pile to another. Then he'd further break down the studs and headers into "door and window packages," which he knew the dimensions and numbers of by rote. We were moving at what I thought was Mach I before either of us took a single handful of 16 penny spikes from the 50 pound cardboard box of nails and dropped them into our leather bags.

My father knew and understood the simplest component parts of a building. More importantly, he made it his mission to understand them, how they worked, how they fit together, and why. So, on a remodel or repair, when it came to tearing a building apart he knew at least what should be there. And if he pulled a house apart and didn't find what he'd been expecting, it didn't take him long to figure out a way to fix it.

After talking with Rachael, after hearing the emptiness in her voice—and knowing that I played a big role in her pulling away from me—I couldn't say that I knew how to fix it like my father could fix a house. What I did know was that Rachael and I were apart. Even though I was back at my childhood home, protected and safe, our worlds were upside down and I felt leagues from a life of contentment and peace. I was leagues from a wife who would put our marriage first. Leagues from passion and romantic love. I remembered what passion felt like—passion built our marriage— and I refused to go to my grave without that feeling again.

Then, like you notice it's suddenly high tide, or that it's about to rain, I heard my own voice inside my head say, "I'm going to Lavallee's tomorrow for breakfast."

* * *

Idling at the red light in my father's truck on my way to the coffee shop, I anticipated the pretty waitress's smile and warm conversation, and I looked forward to her leaning closer to me than she needed to.

"You new to town?" she asked in a lilting, disarming timbre.

"I'm old to town," I said. "I grew up here," and was secretly happy I hadn't replaced my wedding band after the last blow-out with Rachael two months back. "You?"

"I wish I could say I came here to find myself," she offered, standing a little closer to the laminate counter than she had been a moment before, "and tell you some terrific story, but I can't; I live in an apartment by the river," and a ruffle in her smile curtained the window of a story she'd rather not tell.

"Make a decision, and the rest will follow," goes an ancient Chinese proverb I once read on a study desk in my college library. It had been carefully written with a blue felt-tip pen. I always remembered it and hoped they still had the desk. Whatever I was supposed to be studying when I learned the aphorism is long gone.

I felt myself make a decision in this second, a decision about as voluntary as breathing, blinking, or dreaming. I not only wanted her, to touch her skin, to examine the pattern in her sunlit eyes, I wanted to see where this tingling conversation might head. Rachael had pulled too far back over the years, holding me too much at the periphery of her life. The counseling we were in for months prior to my departure only made us both more certain that our marriage was increasingly a partnership in parenting, not a romance that could be resuscitated. Still, at night, in the dark, before falling asleep, I would hug myself into my pillow wishing it was Rachael, and for a moment I'm reminded of the way it had been once. Somehow, after all this, I still hope.

While talking with Rachael on the phone the day before and while searching her eyes before I left, I could sense no feeling from her other than the duty of speaking to me. Our separation only made us more separate. I felt the division in her voice and her words like I felt it in my own heart.

But in the absence of her desire, I had pulled back, too. Separate now, we lived on the verge of waiting—waiting for something to grow, as recommended by our counselor. Meanwhile our daughters sent us cards from camp that they signed with love, a love I knew they had for us and that we shared for them. The weight of the obligation to our beautiful, funny, sometimes frustrating creations hung like a wrecking ball over my heart.

A year ago, a conversation with a woman this attractive whose name I hadn't even asked yet would've been harmless; tempting maybe, but harmless. Today, I decided to let myself feel the joy of it—I could have resisted, but I didn't want to, and I found myself wanting to know more.

"My name's Jesse."

CHAPTER 7

DIG IN

*Risking a look into the Abyss
is part of living a fulfilled life.*

I nside a torn piece of packing paper from an entry door, my father had scribbled this marginalia before making it a page in his notebook:

LIFE HAS A WAY, SOMETIMES, OF GIVING YOU WHAT YOU NEED; JUST WHEN YOU NEED IT, SOMETIMES YOU CAN UNDERSTAND WHAT IT MEANS, SOMETIMES YOU CAN'T, SOMETIMES YOU ARE PARALYZED BY DOUBT.

RECOGNIZING THAT THERE ARE SIGNALS AND LESSONS ALL AROUND US IS THE POINT, IN THE DETAILS OF OUR DAILY LIVES THERE ARE THINGS WE CAN LEARN ABOUT OUR EXISTENCE, FOR ME IT IS CARPENTRY, FOR OTHERS IT IS SOMETHING ELSE, I KNOW THAT SURROUNDING US ALL OUT THERE, SOMEWHERE, THERE'S ENOUGH INFORMATION TO HELP SHOW THE WAY. SOMETIMES THE GIFT FROM THE UNIVERSE IS NICE, A METAPHYSICAL FREE LUNCH, OTHER TIMES, THE GIFT HAS JUST AS MUCH MEANING, BUT YOU MUST EVOLVE THROUGH A GROWTH PAIN THAT COMES WITH IT TO SEE ITS VALUE, THE POINT IS, THE GIFT IS THERE.

My first thought, mixing with pre-dawn semi-consciousness like a drop of cream mushrooming in a cup of black coffee, was how empty and inert the pillow I clutched to my chest felt, and how full of life and vigor I wanted this surrogate to be. The pillow had become my substitute over the past three years for what was once Rachael's supple skin and I had to think back too far to recall the memory of waking to the sensation of her, of her closeness, her skin on mine, the warmth of her affection, even making love early on a Saturday morning before the kids got up, before they ran amuck in the house while Rachael and I sat at the kitchen table near the bay window and shared sections of the newspaper. I had to think back too far to the fulfillment of being needed. Instead, my recent memory was of a new status quo, one not of embrace and acceptance, but of Rachael's growing reluctance to be close, one of distance and dismissal.

For a year and a half I tried to woo Rachael back into our pleasant pattern of starting the day close and together. Maybe I tried too hard. Maybe I didn't ask her what was wrong the right way. Maybe I didn't ask at all. Maybe I was the one who was insensitive. Maybe I missed some important signal and obtusely kept doing the wrong thing. Maybe it was me who hurt Rachael. But I could no longer take the tiny, daily rejections as what once was an embrace from her body and senses transformed microscopically—but steadily—into a stillness that meant rejection and nothingness, a stillness that broke me. I began to feel a meaninglessness in our once sacred union.

Bearing with just as much live load on the other side of this equation was my overwhelming love for my daughters, my role as a present and engaged father, and my utter unwillingness to hurt them.

The second—almost simultaneous—sensation I woke with was the side order of pheromones I had for breakfast with Jesse the day before.

Finally, forms of the building project emerged in my weather system of thoughts. The day turned out to be a wash because a truculent rain punched and gouged the earth, turning it to mud as the water racing across the ground on its inevitable search for the lowest point cut a miniature Badlands of temporary canyons, cuts, and culverts. I worked as much as I could through the drizzle but the rain soon hit so hard I had to run for cover. The upside of the storm delay was that this was the first time my schedule matched my mother's schedule; she was typically busier than a pretty cheer leader with her own car and no curfew.

I sat in the "parlor," as she still called it (most people call it the living room), while she cooked us lunch.

"You look good," I heard her say from the kitchen. "You're losing weight sweating out there," echoed somewhere off the parlor's plaster walls. Louder was the oxygen passing through my lips, across my dry tongue and down my parched throat. I hoped it would ignite my smoldering courage so that I could say the words I'd avoided since arriving here.

"Rache and I are having problems," I blurted through the doorway into the kitchen, staring down at my shirt as I slumped on the couch. No sooner had the words left my mouth than she appeared in the opening with leftover meatloaf and gravy-soaked mashed potatoes. Steam rose from each plate and even though it was one o'clock in the afternoon, I was drinking a beer.

"Do you want to talk about it?" she inquired, her face softening and filling with emotion.

"Yes," I replied, "but I don't know what to say."

"Why aren't you happy?" she asked, and her cerulean eyes found a place in mine that made me feel safe, made me feel loved.

"We had something once," I said. "...Something...something so good... I used to feel complete with her, and felt that our lives were headed toward the same place. Somewhere other things became more important to her—more important than us. She...." I felt myself coming unglued.

"Do Laura and Kelly know?"

"Not yet.

"There's nothing left now, Mom, except pleasantries and "how's the weather" chitchat. It's like we barely know each other. I can't take it anymore, Mom. I don't think I want to be married to her anymore, and it's ripping me in half."

Neither of us touched a bite of the food; its gray wisps of steam dissipated into nothingness. I scrubbed my eyes with my fists and kneaded my eyebrows with my knuckles like a cut man working a fighter in the losing corner of a boxing match. I tried to keep the tears back. The secret, once allowed a foot out of its cage, immediately doubled in size and power and I sobbed for the first time, nearly crushed by the gravity of it all. I looked up and saw, in my mother's eyes, that her heart broke for me in that moment. She wished I was young again so that if she just held me long enough she could distract the hurt away.

Passing time (and a few more beers) brought me some comfort, or anesthesia anyway. This was the first day I had really slowed down in three weeks and it was nice to be still again. My mother and I talked so long that we ended up eating the lunch leftovers for supper. She gently probed me for important details about the feelings in my heart and the thoughts in my head that would help make sense of the situation. I even made mention, in passing, of Dad's notebook. When her eyes brightened with curiosity for what Dad kept in that old notebook, I had to admit that I hadn't paid enough attention to it to really tell her anything. Too spent to talk any more, even to my mom, I retired to my room and found my free lunch from the universe, deep in my father's tattered words.

I stood at my old desk below the waning light of a leaden day and rolled the project plans out of the way, replacing them with the aluminum clipboard. As I did every night since I had found it, my mind usually scattered from the fatigue of a hard day, I flipped through the seemingly random pages hoping perhaps to find a tip that would help make my work on the studio easier. I looked at his notes instead of reading from beginning to end, and I leafed through, noticing the pictures and drawings as I scanned his words without sinking into them. I peeled the old photos carefully off the thin ledger paper and held them gently between my thumb and forefinger, remembering but not understanding. Not until that night.

Holding an old photograph, feeling the paper in my hands, and examining his drawings, the thoughts that filled my mind were no longer of his words on the page or the how-to instructions. They were of him in my life. I'd read my dad's words about digging a hole or truing-up a fence gate but I'd lose focus on the page and instead remember him loading tools into his truck or prayerfully rolling up cords while telling me one of his many aphorisms in an attempt to get me to do things right: "It's important to care for your tools, Brendan, and to store them neatly so that they're ready to go the next time. It's easier to coil a cord or hose now and hang it up than it is to pile it in the corner and untangle it later."

I'd read a few more words and recall the memories of a summer long ago. Feelings of how much I desperately missed him, how much I'd love to hear what he'd say right now, filled my mind. Reading his stories about how much he loved my mom, and things he tried to teach me were washed inside the memory of related events and created an irrational hope. I hoped that I could hear his voice just one more time and see him, so that I could hold this notebook in my hands like an 8-year-old, look up at him, and tell him that I love him.

Despite what my heart tried to make my head think, he was gone and all that was left were his pages, his words, and how much he loved me when he was here, right until the end. I picked the notebook up from the desk, turned the pages back to the beginning, and I started reading—not looking this time, but reading.

I pored over sections I had already seen. I reached past the pictures and drawings, past the memory of him in our lives. I saw that he had written about more than just carpenter's tricks that could help me with the studio. I saw that it wasn't just that my mother and I were mentioned. I discovered something else. I reached inside his comments. There, wound through the how-to of cutting crown like a craftsman and roofing like a mad-dog, wound through the stories of his life and what he wanted from it, I discovered the book my father wanted to write, the message he was trying to deliver, and who he was delivering it to.

There, in every comments section, his how-to tone flip-turned from jobsite drawings and site-proven know-how and it became clear these notes weren't just about jobsite wisdom—about tricks carpenters learn—they were about his life's experience and a search for meaning. They were about loving and being loved by his wife. And they were about me.

This was Gideon Herlihy's Carpenter's Notebook, a carpenter's curriculum on living a meaningful and happy life, told with his hard-won wisdom. What began as how-to instructions for fixing a house ended with a how-to on living a good life. His passion for doing his best exceeded his work. As he wrote this secret journal, this clandestine exegesis about living a well-cared-for existence, I couldn't know until now that his passion for living well, for being enlightened, ran this deep because I wasn't ready to see it. I opened my eyes to the pages before me and I loved him for even having the thoughts.

JOB NAME: MACROPOLIS
PROJECT: FENCE POSTS

DIGGING HOLES IS NO HIGH INDUSTRY. IT'S
USUALLY BRUTAL. AFTER ALL THAT
EFFORT, THE FIRST THING YOU DO IS FILL
THE HOLE BACK UP AGAIN. BUT
CARPENTERS MUST OFTEN TAKE OFF
THEIR TOOLS, PICK UP A SHOVEL, AND
PREP A SITE. IT'S USUALLY NOT FUN, BUT
IT IS NECESSARY. THAT'S HOW IT GOES.
IGNORING THAT THIS WORK MUST BE DONE,
AND BE DONE WITH DIGNITY, ONLY
RESULTS IN LOW-QUALITY WORK. THAT'S
NOT GOOD ENOUGH ON MY JOBS. DIGGING
A PROPER POSTHOLE IS EASY TO
UNDERSTAND. GENERATING THE WILL
AND ENERGY, DOING IT OVER AND OVER—
ESPECIALLY WHEN YOU DON'T WANT TO—
THAT'S THE PART THAT TAKES COURAGE.

HOW-TO:

A PROPER POSTHOLE IS A SHAFT IN THE
GROUND, NOT A BOWL-SHAPED
EXCAVATION LIKE I'VE SEEN A HUNDRED
GREENHORNS TRY TO GET AWAY WITH. TO

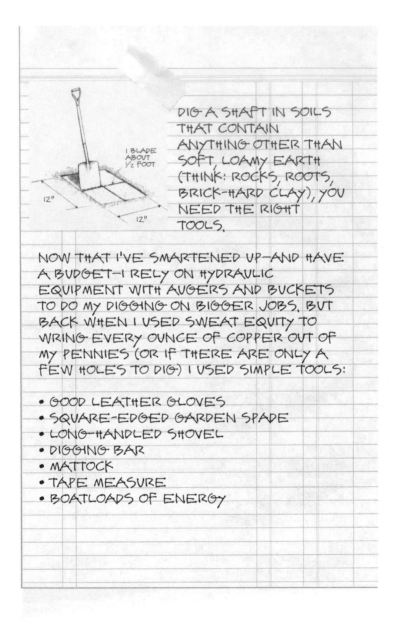

DIG A SHAFT IN SOILS THAT CONTAIN ANYTHING OTHER THAN SOFT, LOAMY EARTH (THINK: ROCKS, ROOTS, BRICK-HARD CLAY), YOU NEED THE RIGHT TOOLS.

NOW THAT I'VE SMARTENED UP—AND HAVE A BUDGET—I RELY ON HYDRAULIC EQUIPMENT WITH AUGERS AND BUCKETS TO DO MY DIGGING ON BIGGER JOBS. BUT BACK WHEN I USED SWEAT EQUITY TO WRING EVERY OUNCE OF COPPER OUT OF MY PENNIES (OR IF THERE ARE ONLY A FEW HOLES TO DIG) I USED SIMPLE TOOLS:

- GOOD LEATHER GLOVES
- SQUARE-EDGED GARDEN SPADE
- LONG-HANDLED SHOVEL
- DIGGING BAR
- MATTOCK
- TAPE MEASURE
- BOATLOADS OF ENERGY

1. THE FIRST THING TO DO IS LOCATE THE CENTER OF THE HOLE.

2. NEXT, GET YOUR HEAD IN THE GAME AND USE YOUR MIND TO PREPARE YOUR BODY. DIGGING IS NOT TENTATIVE WORK. NOW, PUT YOUR GLOVES ON. YOUR HANDS WILL GET TRASHED ANYWAY, BUT THE GLOVES DO HELP, FOR A WHILE.

3. USE THE GARDEN SPADE TO MARK A SQUARE AROUND THE HOLE'S CENTER POINT ABOUT TWO BLADE WIDTHS (THAT'S ABOUT 1 FOOT) ON EACH SIDE. I DO THIS BY CREATING A CROSSHAIRS AT THE CENTER POINT OF THE HOLE BY PUTTING THE BOTTOM-LEFT CORNER OF MY SPADE ON EACH "COMPASS HEADING" OF THE CENTER POINT; I THEN CUT INTO THE SOIL A FEW INCHES TO LEAVE A LINE. NEXT, I USE THE SPADE TO MARK A SQUARE AROUND THE CROSSHAIRS. THIS CREATES THE HOLE'S PERIMETER. THIS PROCESS MIGHT TAKE 120 SECONDS AND IS WORTH THE EXTRA TIME. IF YOU JUST DIG WILLY-NILLY NEAR THE CENTER POINT OF YOUR

HOLE, THE POST PROBABLY WON'T SIT IN THE CENTER. CARELESS DIGGING ALTERS THE HOLE LOCATION. IT'S BEST IF THE POST SITS IN THE CENTER OF THE HOLE.

4. ONCE YOU'VE MARKED THE SQUARE, USE THE GARDEN SPADE TO CUT THROUGH THE TOP LAYER OF SOIL. THIS IS WHERE YOU MUST BRING YOUR BODY TO BEAR IF YOU'RE EVER GOING TO FINISH. START FAST AND WORK HARD. PUT THE SPADE EDGE ON YOUR LINE AND DON'T JUST JUMP ON IT—JUMP ON IT!—WITH BOTH FEET, LIKE YOU'RE TRYING TO DRIVE A POGO STICK TO CHINA. THE FLAT SPADE EDGE CUTS INTO THE EARTH BETTER AND FASTER THAN A POINTED SHOVEL, AND IT LEAVES A CLEANER EDGE. USE THE SPADE TO REMOVE THE "PLUG" YOU CREATE.

5. NOW COMES THE "FUN PART," GOING DOWN. IF THE SOIL IS HARD, ROCKY, OR ROOTY, PULL OUT YOUR DIGGING BAR AND USE IT TO LOOSEN THE SOIL. TRYING TO DO

CONING

SO WITH YOUR LONG-HANDLED SHOVEL OR SPADE IS JUST A WASTE OF TIME. SPEAR THE DIGGING BAR DOWN THE EDGES OF THE HOLE YOU'VE STARTED. ANGLE IT AT THE SHAFT-WALL BEING CREATED SO THAT THE HOLE GOES DOWN STRAIGHT. IF THE HOLE IS "CONING" TO THE CENTER IN THE SHAPE OF A WINEGLASS, YOU'RE DOING IT WRONG. DON'T DO IT THAT WAY. A SHAFT HAS STRAIGHT SIDES AND A STRAIGHT BOTTOM. DRIVE THE BAR INTO THE CENTER OF THE HOLE, THEN CRANK IT AGGRESSIVELY BACK AND FORTH TO PRY COMPACTED SOIL APART. ONCE THE SOIL IS LOOSENED, REMOVE IT WITH THE SHOVEL.

6. FINALLY, THE HOLE MUST BE DEEP ENOUGH WITH A CLEAN, FLAT BOTTOM. WHERE I LIVE 36 INCHES IS THE DEPTH I MUST REACH WITH EVERY HOLE TO KEEP FREEZE-THAW CYCLES FROM HEAVING THE POST OUT OF THE GROUND AND RUINING MY STRAIGHT RUN OF FENCE.

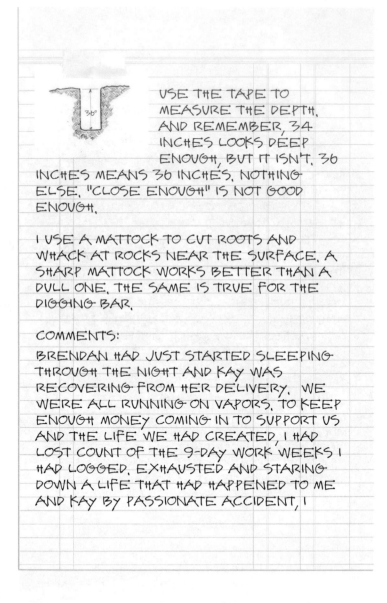

USE THE TAPE TO MEASURE THE DEPTH, AND REMEMBER, 34 INCHES LOOKS DEEP ENOUGH, BUT IT ISN'T. 36 INCHES MEANS 36 INCHES, NOTHING ELSE. "CLOSE ENOUGH" IS NOT GOOD ENOUGH.

I USE A MATTOCK TO CUT ROOTS AND WHACK AT ROCKS NEAR THE SURFACE. A SHARP MATTOCK WORKS BETTER THAN A DULL ONE. THE SAME IS TRUE FOR THE DIGGING BAR.

COMMENTS:

BRENDAN HAD JUST STARTED SLEEPING THROUGH THE NIGHT AND KAY WAS RECOVERING FROM HER DELIVERY. WE WERE ALL RUNNING ON VAPORS. TO KEEP ENOUGH MONEY COMING IN TO SUPPORT US AND THE LIFE WE HAD CREATED, I HAD LOST COUNT OF THE 9-DAY WORK WEEKS I HAD LOGGED. EXHAUSTED AND STARING DOWN A LIFE THAT HAD HAPPENED TO ME AND KAY BY PASSIONATE ACCIDENT, I

ACCEPTED A FENCE PROJECT. IT WAS
DOWN THE ROAD FROM THE SMALL
APARTMENT WE RENTED AT THE TIME. IT
WAS A BIG JOB, BUT I NEEDED THE
MONEY MUCH, MUCH MORE THAN I NEEDED
ANY HELP I WOULD HAVE TO PAY.

EARLY ONE SUMMER SUNDAY, I PULLED A
ROLL OF YELLOW MASON'S STRING
BETWEEN MY CONTROL POINTS AT EACH
CORNER OF THE SQUARE BACKYARD TO
BE FENCED. PULLING A STRING TAUT
CREATES A STRAIGHT LINE BETWEEN
TWO POINTS. THE STRING GUIDED ME, SO
ALL MY POSTS WOULD RUN AS STRAIGHT
AS THE STRING. WHEN I PULLED THE
STRING ALL THE WAY AROUND THIS
BACKYARD I HAD A GOOD LOOK OF THE
WEATHER OFF MY BOW. I HAD BARELY
THE TIME TO THINK ABOUT HOW BIG THE
JOB REALLY WAS WHILE I PLANNED IT.
ALL I COULD SEE WAS MONEY.

BEFORE THE SUN EVEN CLIMBED ABOVE
THE HUGE TREES SURROUNDING THIS
YARD, IT WAS JUST DISGUSTINGLY HOT. I

FELT THE HUMIDITY IN THE AIR CLING TO
MY SKIN LIKE SMOKE AND MY HEART SUNK.
THEN, THE QUESTIONS CAME. "HOW AM I
EVER GOING TO GET THROUGH THIS?"
LEAKED INTO MY MIND. THE WILL TO
CONTINUE DRIPPED OUT OF MY SOUL.

BUT I BEGAN. THREE STRIKES LATER IF
MY SPADE DIDN'T HIT A ROCK THAT JARRED
ME TO MY BONES AND SAPPED ME LIKE A
HEAVYWEIGHT WHOSE OPPONENT IS
SUCCESSFUL WORKING THE BODY, IT HIT A
ROOT THAT HURT ALMOST AS MUCH. THE
PROJECT WENT FROM BAD TO WORSE. I
WENT FROM TIRED TO DESPERATE. THE
QUESTIONS ABOUT HOW COULD I DO THIS
WOULDN'T LEAVE ME ALONE.

THE SUN LODGED BEHIND THE GRAY,
MOTIONLESS HUMIDITY AND IT WAS ABOUT
AS COMFORTABLE AS WEARING A WOOL
COAT IN A HEAT WAVE. I CONTINUED
SINKING HOLES. THE DIRT WAS DRY AS
CHALK. BEFORE LONG I COULD SMELL IT
AND FEEL IT IN MY TEETH. MY SHIRT HAD
LONG BEEN OFF AND SWEAT COATED MY

BACK IN MY BODY'S POINTLESS ATTEMPT TO COOL ITSELF. SWEAT AND DIRT MIXED ON MY SKIN, TURNING IT BROWN. I LOOKED DOWN THE STRING AND MY QUESTIONS TURNED TO RAGE.

I DUG MORE. I JUST KEPT DIGGING. THE SKIN BEGAN TO WEAR OFF MY HANDS AND MY BODY STARTED TO BREAK DOWN. SO DID MY MIND. I WAS 19-YEARS-OLD, WITH A WIFE AND CHILD AT HOME DEPENDING ON ME. I COULD BARELY GET THE RENT PAID AND FOOD IN THE ICEBOX. FORGET ABOUT MY BOY'S CHANCES OF COLLEGE OR A LIFE BETTER THAN MINE. SHIT, IT WAS ALREADY WORSE. AND MY LIFE WAS NOT GOING TO BE WHAT I HAD THOUGHT, NOT BY A LONG SHOT. I LOVED KAY, THERE WAS NO DOUBT OF THAT. I DID LOVE HER, BUT CHRIST! I DID NOT KNOW YET THAT I WOULD LOVE BRENDAN. I SAID I LOVED HIM AND I ACTED LIKE I DID. I KISSED HIM AND HUGGED HIM AND ROLLED AROUND ON THE FLOOR WITH HIM. BUT REALLY, I DIDN'T KNOW IT. I WOULDN'T KNOW IT FOR

A VERY LONG TIME EITHER. ON TOP OF
ALL THIS, THERE WAS THE MONEY.

I WAS LOSING HOPE.

THE MORE HOLES I DUG, THE FUCKIN'
ANGRIER I GOT—AT ME, AT MY MISTAKE,
AT MY LIFE, AT JUST ABOUT EVERYTHING.
BUT I KEPT DIGGING. THERE WERE SO
MANY ROCKS IN THE LAST THREE HOLES,
SO MANY ROOTS, THAT I THOUGHT THE
STEEL IN MY DIGGING BAR WOULD CRACK
AS I SMASHED IT INTO THE GROUND. I
RAMMED THAT BAR IN THERE, THOUGH, AS
HARD AS I COULD—WITH ALL THE DAMNED
VENGEANCE I HAD. I GAVE EVERY
OUNCE OF ENERGY TO SMASH THOSE
ROOTS EVEN AS MY HANDS BLED UNDER
THE ELECTRICAL TAPE BAND-AIDS I
MADE WITH A RIPPED T-SHIRT AS GAUZE
TO KEEP THE GLUE FROM STICKING TO
THE OPEN BLISTERS. AND WHEN I RAN
OUT OF ENERGY, I DRANK FROM THE
BRASS HOSE BIB ON THE SIDE OF THE
YELLOW HOUSE. I TOOK A BITE OF THE
SANDWICH KAY SOMEHOW FOUND THE

ENERGy TO MAKE FOR ME, AND WENT
BACK AND GOT SOME MORE.

THE 6X6 SPRUCE POSTS HAD BEEN
DELIVERED IN TWO GIANT CUBES. My
NEXT STEP WAS TO LUG EACH ONE OF
THE KNOTTy MONSTERS FROM THE
DELIVERy LOCATION IN THE DRIVEWAy,
AROUND THE BACK OF THE HOUSE, AND
DROP IT INTO ITS HOLE. THE SUN BURNED
BEHIND THE GRAyISH WHITE CLOUDS AND
COOKED THE THICK AIR. THE GRAy WALL
REFUSED TO LET A BREEZE PASS. AS I
HOISTED A POST ONTO My SHOULDER, ITS
CORNER CUT INTO My NECK AND THE
COARSE SURFACE OF THE HEAVy TIMBER
WORE THROUGH THE SKIN ON My
SHOULDER.

I RAMMED EACH POST INTO A HOLE WHILE
A FEELING AND THOUGHT CAME
TOGETHER INSIDE ME. I COULD SMELL
DINNER COOKING THROUGH My
CUSTOMERS' OPEN KITCHEN WINDOW.
THEN I SAW SOMETHING INSIDE THOSE
POSTHOLES, SOMETHING THAT I HAD READ

ABOUT ONCE IN MY HIGH SCHOOL ENGLISH CLASS. A PLACE THAT SEEMED SO VERY FAR AWAY FROM ME NOW: I LOOKED INTO THE ABYSS.

YEARS LATER, AFTER READING SOME OF THE PHILOSOPHY BOOKS MY BUDDIES COMPLAINED ABOUT HAVING TO READ IN COLLEGE, BOOKS I COULD BARELY UNDERSTAND, I CAME TO UNDERSTAND MORE ABOUT THE ABYSS. I SEE IT AS A REALM PHILOSOPHERS VIEW AS THE PURE ABSENCE OF REASON, OF THOUGHT AND OF FEELING. IT'S A REALM OF PURE HOPELESSNESS, OF JUST SHEER NOTHINGNESS. I'VE READ THAT IF YOU STARE TOO LONG INTO THAT ABYSS, IT TAKES PART OF YOU. IT STARES BACK AT THE WORLD THROUGH WHAT IT SNATCHES FROM YOUR SOUL—AND DOESN'T GIVE IT BACK.

I LOOKED INTO THE BOTTOMS OF THOSE POSTHOLES, DOWN THE STRING THAT WRAPPED THAT BACKYARD IN A THIN YELLOW LINE. I WANTED TO JUST GIVE IN

AND EVERY CELL IN MY BODY SCREAMED
AT ME LIKE ITS THUMBS WERE PINCHED IN
A VICE, THEY SCREAMED AT ME TO QUIT
THIS POINTLESS EFFORT, THAT I COULD
NEVER MAKE IT, THAT I WAS STUPID FOR
GETTING INTO THIS MESS. I BELIEVED AT
THAT MOMENT THAT I WAS WORTH HATING
FOR THE MISTAKES I'D MADE. I BELIEVED
THAT I WAS A FAILURE.

BUT EVEN AS I THOUGHT THIS, I FELT MY
BODY (AS IF IT HAD SOME KIND OF LIFE OF
ITS OWN,) LIFTING ANOTHER POST OFF THE
PILE, WALKING WITH IT, PASSING THROUGH
THE HEAT AND EXHAUSTION. WHEN I GOT
TO THE HOLE, I SPEARED THE POST INTO
THE EARTH. I RAMMED IT INTO THE
BLACKNESS AT THE BOTTOM. I TRIED,
WITH THOSE BLONDE SPRUCE TIMBERS, TO
FILL THE VOID WITH MY RAGE. BUT RAGE—
RAGE AT MY MISTAKES, FOR HAVING TO
MARRY MY HIGH SCHOOL SWEETHEART
INSTEAD OF GOING TO COLLEGE, AT MY
LIFE GONE WRONG—PROVED A FAITHLESS
COMRADE-IN-ARMS. NO MATTER HOW HARD
I THREW THOSE POSTS INTO THE BOTTOMS

OF THOSE HOLES, THERE WAS NOTHING DOWN THERE TO FIGHT AGAINST, THERE WAS JUST MORE HOLE.

BUT TIME PASSED. WHILE THE LOOSELY PLACED POSTS DANGLED ALL CATTY-WHOMPUS OUT OF THEIR HOLES LIKE SOMETHING DR. SEUSS MIGHT'VE DRAWN, THE FENCE STARTED TO TAKE SHAPE. I ALIGNED AND PLUMBED EACH POST WITH MY NEW 4-FOOT LEVEL, THEN BRACED AND ADJUSTED THEM INTO A PERFECT LINE. I WORKED, LIFTED, TUGGED. I MOVED. THE POSTS SCRAPED MY CHEST AS I BEAR-HUGGED THEM TO ADJUST THEM IN A HOLE. THEN, AS HOURS FELL AWAY LIKE DROPS OF SWEAT, I LOOKED DOWN A ROW OF PERFECTLY ALIGNED FENCE POSTS AND SAW SOMETHING I HAD LOOKED AT EVERY DAY IN MY YOUNG WIFE AND BEAUTIFUL SON. I NEVER REALLY SAW IT, THOUGH, UNTIL I WAS MUCH OLDER.

THERE, IN THOSE PERFECTLY ALIGNED FENCE POSTS, I SAW BEAUTY. NOT SOMETHING BEAUTIFUL, BUT BEAUTY

ITSELF, I SAW REASON AND THE POSSIBILITY THAT THIS MIGHT ALL BE WORTH IT AFTER ALL. I SAW THAT I COULD FINISH THIS PROJECT. I COULD GET PAID. I SAW THAT TOMORROW WOULD COME, AND IT WOULD BRING A NEW CHANCE.

THAT LIFELONG DAY BROKE ME. ALL THE WAY. I WAS ALMOST BEATEN AND I KNEW IT. I LEARNED SOMETHING, TOO. I LEARNED THAT RISKING A LOOK INTO THE ABYSS IS PART OF LIVING A FULFILLED LIFE. KNOWING HOPELESSNESS TEMPERS WISDOM LIKE HEAT TEMPERS STEEL—IT MAKES IT HARDER, STRONGER, AND LONGER LASTING. KNOWING HOPELESSNESS, AND BELIEVING YOU CAN MOVE BEYOND IT, MAKES A WISE PERSON APPRECIATE EVEN MORE THE HOPE THAT ONE DAY GROWS INTO FAITH. THEN, AFTER THAT, HAPPINESS.

I LEARNED THAT MY FAMILY AND I COULD FIND PEACE.

My first thought before opening my eyes to the world the next day was of my father and his words, his struggle, and how much I fucking needed him. I woke with a new understanding and comradeship on my journey. No, my dad was not standing at the wheel with me watching the waves batter the pulpit of a boat too little for these seas washing across its deck. He had sailed here once before, over these same dark waters. But I never knew that; he never told me. While he may have reached the edge of the world, he never poured off the falls into oblivion. Instead, he made landfall, and ultimately found a safe harbor, which I think he would've named Meaning Bay on his charts. I closed my eyes again for a second, and looked up through my eyelids, past the ceiling, and into my past, into my future. My mother was here and I was protected in this place. And he was here, somewhere, too. For the first time in this journey through my sinking marriage, I finally felt that I was not alone.

* * *

Because so much time had been lost during the rainstorm, I left the job spring-loaded for that day, which I could tell in the murk of the pre-dawn was clearing to be one of those summer days you remember in your skin cells more than your brain. Every extension cord was laid out, my cut station was set up. The lumber package was broken down and good to go. The only thing I was able to build the day before was the three-piece sill plate. I had squared it, leveled it, and locked it in. Today was all about running joists, dropping decking, and nailing the piss out of this place.

It was still early and we had neighbors, so I started slowly and quietly; yet I could feel the energy already boiling inside and the minute I pulled out my tape to lay out the sill plate for joists, the frenzy began.

My tools rattled in the pouches that slapped against my thighs as I marched the site. My feet slid in the mud, my hammer swung like a chaotic pendulum in its loop, tapping my thigh, and I could feel the belt I had cinched down a notch tighter press against me as I bent to work. My mind threaded itself through the fibers of this project like a screw turning through a piece of softwood. The building would take its first blonde-haired steps out of the ground, and all the emotion that had slagged me down lifted as the sun poured over the horizon into my mother's backyard like a torch sent from Olympian gods to light my way. I peeled my shirt off and grabbed the rim joists, beginning an old dance to new music.

For the first time since I had envisioned and anticipated this job over the winter, I was positively consumed with something outside my job, kids, and dissolving marriage; something that was essentially me, that made me feel valuable, wanted even needed—on the planet. My pencil slashed graphite lines across the rough face of the rim joist stock along the face of my speed square and I cut the board to length with the circular saw, letting the waste drop to the soft, muddy ground before the blade stopped spinning. Since I had leveled and squared the sill plate already, I could follow its shape and move quickly through the next stages.

For the first time that summer the pouches of my tool bags were filled with fistfuls of 16 penny bright-basics, the framing spikes that would hold the place together. While using one of my father's many nail guns would've been easier, it wasn't possible because the air compressor that powered them wasn't working properly. When I first plugged it in to prepare for my framing the coiled copper hose that ran between the pump and the tank that held the pressurized air hissed so much air that the pump never shut off. As I rolled the 2-wheeled, 25-gallon unit to the corner of the yard to deal with later, words my father said every time we packed the truck together stopped me in my tracks: "It's better to have it and not need it, Brendan, than to need it and not have it." So, without giving it another thought, I stopped what I was doing and drove the unit to the shop in the next town where he had his tools repaired for as long as I could remember.

The key to driving nails well is setting them hard. An aggressive first shot gets the nail started commandingly—and tells it exactly who the fuck is in charge. A solid set means you can really unload on the second, third, or even fourth shots. A solid set takes some faith that you won't smash your fingers, but when you're staring down thousands of nails to be driven home, you quickly learn that little ineffective whacks waste valuable time. And you quickly learn to see the head of the nail clearly before that first heavy whack with your hammer.

I built the perimeter box, called the rim joist. Once nailed in place and scribed with layout marks, I ran the light and floppy—but strong—I-Joists between, spanning foundation wall to foundation wall.

I moved like a pro, like I hadn't taken more than two decades away from this work. My father's blood galloped in my veins, moved to the top of my skin like it hadn't done in too long. I could see the shape of my muscles re-building themselves under my skin and I wondered—more like hoped—Jesse would be impressed, maybe even more attracted to me than she had been before. I also recalled that Rachael had once been impressed by me, that she liked the way I looked and I could almost feel the trace of her polished fingernail on my chest from a moment of closeness whose where and when have been lost to history. All that survives now is the memory of how we once felt for each other.

In two hours of lugging, tugging, hoisting, and nailing, I had the joists crossing the opening like a great ladder laying flat on the ground. Without taking a breath, I dumped what was left of the 16 penny spikes in my pouch back into the white cardboard box, then replaced the empty pouches with 8s, for nailing down the ¾inch plywood deck.

I threw sheets up from the pile, positioned them, then tacked the corners before lunging for another sheet. My hands, this time, instead of growing blisters and bleeding like they did when I tore the shingles off the shop roof, grew stronger, and calluses already forming thickened and protected them more; yet I could still feel every detail of the work I needed to. The sun positively gushed down onto the deck and I was pumping nails faster and faster, moving in perfect concert with the beauty of the day, the momentum of the project, and the joy of creation. I left the pain of my life stranded on another plane and I felt, somewhere at the core of my being, something my father had said once years before. I didn't remember it; I felt it. And the sensation made me invincible, like the day would never end, the high would never fall, that the moment was immortal.

"Building is a search for what's best in us," he told me once, long after I had moved out of the house, married, and our first daughter Laura was beginning pre-school. I remember, too, that for the first time that day he had looked old; not weak, but old.

We were having a beer on my porch long after an Indian summer day had waned and our wives were busy with something else. We sat with our feet up, drinking as much autumn air as we did beer. "Think about it. Before you build, you dream of how something can be better: whether it's something as basic to the human race as shelter or as frivolous as finishing a basement or re-styling a kitchen. In either case—and in most cases in between—someone looks at something and asks, 'How can this be better?'

"I've always liked this business, because its very nature is basic, visceral, and totally essential. We're the only creatures on this rock who design and build our own permanent shelter. If some disaster happened tomorrow, we'd do two things before anything else: find food and build shelter. Then we'd surround ourselves with those we love. Everything else comes after that.

"When we as a society build our institutions and memorials, the building's job is to embody the public's opinion of itself, to illustrate a people's spirit and attitude, and to endure. That's asking a lot out of lumber and limestone, but when an architect goes to work with the real sense of what a building can be, he sees things that others might miss, but certainly can feel. A building holds power and it can inspire the people who look at it, who don't see the construction details, but who do feel the story the building tells. When he designs this building, he is locked in a search. He asks, 'What can this building do besides stand up and keep the weather out?' There is no right answer to that question, at least no answer everyone agrees to. But you know it when you see it. A building with power, mass, balance, brawn, and detail is something people notice. And they feel better for having experienced it, even proud that they live near it.

"This search is a responsibility, like living your life. You can half-ass it and you'll get out of it exactly what you put in. Or, you can dig in and believe that by undertaking the full breadth of the search—'How can this be better?'—you will succeed. Even if you feel you have only gone part of the way, going at all takes courage. And if you are to embark on a journey, don't just embark. Plan to go all the way. Your chances of getting hurt go up exponentially by playing at half-speed, and by moving in half-measures.

"Half-measures are not commitments. Half-measures show that you don't really believe in your search, or that you do not really believe in yourself.

"Believe you can do it, Brendan. Believe it. Believe that if you're wrong, you will rise from whatever fall being wrong causes, and find a way to get back out there.

"I believe it, Boy. I believe it with all the stuff in my guts. And I hope I've taught you that somehow, because, maybe it's this fancy micro-beer you've got here, I just figured out right now how to say it."

I sat in the pale light of a ceiling fan I had someone else install in my porch and I stood in awe of my father.

While I didn't know it then, he had plucked a chord deep inside me that resonated, vibrated, and quivered until I was ready to hear it. I felt the music as I ran with sheets of plywood across the deck of the building that would be. Crosby, Stills & Nash's "Southern

Cross" thrummed from my jobsite radio and I tried to sing the lyrics despite the fact I had no idea what they were. I devoured a peanut butter and jelly sandwich standing up at my mother's kitchen counter and poured a quart of thick whole milk out of the carton and down my throat before running back out to sling my bags on again.

The days were getting longer and the skin on my back was tight from the beginnings of a sunburn that made me feel young. I anticipated the freedom of the coming warmth like a college kid looks ahead to summer as I reached down into the perfect stack of 2x4 studs to throw the first wall parts up on the gleaming plywood deck. Seeing those first wall parts laying there, waiting to be built into something made me believe—like nothing I had ever done before—that the future was upon me. I believed that, for the first time in too long, that my life was going to be good.

I believed this through the entire day, letting it soak me, letting it mix with me, letting it become part of me, letting it somehow find its way through me all the way down into the bottom of my feet, and into my soul. I was euphoric as the sun went down, as I stripped off my tools and took off my boots before heading into the house. I felt good as I crunched into a Granny Smith apple and sat down at the kitchen table where my mom had left the packet of mail that Rachael had forwarded me. I even felt good as I opened the curious envelope from Howe & Partners, Attorneys at Law. The feeling lasted until I saw the sheaf of divorce papers already countersigned in Rachael's hand stating that she had filed for divorce. Then my soul collapsed around itself, imploding like a building wrapped with dynamite.

CHAPTER 8

PLUMB, LEVEL, & SQUARE

There are rules.
There are answers. There is truth.
It's just the way life on a jobsite works.
And it's the way life works.

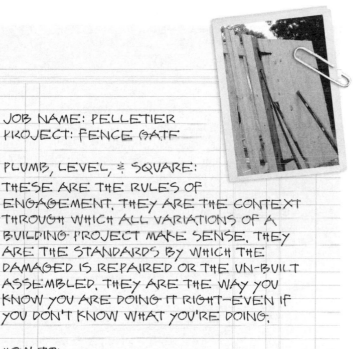

JOB NAME: PELLETIER
PROJECT: FENCE GATE

PLUMB, LEVEL, & SQUARE:
THESE ARE THE RULES OF
ENGAGEMENT. THEY ARE THE CONTEXT
THROUGH WHICH ALL VARIATIONS OF A
BUILDING PROJECT MAKE SENSE. THEY
ARE THE STANDARDS BY WHICH THE
DAMAGED IS REPAIRED OR THE UN-BUILT
ASSEMBLED. THEY ARE THE WAY YOU
KNOW YOU ARE DOING IT RIGHT—EVEN IF
YOU DON'T KNOW WHAT YOU'RE DOING.

HOW-TO:
STEP 1. DETERMINE HEIGHT AND WIDTH

- DETERMINE FRAME HEIGHT. THIS CAN
ALMOST ALWAYS BE DONE BY MATCHING
THE DIMENSION OF THE FENCE RAILS.

- DETERMINE WIDTH BY MEASURING THE
SLAT STOCK (DRAWING ASSUMES 1X6):
LINE UP SEVEN SLATS EDGE-TO-EDGE
TO FORM A LOOSE PANEL. SQUEEZE
THEM SNUG AND MEASURE THEIR WIDTH
AT THE TOP AND BOTTOM. THE FINISHED

GATE SHOULD BE 36" OR WIDER. (FOR VERY WIDE OPENINGS, SAY FOR A LAWN TRACTOR, BUILD TWO GATE PANELS.) ONCE THE PANEL DIMENSION IS KNOWN, MAKE THE GATE 1/2" THINNER THAN THE SLAT'S OVERALL MEASUREMENT.

STEP 2. CUT PARTS
- I USE A MITER SAW TO HELP ME REALLY GET THE CUTS RIGHT, ESPECIALLY ANGLES ON THE X-BRACING, THOUGH A CIRCULAR SAW WORKS. I USE A TABLE SAW AND HAND SAW TO CUT THE LAP JOINTS FOR THE GATE ASSEMBLY.

STEP 3. DRY-FIT PARTS
- ON A FLAT, LEVEL SURFACE (LIKE THE DRIVEWAY) LAY OUT THE RAILS (HORIZONTAL PIECES) AND THE STILES (VERTICAL PIECES) AS THEY WILL FIT TOGETHER ONCE FASTENED.

PULL DIAGONALS

STEP 4. CHECK FOR SQUARE
- SQUARE THEM BY "PULLING DIAGONALS" WITH A TAPE

MEASURE. A SQUARE STRUCTURE
MEASURES THE SAME DIMENSION FROM
OPPOSING CORNERS.

- ADJUST THE GATE PARTS AS SQUARE
AS POSSIBLE (WITHIN 1/8" IS GREAT
FOR A FENCE GATE).

STEP 5. APPLY GUSSETS
- TEMPORARILY SECURE THE CORNERS
WITH GUSSETS AND SCREWS.

- PRE-DRILL THEN SCREW ALL GATE
PARTS TOGETHER.

STEP 6. FIT AND INSTALL X-BRACING
- LAY A LONG PIECE FOR X-BRACING
FROM CORNER TO CORNER AND SCREW
TO THE GATE FRAME.

- FLIP THE GATE OVER AND SCRIBE
ANGLES.

- CUT AND INSTALL X-BRACE. I USE 2
"POCKET" SCREWS ON EACH END TO
FASTEN THE BRACE TO THE FRAME.
THIS MEANS I PRE-DRILL 2 HOLES IN
EACH END OF THE X-BRACE AT A

SHARP ANGLE. I DRILL THE HOLES
PARALLEL TO THE WOOD GRAIN SO THAT
THE SCREW PASSES THROUGH THE END
OF THE X-BRACE AND INTO THE GATE
FRAME. A COUNTERSINK BIT WORKS
WELL FOR THIS BECAUSE IT KEEPS THE
END OF THE X-BRACE FROM SPLITTING
WHEN THE SCREW HEAD SINKS.

- REPEAT PROCESS FOR SECOND X-
BRACE (WHICH INSTALLS IN TWO PARTS).

- REMOVE GUSSETS.

STEP 7. PLANK THE FRAME
- UNLESS USING 6' HIGH PLANKING, RUN
8' STOCK WILD OVER THE TOP AND
BOTTOM OF GATE.

- CAREFULLY APPLY THE HINGE-SIDE
SLAT FLUSH TO THE EDGE OF THE GATE
FRAME.

- APPLY PLANKING TO THE REMAINDER
OF THE GATE FRAME USING NAILS OR
SCREWS ON RAILS, STILES, AND X-
BRACING.

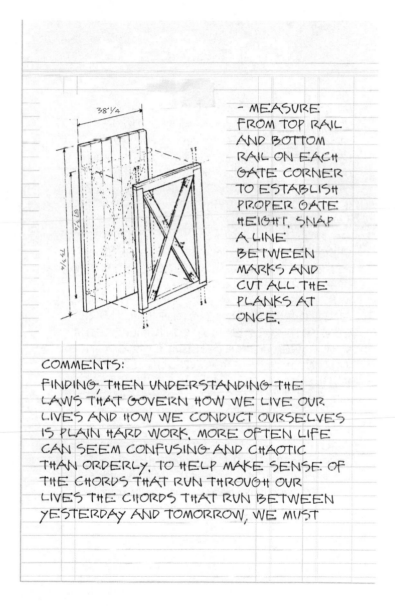

- MEASURE FROM TOP RAIL AND BOTTOM RAIL ON EACH GATE CORNER TO ESTABLISH PROPER GATE HEIGHT. SNAP A LINE BETWEEN MARKS AND CUT ALL THE PLANKS AT ONCE.

COMMENTS:

FINDING, THEN UNDERSTANDING THE LAWS THAT GOVERN HOW WE LIVE OUR LIVES AND HOW WE CONDUCT OURSELVES IS PLAIN HARD WORK. MORE OFTEN LIFE CAN SEEM CONFUSING AND CHAOTIC THAN ORDERLY. TO HELP MAKE SENSE OF THE CHORDS THAT RUN THROUGH OUR LIVES THE CHORDS THAT RUN BETWEEN YESTERDAY AND TOMORROW, WE MUST

FIND THOSE RULES. IT IS IN
UNDERSTANDING THAT—THAT THERE ARE
RULES CO-EXISTING WITH CHAOS, ORDER
CO-EXISTING WITH ENTROPY—THAT WE
CAN FIND MEANING AND REASON IN THE
SHIFTING WATERS OF OUR LIVES. IT IS
HOW WE CAN BEGIN TO SHARE IN THE
CONTROL OF OUR OWN DESTINY.

UNDERSTANDING THAT THERE ARE
INVISIBLE, UNCHANGING RULES THAT BIND
US OVER TIME AND TO EACH OTHER IS
MUCH LIKE TWO SAILORS IN A STORM—ONE
EXPERIENCED, ONE GREENHORN—
SEEKING SHORE IN A HOWLING STORM.
WHILE NEITHER OF THEM CAN CONTROL
THE WEATHER OR WATER, THE SAILOR
WITH KNOWLEDGE OF WIND, TIDES, AND
HIS SHIP CAN STILL NAVIGATE. HE
UNDERSTANDS WHEN TO RUN, WHEN TO
HEAVE-TO, AND WHEN TO POINT STRAIGHT
INTO THE WEATHER. HE UNDERSTANDS
THAT WAVES WILL SWAMP HIS BOAT IF HE
DOES NOT RESPECT THESE TACTICS. HE
KNOWS THAT THEY WERE APPLIED IN
STORMS 500 YEARS AGO AND THEY WILL

APPLY 500 YEARS FROM NOW. HE KNOWS THAT AT THE CORE OF HIS JOURNEY HE IS ALONE. ALL HE HAS ARE HIS WITS, HIS UNDERSTANDING, AND HIS COURAGE TO SEE THE JOURNEY THROUGH. THE NOVICE ON THE OTHER HAND, OR SOMEONE WHO DOES NOT BELIEVE THERE ARE LAWS OF NAVIGATION, SPENDS MORE TIME GUESSING AND HOPING THAN MOVING DEFINITIVELY OUT OF THE HURRICANE.

LIKE SAILORS, CARPENTERS HAVE RULES, TOO. WHILE THEY CAN BE OBVIOUS AND SIMPLE FOR A CARPENTER (PLUMB, LEVEL, AND SQUARE), THE PROBLEM IS THAT A CARPENTER'S RULES AREN'T THE SAME AS LIFE'S RULES. THAT'S NOT THE POINT. THE POINT IS: THERE ARE RULES, THERE ARE ANSWERS, THERE IS TRUTH.

THEY'RE NOT THE SAME FOR EVERYBODY, BUT THEY'RE THERE TO FIND, LIKE THE LAWS OF GEOMETRY OR ALGEBRA. THEY'RE THERE FOR EACH OF US TO EXAMINE AND MAKE SENSE OF INSIDE OUR OWN SKIN. THEY MUST BE

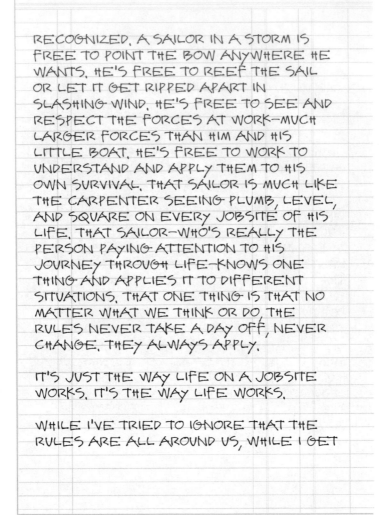

RECOGNIZED, A SAILOR IN A STORM IS
FREE TO POINT THE BOW ANYWHERE HE
WANTS. HE'S FREE TO REEF THE SAIL
OR LET IT GET RIPPED APART IN
SLASHING WIND. HE'S FREE TO SEE AND
RESPECT THE FORCES AT WORK—MUCH
LARGER FORCES THAN HIM AND HIS
LITTLE BOAT. HE'S FREE TO WORK TO
UNDERSTAND AND APPLY THEM TO HIS
OWN SURVIVAL. THAT SAILOR IS MUCH LIKE
THE CARPENTER SEEING PLUMB, LEVEL,
AND SQUARE ON EVERY JOBSITE OF HIS
LIFE. THAT SAILOR—WHO'S REALLY THE
PERSON PAYING ATTENTION TO HIS
JOURNEY THROUGH LIFE—KNOWS ONE
THING AND APPLIES IT TO DIFFERENT
SITUATIONS. THAT ONE THING IS THAT NO
MATTER WHAT WE THINK OR DO, THE
RULES NEVER TAKE A DAY OFF, NEVER
CHANGE. THEY ALWAYS APPLY.

IT'S JUST THE WAY LIFE ON A JOBSITE
WORKS. IT'S THE WAY LIFE WORKS.

WHILE I'VE TRIED TO IGNORE THAT THE
RULES ARE ALL AROUND US, WHILE I GET

UPSET AND THINK THEY'RE A PAIN IN THE
ASS, THEY CAN ALSO GIVE OUR LIVES
MEANING. WE MUST HAVE THE COURAGE
AND VISION TO SEE THEM AND THEIR
POWER. WE MUST HAVE THE COURAGE TO
EMBRACE THEM.

ANY GOOD CARPENTER KNOWS THE
PLUMB, LEVEL, & SQUARE RULE. PLUMB,
LEVEL, & SQUARE ARE THE THREE MAIN
CRITERIA BY WHICH A CARPENTER
JUDGES THE QUALITY OF A PROJECT.
THESE LAWS FOLLOW HIM FROM THE
FIRST DAY HE TAKES OUT HIS TOOLS UNTIL
HE PACKS THEM UP AND BACKS OFF A
JOB. THE RULES NEVER TAKE A DAY OFF,
NEVER HIDE THAT THEY ARE THERE, AND
THEY EMBODY AN IDEAL—THE IDEAL OF A
JOB DONE RIGHT.

I met Jesse for a beer a few doors down from Lavallee's. A guy of French-Canadian descent named Manfred Lucier (pronounced Lucee-yay) owned the place. Since no one in town spoke French, the place had come to be known as Man Lushee's, and it was one of those friendly old-town pubs where the floors were dirty, but the beer was cold, and when the guy behind the bar asked you how you were doing, he was expecting an answer—not a long answer, but the answer. The people in this town had good energy, and cared that its citizens and customers shared the same oxygen supply on the planet.

I pulled two wet pints of suds off the bar and walked across the shotgun-style building to the softly lit booth where Jesse sat wearing a black shirt that highlighted the fullness and shape of her breasts—and highlighted the self-confidence inside her to wear such a featherweight fabric in a jeans-and-workboots bar.

She told me her story, about the marriage that almost was, about the man for whom she had come to town, and about the love she had lost when the relationship tanked. About her destroyed heart. Beneath those words I could feel that she still mourned the loss of her dream, of her marriage to a man who would love her. I knew that's how she felt. Beneath her words was a current of feeling I knew was there as sure as I knew a river cut through this old mill town. And I knew her pain, because it was my own.

Normally, this wouldn't be first date stuff, but we'd already shared what amounted to a couple of hours of conversation over a couple of weeks of breakfasts at Lavallee's when my mom had early morning plans. I'd go in the coffee shop and sit in her section and she'd come over with a steaming cup of coffee, then only leave to wait on other customers. We both felt the pull, the attraction, and had small-talked enough to have this conversation.

"I know how you feel," I told her as much with the painful look in my blue eyes then as with the words I said—and in an instant I knew she understood. I was no longer able to live with my false pretense of bachelorhood, and I experienced a new feeling for

Jesse. Not just lust and desire to trace the lines of her body, to touch her, but a desire for connection and an appetite to know more. Not only was she beautiful on the outside, I found myself hoping— anticipating—that she was beautiful on the inside, and as I thought that, I forced the rest of the sentence from my mind that otherwise would have finished, "...beautiful on the inside, like Rachael."

"I know what it's like to mourn the death of a relationship," I shared. "I know what it's like to live with someone and still feel desperate and alone." Rather than cringing from my circuitous confession, she softened, her arms opened a little, and she leaned into the table just so slightly. Then, she told me more. As she spoke— and as she let me speak—I almost immediately realized that Jesse seemed interested and wanted to share more of her story with me. My shoulders, normally somewhat tense, seemed to relax while my toes, which I cross or make into little fists when I'm anxious unraveled and laid calm. I felt closer to being free and unburdened than I had in years.

Our connection didn't feel like cheating, either. When my boiling desire to reach across the time-worn wooden booth table and hold her hands fed the steam engine of my heart, it didn't feel like infidelity. To be unfaithful, there must be something to be unfaithful to, something more than a platonic, unstated agreement between people who share the same duty and daily routines as co-residents and co-parents. There must be a love to betray.

Jesse and I got ready to leave. We walked over to the bar. She hung her small purse on a hook below the elbow rail and excused herself to the restroom while I waited for the barman to finish with some other customers and come collect our tab. The bartender, a round guy who had worn tracks in the orange rubber floor mats behind the taps pouring drinks and punching plastic number keys on his office-supply store cash register, had just popped my change down on the bar with a "tanks" when Jesse returned from the ladies room. She stood dangerously, surprisingly—but so naturally—

close. Between both the reflection in the mirror behind the courses of liquor bottles and my peripheral vision when we spoke, I could see the racetrack curves of her body, the form of her brown hair catching what little light was in the dark room, and I felt increasingly alive, totally aware of every speck of detail.

"Let's walk," I said, "to the river." She turned and bent down to retrieve her purse from the hook under the bar. As her beltless blue jeans pulled away from her back I could see that she wore a Valentine's Day-red, satin thong.

Man Lushee's to the river was a short walk. I had spent so much time by the abandoned mill along its shores as a child that I could still point out the windowpanes I had broken with rocks. We stood on the bridge, talking gently, watching the black water slip beneath it into the oblivion of eternity. Next thing I knew, she was in my arms. For the first time in a dozen years I was holding another woman—a beautiful, supple woman—and the electrical impulses tripping through the nerve endings in her skin arced through space and time to mine as I pulled her to me.

Her waist was so thin and perfect, her body so receptive. She pressed herself into me as our mouths found one another's. Our lips touched—gently at first, making sure this was real—in a wordless statement that the other's safety was sensed and vital. Jesse, perceptive to my role as a husband and father felt what this could mean to me; I was aware that grief followed her. Then, when we were safe, when we were sure, we kissed at full speed. Her lips opened and I felt her soft, wet tongue searching for mine. Her eyes shut, her back arched into me, and I felt her giving part of herself to me, opening a valuable part of her life to me. And the way her body pressed to mine as I wrapped her safely in my arms made me feel wanted, made me feel desired, made me feel truly like a man. We kissed and I held her steadily, carefully, tightly to my chest. The pain of the day, and of our lives, swept itself down river as we guiltlessly salved the aches of loneliness in one another's hearts.

"I want you," I whispered. "I want this…," and she hugged me, held me, stared into my eyes with a knowledge and confidence that said the same thing without using any words. We walked toward her apartment, the energy coursing between us, the fever growing carefully but quickly as we neared her door. The mutual wish for a single night of unity expressed in physical passion became inevitable. I hoped that sharing this night would heat back the loneliness and grief that filled our daylight hours, and simply by the way her body nestled into mine and the ease with which her head laid on my shoulder. As we slowly arrived at her front door, I knew I wasn't going home that night.

Her taste was on my lips and her smell in my clothes when I thought of Rachael and how much this would hurt her if she knew. As bad as things had become between Rachael and I, she was a good person with a tender heart. While our marriage was gone and the pain that goes with it was present in my waking hours and in my dreams, she was still the last person on the planet that I would seek to hurt. We loved each other once and walked the same path in our lives. We were parents to the same beautiful girls and forever we were bound together through them. I thought of how much this would hurt her—and how much it hurt me to see this kind of passion toward her be disposed of—as though loving me was something she had already done and could check off her list as she moved on to accomplish something else. Yet, I still didn't feel like I had betrayed any trust. I felt like this night with Jesse was right—because it was. Rachael had already abandoned the "us" in our marriage, content with the platonic routines of working, parenthood, and cursory conversations. Rachael had stopped intimacy, emotional closeness, and sex with me; slowly but surely slowed each one to a complete halt. But I hadn't stopped wanting to be intimate and close and sexual with her.

Mine, I suppose, now that I was on my way to doing it, was a sin of commission. Rachael's, a sin of omission. Her crime was that instead of doing something, she did nothing. And how she felt about the way we lived before I left was one of the many secrets she guarded behind the cold courtesy of the conversations we now shared simply out of necessity, and old habit.

Jesse only left the shelter of my embrace to pull her house keys from her purse and open the door. The last thing on my mind was the notion that crossing over this threshold meant entering a new tomorrow, a tomorrow with another woman in it. Instead, my eyes followed the details of her body while both my skin and my soul relished that someone with a gentle touch had reached out and tried to become part of both. Even after she had walked ahead of me into her apartment to turn on a light, I could still feel her touch on my skin, almost as a subtle imprint of her body on my cell structure, and there was a muscular memory of how we walked down the brick sidewalk together at the exact same stride, the exact same speed. It had been so long since closeness was effortless like this, and I saw something in the moment, a dream I had long since retired with Rachael. I saw possibility. And I even found myself wanting to hope again.

As I entered Jesse's neatly kept apartment, the vibration inside me quickened and the inevitability of togetherness—even temporary—searched for its place in each of us. The towering ceilings made the room feel endless, and I found her eyes with mine, almost as if to reassure her, as if to say, "This is OK, for both of us." The huge old windows looked out over the river, which was hidden in the darkness of the new-moon night. She stood in the middle of the white room under the yellow glow of the red-shaded lamp she had just turned on. She stood in a part of the room meant to be walked through, not stood in, and she waited for me, meeting my reassuring eyes with acceptance and a tender understanding of the gift we were about to share.

This time, there was no gentle start. We kissed deeply enough that I could feel our separate pain drain away. She pressed her body to me and I could feel the muscles in my chest firm up, accepting her. They flexed and grew, not to hold her away, but to give her something strong to push against. I could feel through her skin that that was what she wanted—her soft breasts against me, her mouth on mine, my hands finding their way around her body. This was not a goodnight kiss.

Our mouths found solace, tenderness, and the real hope of relief in each other as I held her. I ended the kiss, held both her shoulders, and looked into the maze of her gentle eyes to signal to her that I wanted to stay. "This way," she said and took my hand.

Standing at the foot of her bed, in the dark, our mouths met while she waited for me to ease her down to the linens. My knee found the edge of the mattress to hold us both up, and our mouths never parted as I cradled her thin waist in my right arm and lowered her quietly to the bed. She raised her back just enough so that I could free my arm, bring it alongside her skin, trace her, find her, reach for her. Exploring her body was like being young again. I felt young not because I felt old, but because when I touched her, Jesse's body responded, and I rejoiced that this long-ago feeling could exist once more in my lonely life.

My hands were rough from building but they felt powerful, and Jesse sensed it. I carefully cupped her tender breast to my lips. She sucked air through her lips as if she was surprised at how good it could feel, and our clothes dissolved into the night. And we dissolved into one another, finding, at last and by twist of fate, the oasis of intimacy for which we both journeyed too many lonely nights.

Holding Jesse after we made love, holding her to me, pulling her to my skin was the final piece of heaven. Instead of shrinking away, instead of an awkward elbow in my kidney, Jesse not only accepted my embrace, I could feel her push back, press the fullness of her body into me. She clutched my hands and arms to her chest and I could feel her want to be hugged. I felt whole again.

I felt whole.

* * *

The thin, worn streets of my old town were empty except for me and my father's truck, the headlights carving new tracks in the black powder of a perfect pre-dawn hour. The air was cool and hinted of summer just beginning, of newness, and of new possibility. The weather report crackling out of my father's single dashboard speaker above the radio called for a clear, sunny week. With the rain over, I could build again.

Feelings breezed around inside me in a nice mix, like a summer zephyr that carries honeysuckle, freshly mowed grass, and a hint of late evening rain. The hours with Jesse had changed the paradigm of my life. I had made a decision, the rest had followed just as the old saying said; but the "rest" was all new. My role as a husband had forever and maybe irrevocably changed. Had I affected my role as a father, too? Was I forever changed as a person? Had what I'd done risked hurting those I loved? Or had it helped me? Could it even help those I loved by making me happier? I felt guiltless—but the newness of my feelings gave me pause because I had more questions than answers—as my life swerved down a new road.

The headlights on the big, old truck cut across the backyard of my mother's house, giving form to the yet formless building, their candlepower fading into the lightening sky in the incalculable distance. By the time the sun fell tonight, this addition would be here, up, defined by studs, headers, and corner posts—a new place for my mother to be, to spend her time, to enjoy. And for me—a place where I re-built my soul.

Coffee's sweet smell filled the kitchen as I snuck through the back door like a teenager. The lights were off, but the note pinched under a small bottle of Irish Crème flavoring spoke more about my mother in a few words than I could explain in a hundred conversations, and I suppose in that split second I could see clearly why my father loved her so much. It was the little things. In the note, she gave me the distance I needed to move and the closeness I needed not to feel alone on the planet. It also provided an open invitation to tell her anything I needed to—or not. I had told her who I was meeting the night before. "I love you, Brendan. I hope you had a good night. My new studio is going to be great.—m"

I relished my mom's note for a moment, then relished caring for her in a new way by appreciating her and her little efforts that made those around her feel loved and safe and thought of. I tasted the steaming coffee as it passed my lips and warmed my throat. I paused for a moment while a new day's sunlight navigated over the horizon and my mind ramped itself up to working speed: time to build.

* * *

First, I laid out the plates, marking where the studs, corner posts, doors, and windows would go. If my friend, Kevin, were not already on his way over to help me, I would have had to cut the long wall panels into 8-foot sections. I could never tilt them up alone. Instead, while I waited, I built the walls to full length. I laid out all my plates, working my way clockwise around the building.

With all the plates laid out for studs, windows, corner posts, and doors. I set one of the three plates aside. I kept a pair on the floor deck and spread them out. Next, I placed the 2x4 studs between them. I put the studs on the layout lines I had slashed with my carpenter's pencil and drove two sharp 16 penny framing spikes through the soft plate stock into the end grain of the studs using my foot to steady the stud perpendicular to the plate.

My mom's pot of coffee and a half-morning later, Kevin arrived. We had been friends for many years. Kevin moved into town for our senior year in high school, so I barely knew him then. However, we attended the same college and even played on the rugby team together, and became fast friends. While he lives only twenty miles from here, I could do more to keep our friendship strong. He calls me more than I call him, and his Christmas card always arrives before mine is sent. Nevertheless, when we do talk or even see each other—semi-annually at best—we pick up the conversation and laughs right where we left off.

I was glad that he was here that day, too, because, although happy with what happened the night before between Jesse and me, I had one fact to face—I was a married man and a father of two innocent girls. My life had just changed, a lot, and I knew that Kevin (who had helped me through some of the problems Rachael and I were having over the last year) would have a good take on the situation.

Kevin, a fourth grade teacher by profession, had worked on enough building sites during summers off to know what he was in for tipping up, bracing, and plumbing these walls. I heard his car pull up out front, and not only was I excited to see him and have some help, I was doubly fired up because after we greeted and shared a hearty back-slapping guy-hug, he slung a tool pouch around his waist and said—in true Kevin fashion—"let's go."

We tipped and tacked the first wall section, and while Kevin filled his pouch with 16 penny nails, I threw the next set of plates up on the deck. He knew to spread them out and I said, "Man, I wish you could be here the rest of summer." He laughed, and without skipping a beat or looking up from his work, he said with a joke meant to show affection, "I don't."

Kevin and I joked, laughed, caught up, and tipped all the perimeter walls by early in the afternoon. Next, we secured them plumb to the floor with diagonal 2x4 kicker braces. He told me that he and his wife were thinking about moving out of state, that his 90-something-year-old grandmother was planning a family reunion, and that he might be looking to make a career switch when he and his family relocated. We talked and nailed, and I shared with him that Rachael had filed for divorce. I looked for a way to tell him about Jesse and last night's escape. As Kevin slung his hammer back into its leather loop on his brown carpenter's apron after nailing off a brace, I said, "I met somebody."

"By 'met' you mean" and his voice dropped an octave, "met?"

"Yes, the second one."

"And?" his face lit up.

"And," I reported, feeling both nervous and proud that I had done it "she's so hot." I felt like a high school kid bragging about making it to second base with a cheerleader. Kevin could sense that this was not a high school kid going around the bases to the pride and wonder of his other pubescent lads; it was a friend with a wife and children talking about a massive life change.

The glow on Kevin's face subsided and I could see his countenance change and mature as the thoughts coalesced in his refreshingly direct mind. "Good," he told me. "You're OK. Just because it says you're married on a sheet of paper in the courthouse, it doesn't mean anything. Rachael filed for divorce already. She abandoned you while you lived in the same house. That means it's over, my friend. It's just down to the business relationship you have as parents and partners, so I'm glad that you met somebody."

For me to let the words out and share them with another person was a Get out of Jail Free card. I was torn up with anxiety over what I had done and what it could mean. "How's the rest of it going?" he asked as he moved to grab the level for plumbing the next wall section.

Even though the next part of the process was important—plumbing and straightening the walls—we were able to talk while we worked. Kevin listened and shared his opinions as I talked about my divorce. I wished he could stay, but he had to join his family for a Fourth of July barbecue.

As Kevin and I worked like we had been on the same construction crew for our entire careers, we worked to complete the carpenter's triptych: plumb, level, and square. I had squared and leveled the deck already, almost unconscious of the importance of these steps as the building grew. But Kevin held the level on the gleamingly blonde wall studs against the tarnished frame of the old building, and told me with pride in his voice when the air bubble in the liquid vial found its way between the black lines, "It's money." With those words, the ghost of my father appeared in my mind's eye.

My father, Gideon Michael Herlihy, was young and powerful, the way I remember him when I think of him. His veins rose to the surface of his tight skin and wrapped his statuesque physique, the proportion and balance of his body matching the proportion and balance of the building he and I framed together so many summers before.

"Plumb, level, and square," he said to me so long ago while we moved through the maze of studs and braces in Arthur Pelletier's new house. "It's more than something I just say, Brendan. It's a rule we use to measure if we're building this place right. I want you to pay attention to what I'm telling you because you'll work alone some day—maybe years from now—and you have to remember something: the rule never takes a day off."

With each wall section built, lifted, and plumbed, it was time to link them with the double top plate, which Kevin and I whipped through in no time, walking along the tops of the walls like kids on the jungle gym.

Kevin handed me parts as I high-wired on the tops of the walls, and my heart felt light because my friend was here to share my life. Our friendship was honest, time-tested—and he was not a $175-an-hour therapist with too much book learning and not enough life experience. Kevin and I drank a beer before he had to get going. We shook hands hard, and he understood in that gesture just how much his presence, not only today but throughout this process, carried me through impossible times. There was still plenty of sunlight left before my mom and I would hop in the car and go watch the fireworks kaboom over the town green, so I had one more beer sitting in the bright afternoon sunlight. I felt thankful for the kindness in my life. I clinked the glass bottle to the surface of the plastic backyard table and rose to get after another couple hours of work.

But, before I got up, in the quiet and stillness, Jesse came back to my mind. Her smell was still on my skin, or at least I imagined it was there, faintly, gently, indelibly. I wanted to see her again. I thought about my father's carpentry advice, about the invisible laws he taught me that followed us through our days. I thought that these laws might have just changed in my life, because of Jesse and how I had come to feel about her in such a short time. Then I thought that maybe they hadn't.

Before the paralysis of confusion and angst could grab me, before my life moved further toward chaos, I felt a comfort I never felt before. The calm of peace came over me like a gentle wind on a hot day. I felt the presence of an order and proportion that could guide me through the next, undiscovered furlongs of my life. I felt the presence of my father and heard his calm, confident voice.

I didn't hear the words; I heard his tone. I didn't hear the context; I heard that there was one. I didn't see the how-to of the plumb, level, and square lesson in his journal entry; I saw between the lines. And I knew as surely as the sun warmed my skin, and that my hammer would power home nails, that a new order would emerge, that my life could make sense again, and that my family and I could rise from divorce decrees, a dying love, and decimated hearts.

We would be re-born, and, I believed, re-born whole.

CHAPTER 9

MORE ROOF!

*I elect strength over weakness,
energy over stasis,
success over failure.*

JOB NAME:
  PELLETIER
PROJECT:
  CUT STATION

I WILL DO ANYTHING TO AVOID
RUNNING SHEATHING, THE ½-INCH THICK
PLYWOOD "SKIN" THAT TIES A BUILDING
TOGETHER AND GIVES THE STRUCTURE
RIGIDITY AND A NAILING SURFACE FOR
SIDING. I MEAN IT. I'LL GO FOR COFFEE,
START ANOTHER PROJECT—I'LL EVEN
CLIP MY FINGERNAILS IF I CAN. I'D TEACH
MYSELF CHESS IF I WAS SMARTER.
ANYTHING TO AVOID PUTTING THIS CRAP ON
A HOUSE.

THERE'S ALMOST NO CRAFT TO HANGING
IT. IT'S JUST WORK THAT NEEDS DOING.

I HATE SHEATHING SO MUCH, I CAN'T
EVEN THINK ABOUT WRITING A HOW-TO ON
IT. YOU'RE ON YOUR OWN IF YOU HAVE TO
SHEATHE A BUILDING. BRING LOTS OF
NAILS.

INSTEAD, TRY OUT THIS CUT STATION/WORK
TABLE FOR A MITER SAW. IT'S MADE FROM
A SINGLE SHEET OF ³/₄" BIRCH PLYWOOD. I
HAVEN'T SHOWN UP TO A JOBSITE WITHOUT
THIS UNIT IN TOW IN A HUNDRED YEARS.
WHEN IT'S NOT ON SITE, I USE IT IN THE
SHOP FOR MORE THINGS THAN I CAN COUNT.

HOW-TO: STEPS

CUT LIST
  - RIP 4 STRIPS OF PLYWOOD 9" WIDE. CUT
  TWO 16" LONG; LEAVE TWO 8' LONG.

  - RIP 1 PIECE 20" WIDE AND CUT THEM
  34" LONG.

  - RIP 2 PIECES 4" WIDE AND CUT THEM
  16" LONG

LAYOUT
1. MEASURE THE EXACT HEIGHT OF YOUR
MITER SAW DECK. NOTE: I DO THIS OFF A
LEVEL SURFACE WITH A COMBINATION
SQUARE.

2. CUT THE PLYWOOD.

3. MEASURE WIDTH OF YOUR MITER SAW DECK, THEN ADD 6" TO THAT VALUE.

4. FIND THE MACHINE EDGE (THE ONE CUT AT THE FACTORY, NOT BY YOU) OF THE 8' X 9" WIDE PIECES. MAKE A MARK AT 4'. ALIGN THE CENTER OF YOUR MITER SAW DECK WIDTH WITH THIS LINE. MARK THE EDGES.

ASSEMBLY

1. CLAMP OR SCREW THE 8' FOOTERS TOGETHER, ALIGNING THE MACHINE EDGES AND ENDS CAREFULLY. CUT OUT THE NOTCH FOR THE MITER SAW. DON'T BE FAKED OUT: A MEASUREMENT THIS EXACT IS HARD TO GET RIGHT THE FIRST TIME. THINK ABOUT BUYING TWO SHEETS OF PLYWOOD. NOTE: TO GET THIS RIGHT, I SET THE FENCE ON MY TABLE SAW TO THE EXACT MEASUREMENT I NEED, AND THEN RAISE THE BLADE THROUGH THE PLYWOOD. I FINISH THE REST OF THE CUT WITH A JAPANESE PULL SAW.

2. PRE-DRILL AND SCREW THE 8' PIECES
TO THE 16" PIECES. BEFORE SETTING THE
SCREWS, PULL DIAGONALS TO SQUARE THE
BOX. GUSSET THE CORNERS.

3. SET THE SCREWS.

4. SCREW IN THE 4" RIPPERS ON THE
EDGES OF THE SAW DECK NOTCH.

5. APPLY THE 34" LONG PIECES ON TOP OF
THE CARCASS YOU'VE BUILT FLUSH TO THE
NOTCH.

6. INSTALL BRIDGING ACROSS THE NOTCH.

7. ROUT A TINY CHAMFER ON THE EDGES
OF THE TABLE TOP.

8. BRIDGE THE CUT STATION ACROSS SAW
HORSES AND CUT AWAY.

SMART THINKING
   - BUILD YOUR SAW HORSE/CUT STATION SO
   THAT THE TOP OF THE STATION IS THE
   SAME HEIGHT AS YOUR TABLE SAW DECK.
   THE CUT STATION CAN THEN DOUBLE AS
   AN OUTFEED TABLE FOR THE SAW.

- ADD A MULTI-PLUG TO THE CUT
STATION. IT SAVES HUNTING FOR AN
OUTLET EVERY TIME YOU NEED ONE.

- SET NAILS IN THE SAWHORSE LEGS
FOR FREQUENTLY USED ITEMS:
COMBINATION SQUARE, COPING SAW,
BLOW GUN, ETC.

- FINISH THE SURFACE WITH BOILED
LINSEED OIL. IT WILL REPEL WATER IF
YOU LEAVE IT OUT IN THE RAIN.

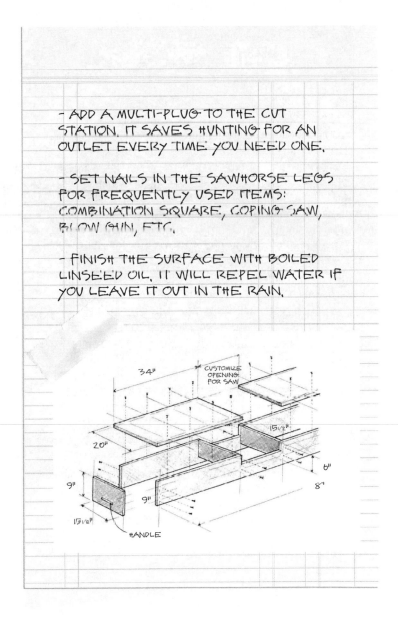

COMMENTS:

NOW THAT I'M THINKING ABOUT IT, THE
THING I REALLY HATE ABOUT HANGING
SHEATHING IS THAT EVERY GODDAM INCH
OF THE BUILDING IS COVERED WITH IT.
SINCE I USUALLY WORK ALONE, THE
SCALE OF THE JOB JUST SEEMS
OVERWHELMING. THE COMBINATION OF
THE LOUSY WORK (DESPITE MY ATTEMPTS
AT TELEKINESIS, PLYWOOD WILL NOT FLY
OFF THE STACK AND NAIL ITSELF TO THE
BUILDING) AND MIND-CRUSHING BOREDOM
(IMAGINE STARING AT YOUR DESK ALL
DAY, JUST YOUR DESK) ABSOLUTELY
SUCKS THE LIFE OUT OF ME. I BECOME A
LUMP.

BUT SOMETHING ALSO COMES OVER ME
ONCE I BUILD THE MOMENTUM FOR
HANGING THAT FIRST SHEET. BEFORE I
KNOW IT, I'M PUMPING NAILS INTO THE
BUILDING LIKE A MAD MAN. ONCE I BUILD
UP THE HEAD OF STEAM TO GET STARTED,
ONCE I BUILD THE ENERGY FOR A POWER
TAKE-OFF, I'M GOING AND I WON'T STOP.
WHILE MY NAIL GUN RAPID FIRES NAILS

THROUGH THE PLYWOOD INTO THE STUDS AND RAFTERS, MY BODY TEMPERATURE RISES, MY BLOOD COURSES LIKE A FREIGHT TRAIN THROUGH MY VEINS, I'M TRANSFORMED BY THE EFFORT OF PUSHING BEYOND MYSELF.

PUSHING BEYOND MY COMFORT ZONE— LUGGING PLYWOOD ALL OVER THE PLACE, SCURRYING IT UP A LADDER TO THE ROOF, NAILING UNTIL I'M DEAF AND VIBRATING FROM THE RECOIL OF MY NAIL GUN— MAKES ME A BETTER PERSON, BECAUSE I CAN BLAST THIS BARRIER IN MY LIFE (I MIGHT'VE MENTIONED HOW MUCH I HATE IT) I CAN SURPASS OTHERS, I CAN ADAPT, I KNOW I CAN JUST DO THE GRUNT WORK OF LIVING DAY-TO-GODDAM-DAY.

I KNOW I CAN DO IT, I KNOW THAT I WILL GET THE WORK DONE, I'M CAPABLE AND PROUD OF THAT, I WILL END THE DAY BETTER FOR HAVING DONE IT, I CHOOSE THIS INSTEAD OF QUITTING. IT'S A CONSCIOUS, KNUCKLE-BUSTIN' CHOICE, BUT IT IS A CHOICE, I ELECT STRENGTH

OVER WEAKNESS, ENERGY OVER STASIS,
SUCCESS OVER FAILURE.

IT'S MY DAY, WEEK, AND LIFE. NOT
SOMEBODY ELSE'S. NO ONE WILL CHOOSE
FOR ME, AND ONCE THE TIME IS GONE,
THAT'S IT. I MUST CHOOSE WELL—AND NOT
JUST FOR ME, BUT FOR THAT BOY OF OURS
WHO NEEDS SOMEONE TO GO FIRST; FOR
MY WIFE WHO LOVES ME LIKE THE HERO I
WISH I REALLY WAS. I MUST DO IT
BECAUSE IT IS THE RIGHT THING; IT JUST
SO HAPPENS IT'S UNCOMFORTABLE, TOO.

Now that I was reading my father's journal every night, poring through the details of a man I wish I knew better, I can't say yet if I'm like him any more than I thought, or if we are totally different people. I do know this, though, and it may have been the same for him: I'm a creature of habit.

I get into a routine that I think works and I really don't change it unless I have to. Life is easy that way and I've lived believing that "easy" and "good" are the same things. I know the steak at my favorite restaurant is good and priced right, so, even though I read the menu every time I go there, I still get the steak. Since our first daughter was born, my body has woken me up about five minutes before she woke up as an infant. She no longer gets up that early, but I do. I've worn a few ruts in the road.

Starting out the "skin job" on the bare-bones studs was no different. In fact, this was a job made for me—a good sheeter is all about head-down production duty; not much thinking, but plenty of busy working. I quickly developed good carpentry habits on the jobsite, too. A good carpenter breathes efficiency and always looks to streamline activity and make those activities accurately repeatable. He does this for two reasons: One, to save time—the longer a job takes, the less money he makes for it. And two, repetition usually leads to increased quality—you don't have to re-invent the wheel every time you need to do something.

* * *

I opened the circ saw box where the thick, black two-prong cord was neatly wrapped around the metal saw body of the tool, closed the tough steel box, and returned the box to its designated spot before plugging in the saw. I loaded my pouch with nails, then sipped coffee from a black-rimmed stainless steel thermos before stepping onto the dry ground and into the cool air of the morning.

I set the first sheet by half-setting two spikes between the foundation and the mudsill and putting a sheet across them. They act as a little shelf and should be level. Next, I lined up the edge of the plywood with the corner of the building and tacked the top corner. If the top edge of the sheet was level, I drove two nails in to each stud—one in the middle of the sheet, one near the top edge—to hold it until I could come back and nail it totally off. Then I set the subsequent sheets by driving tacks in the center at the top edge (and a few in the middle, or "field," to flatten it out), working left to right along the building. Next, I set the following course of plywood, off-set from the first by half a sheet. If the building were a brick walkway, it would look like a running bond pattern, so from course to course, none of the vertical seams line up. This gives the building great strength.

With all the wood hung on the south elevation, I decided to nail it off, placing a nail every 8 inches or so apart to secure the sheets to the building frame. I used to nail a lot like this working with my father, during the summers I worked with him before we started Arthur Pelletier's place, long before he could afford nail guns. Even on Pelletier's house, only he used the nailer while I hand-nailed. I never got the sense that my dad despised installing and nailing sheathing, but as it turns out, he dumped a ton of work on me that he didn't want to do. I didn't mind. I could lose myself in it. I lost myself in the repetition of my duty that summer in Arthur Pelletier's house, and now years later, I lost myself in it again. My mind at once evacuated all thoughts irrelevant to my task but cleared itself to allow new thoughts while my body took over as if on auto-pilot.

While I nailed across each joist, placing nails and smashing them down, my movements almost mechanical, my mind wandered and finally arrived at a thought. I found myself trying to observe something difficult to see, and soon discovered that I was searching to identify something that wasn't there. I knew that Rachael's coldness and distance were there. I knew the heat in her eye had faded. I knew that I tried to reach her in my own way, but I couldn't rememher if I had tried to reach her in her way.

Every morning I'd wake up and want to be close to her. I'd reach out to her and try to be close before words, vision, and the daily grind of reality found its inevitable way to us, like water locating the lowest point. I wanted to be close when it was just the two of us alone in the world—and I only wanted it for five min utes. I wanted us to be two people who—for a single moment during an entire day—could become one, could complete each other. A moment where simply holding and being close was all the peace each of us would need before we left that edge of Eden and entered a world with more facets, people, complexities, and needs. I recalled those desires and wishes, but I couldn't recall asking her to take a walk on a Sunday. I couldn't remember telling her she looked good beyond the dutiful "You look nice," as we got into the car on the way to the office Christmas party. I don't think I ever said, "Hey, let's go on a date," then called a babysitter and swept her off her feet. I never fulfilled a fantasy she had of me taking her to a fancy hotel for the weekend.

The reason those things were hard for me to see is because they weren't there. I didn't do them. There were no reactions against which to measure so I could solve the equation of what was happening to us, so I could finally understand why we fell apart, and why what was once good was gone. Instead, what I found when thinking back, was me doing one more thing in my home office before dashing up to give the kids a bath, or hurry-up-quick reading them a book, or jetting them out to soccer or lacrosse practice. I used to buy her flowers and bring them home. I still did on occasion, but that one-trick-pony was way out to pasture.

I nailed and nailed while this revelation took hold, methodical ly marching across the field of plywood and back. This time, when I felt myself slipping into the haze of routine, I let myself go on purpose, and meekly hid there in that opaque zone of blissful semi-consciousness. The pain of possibly not having done enough—even though I tried the best I could when we lived together, even though I initiated contact, even if it was the wrong kind for her—was too much to take at one shot.

* * *

"More roof! More roof!" my father yelled down from the top of Arthur Pelletier's house. "Move like you mean it. Let's go!" He stood on a collar tie, straddling 2x8 rafters that raced skyward behind him like steepled hands pointing to the heavens. My father positioned himself gymnastically for the next sheet of ½inch plywood that I hauled up the ladder like a one-man bucket brigade. He was on fire, in one of what I called his "lightning moods," where he wanted our two-man crew to work like a high-performance, special-operations machine. In other words, he wanted us to do the work of four men.

I could scarcely get down the ladder and back up with another sheet before he was done nailing the one I had just delivered. In his vein-mapped right hand, his hickory-handled rip claw framing hammer blazed, setting the 8 penny nails in one fearless whack. Then the steel in his hammer head vibrated, causing the tool to sing like a tuning fork as it struck nails, which he drove home in one savage blow. In his mighty left hand, his fingers curled around a bundle of 8 penny sinkers, all aligned heads up, so he could feed them and set them in one mechanical motion.

The roof was simple. There were no dormers or irregularities and it was a walkable pitch. I was exhausted at lunch but his eyes darted over our waxed paper-wrapped white bread and meat sandwiches. He couldn't wait to strike again, couldn't wait to beat back at whatever darkness in him chased him through the sun-drowned day.

"Let's push hard today, Brendan," he said as he led me with steel in his eyes. "Once this plywood goes down, we can roll tar paper on the roof and this place will hold out some rain."

I didn't hear him. Like today, and, I fear, too many days since then, I was happier lost in the patterns of my day. I'm afraid to push any harder than I already push. Easy is good. I'm afraid I'll waste my energy and do the wrong thing if I venture too far past easy and known. I'm afraid that I'll be left with the feeling that I should've just had the steak, because I knew it would be good.

* * *

"We can't get to the phone just now," Rachael's voice announced happily on our voice mail, "leave us a message and we'll call you back." It sounded warm and sang with a happy tone that she hadn't used with me in forever.

"Rache," I stammered. "It's me." Tears punched their way into my eyes and a breath trickled like syrup down my throat toward my lungs. "Maybe more of this is my fault than I ever realized. Maybe I didn't...I don't know...reach out to you in the right way. I meant to. And I'm sorry if I didn't do enough—because I meant to do enough. I did everything I could damn well think of. I wish I could've found a way to think of more, a way to make this work. I miss—"

Rachael picked up. I apologized. I cried. She answered with a long silence. Just still air and the quiet sound of too-little-too-late.

"I'll...think about it," she offered after a brief pause, instead of just hanging up. The numbness in her voice scalded my insides. Invisible to me so many miles away, she was not as numb as she sounded. I thought I heard a subtle trip in her reply, a tiny stammer that meant she did feel us, the loss of us, but it was microscopic and there was no way to be sure. Besides, we needed to make big changes, not little ones, so I gave up even thinking about it. But what I couldn't see as she walked outdoors afterward, with a pile of mail to sort, was that instead of organizing the pile of post, she dropped it carelessly next to her on the wooden deck. Then she stared into the backyard of our home, and a tear slurried her black mascara before skating down her soft, round cheek. It contoured itself over the pores in her supple, gentle skin, and found the corner of her full lips before dripping off into the endlessness of space.

* * *

Two days later, a bundle of letters arrived from Laura and Kelly via Rachael. They were growing up fast at their summer camp and I suspected they'd look different when Rachael and I went to visit them the following week. There were bills and bank statements that I would have to get to work on, but it was the junk mail Rachael sent that caught my attention in a different way. She had become so automatic, so detached from us, so disengaged from thinking beyond her imploding bandwidth, from thinking about anybody but her and what she expected life to be like, that she even sent my junk mail. I was sifting through the stack, flipping computer-printed credit card offers and pennysavers into a pile when my cell phone chirped from somewhere under the rubbish heap of stuff no one would ever read. The caller ID showed a local number and my heart jumped into my throat as I realized it was Jesse.

"I'd love to," I said as the smile climbed up my cheeks and the tension from my desperate conversation with Rachael lost some of its edge. It ebbed, slowly at first. Then as the nearly audible thump in my chest disappeared, I could feel pleasure again and the pain from talking with Rachael drained away.

For the second time, the pattern of my day broke. This time, though, like an ocean wave on a supple, sandy beach.

CHAPTER 10

LIFE IS A TEAM SPORT

We all depend on others.
The risk in depending on them is that
they choose not to play as promised.
It hurts to let them go,
but it hurts more to keep them.

JOB NAME:
PELLETIER
PROJECT:
I-BEAM SAW
HORSES

YOU CAN'T HOLD THE BOARD DOWN AT
BOTH ENDS BY YOURSELF. THAT'S WHY YOU
NEED SAWHORSES. THAT'S WHY YOU
NEED HELP. SINCE THEY ONLY PUT 24
HOURS IN A DAY, THERE'S A LIMIT TO WHAT
ANYBODY CAN DO ALONE. SO, LIKE
EVERYONE ELSE IN THE WORLD, I LOOK
TO SOMEONE ELSE TO COMPLETE ME.

THAT'S WHERE SUBCONTRACTORS FIT INTO
MY BUSINESS LIFE. I FARM OUT CONCRETE
WORK, DRYWALL, PLUMBING, AND
ELECTRICAL. ON THE PROJECT THAT I
HOPE BRENDAN BUILDS ONE DAY, I HAVE
LAID THE FOOTINGS AND FOUNDATION—I'M
RETIRED AND HAVE TIME. I HAVE
ORGANIZED SUBS FOR HIM TO HIRE AND
MANAGE FOR THOSE OTHER TRADES.
BESIDES, WORK KEEPS ME YOUNG EVEN
THOUGH I AM IN WINTER AND MOVING SO

QUICKLY TO A PLACE THAT I FEAR IS COLD AND SCARES ME INTO THE PIT OF MY SOUL.

TEAMING UP WITH SOMEONE ELSE MEANS GIVING UP SOME CONTROL OVER YOUR LIFE. TRUST REQUIRES RISK. IT MEANS TAKING THE CHANCE THAT THE OTHER PERSON WILL CARE AS MUCH AS YOU DO. IN OTHER WORDS, THEY HAVE TO SHOW UP, GET IT DONE, AND DO IT RIGHT.

NORMALLY, SUBS WORK OUT FINE AND EVERYBODY'S HAPPY. HOWEVER, TEAMING UP DOESN'T ALWAYS WORK AND SOMEONE WILL EXPECT A CHECK FOR WORK THAT AMOUNTS TO A DISASTER. I'VE FOUND THAT GIVING MY CREWS UNCOMPROMISINGLY HIGH STANDARDS THAT THEY MUST EITHER RAISE THEMSELVES TO OR FAIL IS THE SUREST MOTIVATOR. I LEARNED THIS TWO WAYS: FROM MY MENTORS, AND WHILE BUILDING THE SAWHORSES I CAN'T LIVE WITHOUT.

HOW-TO:
SAWHORSES HOLD YOUR WORK. THEY ARE

THE GIRDERS UNDER WHAT YOU'RE
BUILDING. TAKING THE TIME TO BUILD MY
HORSES PROPERLY IS AN INVESTMENT.
CARELESSLY MADE, THEY'LL CRUMBLE
UNDER STRESS. THE BEST PART OF THIS
DESIGN IS THAT IT WORKS. IT IS SIMPLE
AND QUICK TO MAKE. AND LONG LASTING.

1. CUT EIGHT 2X4 26" LONG.

2. CUT SIX 2X4 36" LONG.

3. BUILD AN **I** FROM THE 36" BOARDS.

4. NAIL EACH LEG TO THE END OF THE **I**
SHAPE WITH FOUR NAILS. 3" DECK
SCREWS WORK WELL TOO.

COMMENTS:

MANAGE WITH YOUR EYES. MANAGING
WITH YOUR EYES REQUIRES CONFIDENCE
IN YOURSELF AS A LEADER. IT DEMANDS
DETAILED KNOWLEDGE OF YOUR CRAFT.
YOU HAVE TO KNOW WHAT TO LOOK FOR
WHEN YOU WALK ONTO A JOB (PEOPLE
KNOW IF YOU'RE FAKING IT). YOU MUST
HAVE THE WILLPOWER TO LEAD THE
CREW TO THE END OF THE PROJECT—OR
FIND ANOTHER CREW THAT'LL WORK UP TO
YOUR STANDARDS

FOR ME, CONFIDENCE CAME FROM
EXPERIENCE. I HAD TO BUILD IT OUT OF
NOTHING. OVER TIME I SLOWLY LEARNED
THE ART AND SCIENCE OF HOW A
BUILDING WORKS. THE CONFIDENCE
SERVES AS A STABLE PLATFORM, LIKE
GOOD SAWHORSES HOLD A MOUNTAIN OF
LUMBER.

MY MENTORS APPROACHED THEIR
JOBSITES LIKE ATHLETES STEPPING
ONTO THE FIELD. THEY COULD READ

DEFENSES, EYE PLAYERS, AND BE
UNCOMPROMISING IN THEIR WILL TO WIN. IT
TOOK ME MOST OF MY CAREER TO EARN A
TENTH OF THEIR KNOWLEDGE, ABILITY TO
OBSERVE, AND CONFIDENCE TO LEAD,
BUT, TO A MAN, EACH HAD THE SAME
TRAITS: THEY KNEW THEIR TRADE.

WHEN THEY SPOKE, THEIR EYES WERE
ON YOU. THEY DIDN'T LOOK PAST YOU,
AROUND YOU, OR NEAR YOU—THEY LOOKED
AT YOU, INTO YOU. THEY WERE FEARLESS
AND PHYSICALLY ENGAGED IN THEIR
PROJECTS. THEY WALKED SITES AND
LOOKED AT EVERYTHING—THEY MANAGED
WITH THEIR EYES.

THEY ALSO HAD VISION. THEY APPLIED IT
TO OUR WORK, WALKING IN THE SAME MUD
WE WALKED IN. THEIRS WAS NOT A
STRATEGY DEVELOPED ALONE BEHIND
THE CONFERENCE ROOM DOOR OF THE
CORPORATE SUITE OR AT BUSINESS
SCHOOL. THAT STRATEGY JUST DOESN'T
WORK OUT HERE.

BUT I'M LUCKY ENOUGH TO HAVE AN EVEN
BETTER TEACHER, SOMEONE WHO HAS
TAUGHT ME SO MANY IMPORTANT THINGS
ABOUT LIVING A FULFILLING LIFE. WHILE I
COULD NOT DO MY JOB AS WELL AS I DO IT
WITHOUT THOSE WHO CAME BEFORE ME, I
COULD NOT LIVE MY LIFE AS WELL
WITHOUT THE WOMAN WHO SHARES IT WITH
ME. MY WIFE, KAY, MAKES BEING STRONG
AND CONFIDENT AN ART FORM (LIKE SHE
IS), AND SHE FINDS A WAY BENEATH
WORDS TO REACH ME. SHE TOUCHES MY
SOUL AND I AM A BETTER MAN FOR
HAVING SHARED SO MUCH LIFE WITH HER.
IN A WAY NO ONE ELSE COULD, SHE
LEADS ME THROUGH SO MUCH OF MY DAY. I
LOVE HER FOR IT.

MY MENTORS AT WORK EACH HAD
DIFFERENT STYLES: RICK WAS
COURAGEOUS AND FUNNY; STEVE, CALM
AND UNFLAPPABLE; DUNK COULD CHARM
YOU INTO A BLIZZARD WITH A STORY AND
WINK. EACH GUY'S SMARTS AND GRAVITAS
MOVED MEN TO CLIMB RICKETY STAGING,
NAIL SHINGLES ON WINDY DAYS, AND

FRAME LIKE FUCKIN' MANIACS. IT WAS
WITH THESE GUYS IN MY HIP POCKET THAT
I GOT THROUGH ONE OF MY TOUGHEST
DAYS. THEY HELPED ME CLIMB A HURDLE
THAT MADE ME PROUD. IT WAS A DAY THAT
I CONQUERED FEAR. IT WAS A DAY I LED
NOT MEN TO BUILD, BUT FOUND A BETTER
WAY TO FATHER MY BOY.

THE CONCRETE SUB I HIRED TO FORM UP
AND POUR ARTHUR PELLETIER'S HOUSE
WAS A BUDDY. WE HAD GUZZLED PLENTY
OF SUDS TOGETHER AT MAN LUSHEE'S
AND SHARED MEALS IN EACH OTHER'S
HOMES, BUT WE NEVER WORKED
TOGETHER. WE LIVE IN A SMALL,
HANDSHAKE-IS-YOUR-WORD KIND OF TOWN,
SO I TRUSTED HIM, AND STUPIDLY, DIDN'T
PREPARE A CONTRACT. HANK PROMISED
THAT HE'D POUR THE FOUNDATION AS I
ASKED, AS THE PLAN CALLED FOR.

RULE NUMBER ONE FOR BUILDING A
HOUSE IS TO MAKE SURE THE FOUNDATION
IS SPOT-ON. IF THE FOUNDATION IS OUT OF
SQUARE (AND YOU DON'T COMPENSATE

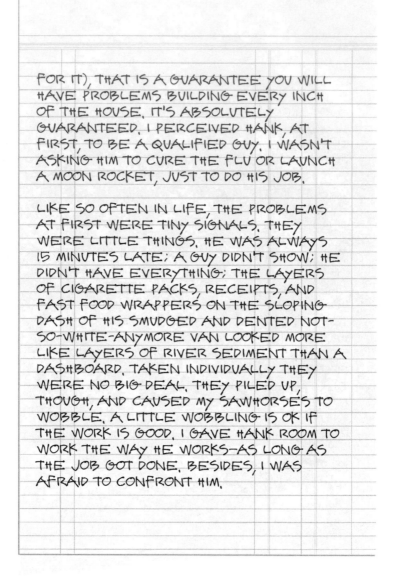

FOR IT), THAT IS A GUARANTEE YOU WILL
HAVE PROBLEMS BUILDING EVERY INCH
OF THE HOUSE. IT'S ABSOLUTELY
GUARANTEED. I PERCEIVED HANK, AT
FIRST, TO BE A QUALIFIED GUY. I WASN'T
ASKING HIM TO CURE THE FLU OR LAUNCH
A MOON ROCKET, JUST TO DO HIS JOB.

LIKE SO OFTEN IN LIFE, THE PROBLEMS
AT FIRST WERE TINY SIGNALS. THEY
WERE LITTLE THINGS. HE WAS ALWAYS
15 MINUTES LATE; A GUY DIDN'T SHOW; HE
DIDN'T HAVE EVERYTHING; THE LAYERS
OF CIGARETTE PACKS, RECEIPTS, AND
FAST FOOD WRAPPERS ON THE SLOPING
DASH OF HIS SMUDGED AND DENTED NOT-
SO-WHITE-ANYMORE VAN LOOKED MORE
LIKE LAYERS OF RIVER SEDIMENT THAN A
DASHBOARD. TAKEN INDIVIDUALLY THEY
WERE NO BIG DEAL. THEY PILED UP,
THOUGH, AND CAUSED MY SAWHORSES TO
WOBBLE. A LITTLE WOBBLING IS OK IF
THE WORK IS GOOD. I GAVE HANK ROOM TO
WORK THE WAY HE WORKS—AS LONG AS
THE JOB GOT DONE. BESIDES, I WAS
AFRAID TO CONFRONT HIM.

POUR DAY CAME AFTER I HAD BEEN OUT OF TOWN FOR SEVERAL DAYS AND COULDN'T MONITOR HANK'S PROGRESS. BRENDAN WOULD BE OUT OF SCHOOL FOR THE SUMMER SOON, SO HE AND I DROVE TO THE SITE TO CHECK IT OUT ONE SATURDAY. WE TALKED ABOUT HIS LAST FEW TESTS, CLASSES, AND THE GIRL HE WOULDN'T SAY MUCH ABOUT. (FOR CERTAIN HIS MOTHER AND I WOULD HEAR MORE ABOUT HER LATER IN THE SUMMER WHEN WE COULDN'T GET WITHIN SIX MILES OF OUR ONLY TELEPHONE).

HANK WAS TO COMPLETE THE LAST BIT OF EXCAVATION WORK WHILE I WAS AWAY, SO I DID NOT SEE THE SITE UNTIL AFTER I PARKED MY TRUCK. I WHEELED IN DOWN THE ROAD A WAYS SO THAT THE CONCRETE TRUCK HAD A CLEAR PATH. LATER, CONCRETE WOULD GUSH DOWN ITS STEEL, SEMI-CIRCLE CHUTES AND FILL THE STEMWALL FORMS ON TOP OF THE FOOTINGS.

BRENDAN CLUTCHED HIS BLUE AND
WHITE WAX-COVERED GO-CUP OF BROWN,
STICKY COLA WE GOT AT THE SODA
FOUNTAIN. WE JUMPED OUT OF THE CAB
AND WALKED OVER TO MAKE THE FINAL
CHECKS. I ENJOYED—REALLY ENJOYED—
WALKING THIS SITE WITH HIM. HE HAD
GROWN STRONG AND CAPABLE. THERE
WAS AN INTENSITY IN HIS EYES WHEN HE
WALKED ON SITE THAT I JUST DIDN'T SEE
IN OTHER BOYS HIS AGE. HE LOOKED AT
ME WHEN I SPOKE, I LOOKED AT HIM, AND
WE COULD BOTH SEE THE ACTIVITY IN
EACH OTHER'S MINDS, BEHIND OUR EYES.

SEVENTEEN YEARS BEFORE, WHEN
BRENDAN WAS BORN, KAY AND I WERE
JUST A LITTLE OLDER THAN HE WAS
THEN. ENVISIONING A MOMENT OF PRIDE
AND POWER LIKE THIS WAS LIKE THE
IDEA OF ORBITING THE EARTH IN A LUNAR
MODULE OCCURRING TO A CAVEMAN. KAY
AND I WERE ALONE WITH BRENDAN IN
THAT HOSPITAL, ON THE DOCK OF OUR
VOYAGE. BRENDAN ENTERED THE WORLD
ON A LEADEN SPRING DAY THAT HELD

MORE OF WINTER'S COLD THAN SPRING'S
SOFT RELEASE, BUT THERE WAS STILL
PROMISE SOMEWHERE IN THE AIR,
BETWEEN THE RAIN DROPS AND BEHIND
THE SKIN-REDDENING COLD, SOME KIND
OF PROMISE WAITED LIKE THE GENTLE
BUT INEVITABLE CROCUS SHOOTS
STRETCHING OUT FROM BETWEEN THE
BLADES OF THE FRESHEST, GREENEST
GRASS YOU'VE EVER SEEN.

KAY'S LABOR CAME ON FAST. AFTER WE
GOT TO THE HOSPITAL, NURSES AND THE
DOCTOR RUSHED TO GET HER TO THE
DELIVERY ROOM. BUT SHE WAS SCARED—
HORRIFIED—AND WOULDN'T LET GO OF MY
HAND. SHE LIFTED HERSELF UP OFF THE
WHITE GURNEY ONTO HER RIGHT ELBOW
AND STARED INTO THE DOCTOR'S EYES
WITH A GRAVITY THAT MADE THE ENTIRE
ROOM FREEZE: "HE COMES IN OR I'M
HAVING THIS BABY RIGHT HERE IN THE
HALL!"

IN EVERY SECOND OF HER LABOR, KAY
WAS HEROIC. HER HAIR WAS WHIPPED

AROUND HER FOREHEAD, AND HER EYES
BURNED WITH A SUN INSIDE THAT SPOKE
TO HER EXHAUSTION AND DETERMINATION
TO BRING BRENDAN INTO THE WORLD.
DESPITE HER AGONY, I SAW LOVE FOR
HER CHILD FUELING THE BURN IN HER
GENTLE EYES. IT WAS A FIRE THAT
MADE THE BRIGHTNESS OF THE HOSPITAL
LIGHTS LOOK LIKE A FLASHLIGHT BULB ON
A SUNNY DAY. WHEN BRENDAN REACHED
OUT THE TINIEST HAND I EVER SAW TO HIS
NEW EXISTENCE, SHE WAS AN OLYMPIC
RUNNER AT THE END OF A GREAT
CONTEST, BUT ONLY AT THE BEGINNING
OF A LEGENDARY CAREER.

ONLY NOW WAS I TRULY PART OF THIS. I
FELT BOTH ALIVE AT THE BIRTH OF OUR
NEW FAMILY, AND CRUSHED BY THE
WEIGHT OF OUR NEW RESPONSIBILITIES. I
CAN STILL FEEL MY PUPILS SHRINK LIKE A
CAMERA LENS FLOODED WITH LIGHT
WHEN I WALKED THE HOSPITAL'S
ENDLESS WHITE-ON-WHITE HALLS. THE
CHILL IS STILL THERE ON MY SKIN AS I
REMEMBER HOW CLEAN AND COLD THE
ASBESTOS TILE FLOORS WERE AND HOW

WHITE THE PORCELAIN WAS THAT COATED
THE TABLES, GURNEYS, AND TRAYS. I
PACED ALONE FOR A WHILE IN THE
HALLWAY WHILE KAY AND BRENDAN
RESTED. THERE WERE NO CIGARS TO
HAND OUT. WE WERE ALONE. I WAS
TERRIFIED. I WAS NOT YET CONSUMED BY
THE LOVE KAY ALREADY HAD FOR
BRENDAN, NOT YET ABLE TO SEE HOW
MUCH I WOULD LOVE THIS BOY. I WAS NOT
ABLE TO REACH PAST TODAY INTO THE
PROMISE OF A BETTER TOMORROW.

THAT DAY, THOUGH, IN THE MUD, BRENDAN
AND I WALKED. THE YELLOW, RUST-
POCKED EXCAVATION EQUIPMENT CAST
MONSTROUS SHADOWS ACROSS THE
BROKEN EARTH AND ROUGH MEN IN
BROWN WORK PANTS. WE WALKED IN THE
SHADOW OF A FUTURE BRENDAN WAS NO
MORE CAPABLE OF SEEING THAN I WAS
AT HIS AGE. MY HEART WAS SO FULL MY
CHEST COULDN'T CONTAIN IT AND I
REACHED OUT TO HIM. I TOUSLED THE HAIR
ON THE BACK OF HIS HEAD, GIVING HIM AN
AFFECTIONATE SHOVE SO HE'D THINK IT
WAS MORE TOUGH-GUY THAN TENDER,

AND NOT THE LOVE FOR MY LITTLE BOY
THAT IT REALLY WAS. WE WALKED AND I
SHOWED HIM WHAT I WAS LOOKING FOR. I
CHECKED THE SITE TO BE CERTAIN
SOMETHING UNEXPECTED DIDN'T HAPPEN
WHILE I WAS AWAY.

THE CONCRETE TRUCK, ITS HUGE STEEL
DRUM PAINTED LIKE A WEIRD LOOKING
BARBER POLE, SPUN A LAKE OF
CONCRETE INSIDE. THE PISTONS IN THE
RIG'S MASSIVE DIESEL ENGINE
THUNDERED THE HUGE, DOUBLE SET OF
DUALLY TIRES OVER THE GRAY GRANITE
CURBSTONE, DEFORMING THEM AS THEY
PUSHED OVER THE SHARP CORNER AND
INTO THE DIRT LOT. THE WORKERS
UNHOOKED THE MAIN CHUTE FROM THE
SIDE OF THE TRUCK AND PREPARED TO
DROP 15 TONS OF CONCRETE INTO THE
HOLE AS INSTRUCTED.

I EYED THE SITE WITH BRENDAN, TOTALLY
ALERT TO DANGER ON MY FIRST SOLO
HOUSE. I THOUGHT ABOUT HOW RICK,
STEVE, AND DUNK WALKED THEIR OWN

PROJECTS WHEN I WORKED FOR THEM. I POINTED TO THE TRUCK READYING ITSELF TO EMPTY ITS CONTENTS INTO THE CAREFULLY PREPARED SPACE. I EXPLAINED TO BRENDAN WHAT WAS ABOUT TO HAPPEN AND WHY. THAT'S WHEN I NOTICED THAT HANK HAD FORGOTTEN TO FORM UP THE GARAGE SLAB.

I STOPPED THE TRUCK FROM DOING ANYTHING FURTHER. I WAS AFRAID. I WAS ALSO ANGRY THAT THERE MIGHT BE OTHER MISTAKES. "WHAT ABOUT IT," I ASKED HANK, LOCKING HIS EYES WITH MINE. I STOMPED ON THE NERVOUSNESS EXPANDING IN MY BELLY LIKE THE BUBBLES IN A SODA LEFT ON THE DASH OF HANK'S TRUCK ON A SWELTERING DAY. HIS EYES DARTED AS HE SEARCHED HIS MIND FOR A REPLY.

SUDDENLY, I WAS TREMBLING. I WAS REALLY AFRAID OF A POTENTIAL CONFLICT WITH HANK. I KNEW HIM TO BE A FIST-THROWING HOTHEAD. BUT WITH BRENDAN AT MY SIDE, AND WITH ALL THE

YEARS I'VE BEEN WORKING TO BE GOOD AT THIS JOB, I COULD FEEL SOMETHING BENEATH ALL THAT THRUST MY CONFIDENCE UP OUT OF THE MUD. I WAS CLEAR THAT HANK HAD ONE CHOICE: 'FESS UP OR LIE. IT BECAME CLEAR THAT I COULD COMMAND THIS SHIP LIKE THE GUYS WHO TAUGHT ME COMMANDED THEIRS. I KNEW I SHOULD SET A STANDARD FOR HANK TO RISE TO, NOT LOWER ONE AND HOPE HE'D COME THROUGH. I WALKED THE EDGE BETWEEN THE CONCRETE TRUCK AND THE FOUNDATION PIT WITH BRENDAN WHERE I HELD THE TRUCK CREW OFF.

HANK SEARCHED FOR AN ANSWER. WE HAD LAID OUT THE GARAGE SLAB TOGETHER BEFORE HE BROUGHT IN HIS EXCAVATION EQUIPMENT TO DIG THE SITE. WE WALKED THE PROJECT. STRINGS WERE NAILED TO WOODEN STAKES (CALLED BATTER BOARDS) IN THE GROUND THAT OUTLINED THE BUILDING. HANK SIMPLY (AND THIS FLOORED ME) SCREWED IT UP. IF THIS

WAS ALL FOULED UP, IT WAS MY JOB AS
SOMEONE ENGAGED IN MY OWN
SUCCESS TO FIX PROBLEMS—BEFORE
THEY STARTED. THERE IS NO SUBSTITUTE
FOR PREPARATION AND PLANNING; NONE.
NOT ONE.

HANK HAD ALREADY COST ME A WEEK—A
TON OF MONEY TO ME—BUT THE WHOLE
PROJECT WAS MORE IMPORTANT THAN
THIS SINGLE PART.

"FORGET IT HANK," I TOLD HIM. "CALL OFF
THE POUR."

WHEN HANK MOVED A STEP TOO CLOSE TO
ME, WHEN HE GOT IN MY FACE, I FELT
LIGHTNING STRIKE INSIDE ME. ON
ANOTHER DAY, MY FINGERS MIGHT'VE
FOUND THEMSELVES CLAMPED AROUND
HIS THROAT AND HE WOULD'VE FOUND
HIMSELF IN THE MUD WONDERING WHERE
HIS NEXT BREATH WAS GOING TO COME
FROM. I HAD THAT IN ME AND PART OF ME
LIKED IT WHEN IT CAME OUT. I COULD ALSO
FEEL BRENDAN. HE SENSED THE

ENERGY. HE WAS WATCHING. I OWED HIM
MORE THAN A CRAZY BRUISER. I OWED
HIM MY SINGLE BEST. BRENDAN
WOULDN'T REMEMBER THE SPECIFIC
EVENTS OF THIS MOMENT AS MUCH AS
HOW IT PLAYED OUT. I SENSED THE
EVENT WOULD BECOME A PART OF HIM
AND I FELT MY SPIKING BLOOD PRESSURE
GO DOWN QUICKLY. HANK HARD-CHARGED
ME A LITTLE MORE AND, LIKE MY
MENTORS, I FOUND THE CONFIDENCE TO
LOOK UNCOMPROMISINGLY, UNFLINCHINGLY
INTO HIS EYES. THAT OPENED HIM UP
MORE THAN ANY PUNCH I COULD EVER
THROW.

I KNEW HANK WAS WRONG, AND AS SOON
AS THE LIGHTER FLUID BURNED OFF HIS
BRIQUETTES, HE KNEW IT TOO. "YOU'RE
OFF THE JOB, HANK."

WITHIN A WEEK, I HAD ANOTHER CREW IN
THERE THAT FINISHED THE JOB RIGHT.
AND THREE MONTHS LATER, I SAW HANK
AT MAN LUSHEE'S. "I'M SORRY," HE SAID
AND TOLD ME A LONG STORY EXPLAINING

WHY AS WE DOWNED A FEW PINTS
TOGETHER.

LIKE THE GUYS WHO WENT BEFORE ME, I
FOUND THE COURAGE TO SET A
STANDARD. I BELIEVED IN THE WILL TO
CUT LOOSE PEOPLE WHO COULDN'T MEET
IT. MY EXPERIENCE IN THE TRENCHES
GAVE ME THE CREDIBILITY AND
KNOWLEDGE TO SET A REALISTIC
STANDARD. MY LOVE FOR MY SON GAVE
ME THE FOCUS TO MEET THE STANDARD
IN EXCELLENT FASHION.

LIFE IS A TEAM SPORT. THOSE WHO COAST
GET CUT AND DON'T LIVE TO THEIR FULL
POTENTIAL. FOR ME, LIVING TO MY FULL
POTENTIAL—DOING MY BEST, THEN A LOT
BETTER—IS THE POINT. WHY MERELY
EXIST WHEN YOU CAN LIVE!

WE ALL DEPEND ON OTHERS. THE RISK IN
DEPENDING ON THEM IS THAT THEY
CHOOSE NOT TO PLAY AS PROMISED. IT
HURTS TO LET THEM GO, BUT IT HURTS
MORE TO KEEP THEM.

Rachael and I had only spoken long enough to plan where we would meet before Parent's Weekend at summer camp. We would wait until Laura and Kelly got back from camp, and I was finished at my mom's, to tell them we were divorcing. But for this weekend, for this quick dash into the kids' lives, we decided to put on our brave faces and hold the line.

Seeing Rachael before we got in the station wagon to go from the motel down the two-lane country road to the camp entrance filled me with apprehension. The thought that nothing was going to come out of her—no feeling, no emotion—made me feel lonelier and angrier than I had ever thought possible.

My father had my mother, and she had him. They were in each other's lives and they did things together besides the day-to-day routine in order to give their life meaning. The note my mom left with my coffee was just like the ones she also left for my father. My parents were people who hugged and touched each other when I was around. Affection wasn't assigned to a time or place. But with Rachael, whose orderliness had replaced the affectionate patterns we once shared, my vigor and hopefulness for a long love affair with her had been transplanted with apathy. We were in for two sterile days.

"I don't want to argue with you," she started before I had said a word. She locked her motel room door before slipping the motel key into her purse and handing me the car keys.

"Rachael, I haven't even said hello yet. Is it possible I can have a chance before you assume I'll fail to live up to whatever impossibly narrow standard of conduct you've established for us this weekend?" Seven words out of her mouth instantly created the kind of tension that she carries with her and exudes all day. I hadn't missed it.

We got in the car and I turned the key in the ignition. I tried hard not to look at Rachael's legs and how good they looked. Her shorts were short and her shirt tighter than normal. Uncommonly, she wore red lipstick and I did all I could to not let old feelings come back, feelings that she gave no signal would ever be reciprocated again. I backed the car out of the space in front of my room and turned out of the motel's driveway.

The country lining the road along the basin of the big lake, on the shores of which Camp Wequaquet made its home, was gorgeous and green. Mountains charted a lumpy, stunning horizon in the distance while huge, ancient firs, pines, and hemlocks stretched skyward and reminded us of what forests were like before people came and logged them to build ships, homes, and textile mills. But try as I might to lose myself in all this beauty, Rachael's silence screamed at me. The mixture of her body sitting there in prim, antiseptic quiet as we wound down the road on the way to lie (at least to postpone the truth) to our children was too much. I stopped the car in a gravel turnout.

I shoved the gear into park, sat a moment to gather my racing thoughts, drank in a breath of thick, humid air, and turned to her. "Love matters," I said, finding her shifting eyes with mine.

Her reply was as evasive as her eyes as she tried her hardest not to turn in her seat. "I'm not sure what you're talking about, Brendan."

"I'm going to do my best here, Rachael, and that's either good enough for you or it's not. I'm going to try one more time to tell you how I feel, what I want, and what I hope for. I will be blunt, because we are past niceties and the whole game is on the line here. And what you need to do is not pick my words apart, Rache. Rather, we need to look at the big picture before we can even think about details. If you're unwilling to see the spirit in what I'm about to say, then our marriage has no future and I will never, never talk to you about it again."

She sat in expectant silence, as she always does when conversations get uncomfortable for her, and I ended my pause.

"No silence this time, Rache. I'm reaching out to you now the best I know how. You either reach back—with words so I know your heart's in this—or the love we once shared is truly dead." With the car at a standstill, I could see the lake glittering through the green needles and brown, scaly trunks behind Rachael and knew that to be the place where our girls were growing up that summer.

Something happened in Rachael's eyes that made me think she had really understood. I saw a fleck of desire and the softness of emotion in the green sea of her gaze, so I continued.

"My father taught me something a long time ago. I only really understood it while reading a journal of his this summer that I found in his shop. I thought a lot about it while driving his truck up here this weekend. He taught me that in order for a team to work, there must be risk of failure for both parties. And both parties must try their hardest to raise a standard from which their lives can evolve together. Without this—without this unified travel along life's path—the partnership will fail and the team will fall apart.

"Somewhere we started to fall apart, Rache. We drifted away from each other. It happened before we ever talked about a third baby, not because of it." Rachael's gaze broke from mine, she softened her turgid posture, and shifted uncomfortably in the passenger's seat. I went on, "As I build this new studio for my mom, I think about being a new dad again and how much fun it is being Laura and Kelly's old man. I think about how my father loved me, how he loved my mother, and how I loved you once. I think about how much I love Laura and Kelly and how much I want them to be safe and whole with us. Then, I think about all the ways I've tried to reach out to you, Rachael, only to have you slap my hand.

"I will not reach out another time. I want you, Rachael Herlihy. I've wanted you since the first day I met you. I will have to live with that for the rest of my life, whether we save our marriage or let it drown. And what I learned from my father, I have now shared with you. It's my last effort to save what we had and grow into a tomorrow that I am willing to believe in and strive for—a tomorrow I want to strive for with you." As the words and the vibrations of my voice echoed and were absorbed into the leather interior of our car, I knew how much Rachael detested ultimatums. She saw them as threats—no matter what they actually were—and she tried to ameliorate and soften them so they were less meaningful. Her first move was always to strike a compromise. I knew as I spoke that I had compromised enough. Not being strong enough to stake my own claim in this marriage was a big part of why it wasn't working. That would end today.

"We must make our marriage a journey together," I said filling my voice with a confident calmness, not threatening, just telling it like it is. "A journey where we share love and where we share sorrow, one where we offer love—a hug, a kind note—a free lunch that you have to ask for is not free—and not enough. I want to love you, Rachael. I want you to let me love you, and hold you, and take care of you. I want to be your champion again.

"But I also want you to love me, to take care of me, to hold me and tell me that it'll be OK when the night is darkest and I forget what I believe in.

"Without that shared responsibility to love one another, our marriage ends here, on this road, right now. No little gesture will save it in a month. No half measure of affection will resuscitate it. We either stand out into new water together—open to the possibilities of a hopeful future or we sink the ship now."

Rachael folded her hands in her lap and looked at me with templed eyebrows that suggested she was unraveling inside, that a storm had brewed in her heart and her belly, and that she was unsure.

"I've lived in agony and stasis and apathy for long enough. Today is the first day of the rest of my life. I want you to come along and share the journey with me—and all the things that come with it, but it is your choice, now. You can see what I want and I will accept nothing less. I know I have failed you in some way, and for that I am sorry. But I cannot undo whatever failure you see in me. The new day is now: come or stay behind."

I turned for a moment, to see the road, to realize that there was more in the world than the inside of our family station wagon and that there were two little girls waiting for us at the bottom of the windy dirt road. I did not give her a chance to reply. She would have to do that herself. I shifted back into drive, and fixed my eyes on the road before us.

* * *

My girls didn't want the giant hugs I wanted to give them in front of their new camp friends—"Daaa–aaad!" they whined as they shrunk away with big smiles. But in the sliver of time I had each one in my arms, I tried to send every joule of good energy I had in me to each one of them.

"Can you show us around?" I asked, and they took Rachael and me on a tour of all the places they spent their days: the field where they were called to assembly, the lake where they took swimming lessons, the enormous spruce tree behind which their favorite counselor caught Patty Riley smoking a cigarette.

Dragging around the secret of our impending divorce like a trunk full of pig iron cut into me. A lie seeping into all this truth was somehow deeply unjust, going against the grain of what I thought and wished should be. But I could make it through this day, because I had said my piece. I had reached out. I shared with Rachael what was in my heart. I had done the right thing, for me, for Rachael, and for my girls.

Rachael and I walked, totally engaged in the lives of our daughters, like we were the family Laura and Kelly thought they had when they left for camp early in the summer. I caught myself wanting to reach out to Rachael and take her hand, like I might have years before. I looked at her as she walked through the just-mowed grass and smelled the inimitable summer smell of grass clippings in the air. If we walked long enough, the toes of our shoes would turn green.

She was still beautiful, but I looked closer behind her eyes and saw not just her bone-crushing absence, but something new—anger at me for ruining her life. I felt for sure that every word I had said in the car was lost on her. Even with all that, I knew she could not envision a life with me other than the single option of three kids and endless lists of things to do, rather than people to love and experiences to be shared. I looked down at my own hand as it rose from my side in mid-reach for Rachael's.

As the girls and their mother talked about the rope swing they had seen while on a boat ride around the point that was wooded with firs and pines, I rubbed my right palm with my left thumb and could feel Jesse's skin on mine. I could feel her smell on my fingers. I sensed the receptive tension in her skin in a zephyr of summertime air that curled around me like an invisible silken veil of calming smoke. I felt whole when I remembered the image of hugging my body into her and without being asked she accepted the embrace, pressing herself back to me, and clutching my hands to her chest as she did so. A secret smile brightened my face and I turned to see the camp from this side of the field, and to hide my joy so that it wouldn't cause Rachael any pain. Across the grass and into the ancient trees, my heart wandered into a garden of sustaining, satisfying fruit until the next story began with the unstoppable energy of youth and the anticipation that life has a lot more summers full of grass clippings, lakes, and friends where it could only get better....

"Here's my cabin, Pop. Laura sleeps two cabins down." I loved being called "Pop" more than anything in my life, and the goodness of the day reached into my darkness, pulling me beyond myself into a place my father traveled more and better than I ever would, but a place I would go. And an expedition I would survive.

I would make it. We would make it. I didn't know what "it" is, but there was a right way to do this and I would find it. I took the first steps, today.

I loved my daughters.

CHAPTER 11

FUCK IT. NAIL IT.

We all need a roof, that hard-edged, take-no-prisoners, first-line-of-defense part of ourselves. We need something inside us that keeps the weather out and that doesn't give a shit if the water gets hurt on its way to the ground.

Good-byes had taken on a new meaning in my life. Clutching each of my daughters to me while Rachael and I omitted the truth of our lives found me hammering back a lake full of tears and the cry of "no fucking fair!" Each girl, so unimaginably small when her mother brought her into the world, now looks so close to shedding the skin of her youth—yet a thousand parsecs from being grown up—and strikes me as a new person, someone different. Older, more knowledgeable, and still Daddy's little girls.

Rachael stood behind me as I hugged them. Her good-bye was quicker, but I knew it was no less heartfelt. She loved them and that was the undeniable truth of her. We walked together back to the car and headed off to the motel together. We would share a breakfast tomorrow with the girls at long camp tables in their cafeteria before heading our separate ways. The drive into camp saw my plea and Rachael's predictable silence. The short drive back, with so much hurt inside, heard silence. I said to myself under my breath as Rachael got out of the car before walking into the motel room, "Well, you're on your own now," and I decided to call my lawyer on Monday to speed up what I now saw as inevitable: divorce.

After breakfast the next day, on the way home in my father's truck, I thought about the weekend, about my girls, and about how Rachael reacted. I tried to reach out to her so many times in our marriage, and now in our separation. She kept slapping my hand with her emotionless absence, with her one word answers, with anger that there wasn't another baby, with the sense of loss that part of her life was ruined, and that I was to blame. Yet, I still remembered the "us" before our life happened, felt the memory of happiness we had once, but lost. And it was with that loss—that unbridgeable distance—that any hope for more babies fell into the chasm. Just then, Jesse's skin raced to my mind and my nerve endings reached for her body. I'd see her, touch her, and be touched by her in just a few hours. I squeezed the hard plastic wheel of my father's pick-up truck, pretending to be something I wasn't, maybe pretending to be him, and maybe pretending everything was OK.

JOB NAME: PELLETIER
PROJECT: BROWN

I LIKE ROOFING. IT'S FAST.
I DON'T HAVE TO THINK TOO HARD AND I
CAN SEE PROGRESS AS I NAIL UP
TOWARD THE RIDGE. I WOULDN'T WANT TO
DO IT EVERY DAY, BUT PUTTING ON A ROOF
CAN BE A NICE CHANGE OF PACE FROM
SWEATING THE DETAILS ON A RAFTER
CUT OR MOLDING DETAIL.

ROOFING MATERIALS GO ON IN A
WEATHERBOARD FASHION. THIS MEANS
EVERYTHING YOU DO ON A ROOF
PROCEEDS FROM THE BOTTOM UP.

HOW-TO:

1. INSTALL ALUMINUM DRIP EDGE AT THE
EAVES.

2. INSTALL BLACK PAPER OVER THE DRIP
EDGE.

3. INSTALL DRIP EDGE ALONG THE
GABLES.

4. INSTALL THE STARTER COURSE.

5. INSTALL THE FIRST COURSE OF SHINGLES.

6. INSTALL THE FIRST "SET" OR HALF-PYRAMID OF SHINGLES.

7. KEEP INSTALLING "SETS" ACROSS THE ROOF AND, LIKE A CARRIAGE RETURN ON A TYPEWRITER, GO BACK AND START AGAIN.

8. INSTALL RIDGE (AND SOFFIT) VENTS SO THE ATTIC CAN BREATHE.

9. INSTALL SHINGLE CAPS.

10. ON THE LAST TWO EXPOSED NAILS ON THE LAST SHINGLE CAP, APPLY ROOFING TAR (WE CALL IT "BLACKJACK" SOMETIMES) TO SEAL THEM.

COMMENTS:
ROOFERS ARE TOUGH. SHINGLES ARE TOUGH. THE PLACE THEY WORK IS TOUGH—HIGH-UP AND EXPOSED TO EVERY DAMN

THING MOTHER NATURE'S GOT, BUT AS
TOUGH AND UNPLEASANT AS ROOFERS
AND ROOFING CAN BE, ANY BUILDING
WITHOUT A GOOD, TOUGH-AS-ASPHALT ROOF
WILL FAIL, IT WILL SINK IN ON ITSELF, IT
WILL BE DEFENSELESS.

REPLACING THAT ROOF WHEN IT NEEDS
CARE TAKES WORK, IT IS HARD,
MERCILESS WORK, BUT, AS I PEER
AROUND THE HORIZON OF ROOFTOPS
STANDING AT THE RIDGE OF MY PROJECT,
I REALIZE THAT WHILE IT'S UNPLEASANT
WORK TO HOLD OUT THE RAIN AND SNOW, IT
IS VITAL THAT WE DO IT, IT'S VITAL TO OUR
HOUSES, AND TO OURSELVES, IT BOILS
DOWN TO ONE THING—OUR SURVIVAL
DEPENDS ON IT.

THIS OCCURRED TO ME WAY UP IN THE
WIND OF A COLDER THAN NORMAL FALL
DAY. I WAS LOADING 80-POUND BUNDLES
OF SHINGLES ON THE RIDGE OF A ROOF
JOB. THE WIND BIT AT THE SKIN ON MY
FACE AND FORCED ITS WAY THROUGH THE
WEAVE OF MY SWEATSHIRT. EACH HOUSE

I COULD SEE HAD A ROOF THAT HAD BEEN UPDATED WHEN THE OLD SHINGLES HAD LIVED THEIR USEFUL LIFE. I IMAGINED THE INSIDE OF EACH OF THOSE HOUSES, THEY WERE DRY. I WAS SURE THAT THERE WAS NO COLLAPSING PLASTER OR DRYWALL. SURELY, THERE WERE NO WATER STAINS ON CEILINGS, NO MUSTY SMELLS IN THEIR SOAKING BASEMENTS. NONE OF THAT COULD BE SAID ABOUT THE HOUSE I WAS STANDING ON TOP OF.

THIS HOUSE HAD BEEN A RENTAL PROPERTY, AND ITS OWNER LET IT GO TO POT. THE SALTINE-BRITTLE SHINGLES COULD NO LONGER HOLD OUT THE WATER SO THE BUILDING LEAKED AND ROTTED INSIDE. WATER IN A BUILDING IS A CANCER. I LOOK AT IT THE SAME WAY I SEE PAIN IN PEOPLE. PAIN ALLOWED TO GROW UNCHECKED WITHIN THE WALLS OF YOUR SOUL IS ALSO A CANCER.

WE ALL NEED A ROOF, A HARD-EDGED, TAKE-NO-PRISONERS, FIRST-LINE-OF-DEFENSE PART OF OURSELVES. WE

NEED SOMETHING INSIDE US THAT KEEPS
THE WEATHER OUT AND DOESN'T GIVE A
SHIT IF THE WATER GETS HURT ON ITS
WAY TO THE GROUND. IT'S GOING THERE
ANYWAY. AT SOME POINT, THAT RAINDROP
OF PAIN MUST HIT A COARSE, THE-BUCK-
STOPS-HERE SHINGLE.

IT'S SIMPLE BUT TRUE, JUST LIKE PUTTING
ON SHINGLES. SHINGLES NEED TO GO ON
THE ROOF PROPERLY, BUT THERE IS SO
MUCH ROOM FOR ERROR THAT A 1/8" INCH
DOESN'T MATTER LIKE IT DOES IN A
WINDOW TRIM OR BOOKCASE. JUST LIKE
THE COARSENESS OF THE MATERIAL,
THE SAYING IS EQUALLY COARSE: WE
'AINT BUILDIN' PIANOS—FUCK IT. NAIL IT.

SHINGLING IS A TOUGH PHYSICAL
PROCESS. THE ONLY WAY TO MAKE MONEY
AT IT IS TO GO AS FAST AS YOU GODDAM
CAN AND GET OFF THE ROOF (USING THE
LADDER.) WE ALL HAVE A ROOF
SOMEWHERE INSIDE US, TOO. WE NEED
IT. IT'S NATURAL. THE DIFFERENCE
BETWEEN A PERSON AND A HOUSE IS

THAT WE CAN DEPLOY OUR ROOF AS
NECESSARY, LIKE AN UMBRELLA IN THE
RAIN. IT'S IN DEPLOYING IT, SHOWING IT TO
OTHERS, THAT WE DRAW THE BOUNDARIES
OF OURSELVES. AND WHEN THERE ARE
THUNDERHEADS IN THE DISTANCE, THE
WIND IS WHIPPING ALL AROUND US, AND
THE MERCURY SINKS LIKE A STONE, ONLY
THE BEST ROOFS HOLD OUT WEATHER.

My return to my mom's house coincided with her summer vacation, an annual pilgrimage planned long before the notion to build her studio even existed. In fact, I raced home to get her to the airport Sunday evening so that she could go, much to my amazement, to the searing summer heat of Florida for a month where she had a time-share condo with friends. She continues to live a happy, productive, busy life—one full not of pain in the absence of my father, but of love for friends, grandchildren, life itself. I was feeling lonely and told her so. "Mom, I'm going to miss you and your lunches on the patio."

"Bren, I really want to be around for you...."

"Mom, come on," I said. "You can't cancel this time with your friends. They've been looking forward to this all year. I'll be OK, and we can talk on the phone."

"You need to promise me something, Brendan," she said as the late summer corn bristled the undulating fields that surrounded the regional airport. "You need to promise me that you will trust yourself as you work with Rachael, the lawyers, and the unknown. You need to promise me that you will believe in yourself as much as I believe in you. Do not betray yourself. You've come too far and life is too short to give it away. I know."

The "I know" tacked onto my mom's sentence caught my attention as intended and my eyes snapped into focus, almost as if that were the cue she needed to begin her story. "Your father and I split up for more than a year when you were young, Bren. We lost sight of why we had fallen in love in the first place, and our obligation to you rasped the joy of our life down to duty. We both saw that our marriage was not a choice, but an obligation.

"Your father worked a lot during those days so that you and I would be OK living in the apartment we rented, but he still came to see you as much as he could. I was all alone in those days with you. I even thought about seeing someone else because I was just so lonely, but it just didn't feel right. It just wouldn't be the same.

"I missed your father. He took care of me. He took care of us,

Bren. Even in those dark days. His eyes were always filled with love and courage, even then. He just had a fire inside him that I never thought would let go," she said, her eyes falling to her folded hands in her lap, which were idly thumbing her plane ticket. She paused a moment before I heard her gently whisper, "I miss him." Her eyelids shut tight and I knew her mind drifted for a moment to a place where my father still lived inside her. I don't know that I had ever seen my mom this unsure about telling me something.

"We lived apart, but there was something neither of us could avoid—or wanted to avoid: we loved you, but we also loved each other. We were young, so you can call it puppy love or whatever you want, but I know this—I loved him, Bren. Splitting up was the right thing for us at that time. It showed us what was truly important in a marriage. And because we lost it, when we got it back we nurtured it as best we could.

"A lot of people don't have what your father and I did. We were friends and we cared. And," she said smirking peacefully as her mind wound back on experiences she missed, "we laughed."

"There were hard days, too; this isn't a fairy tale. But there were good days. He killed himself for us and this family out on those jobsites. You were a surprise, as you know, and your father tried to compensate for what was at its root a mistake," then she looked up and into my eyes, captured them with an emotion there is no label for and added, "A blessed mistake."

"Trust yourself, Brendan. Believe that you can find what is right for your family and stand by it. I believe in you more than I ever have. As I've watched you transform that old shop into the studio your father always wanted to build for me, I can see him in you and he is very much alive."

* * *

When I got back from the airport, my heart felt full inside the quiet, empty house. I was alone, but not lonely. Looking out at the project, I inventoried what was next. I had finished what work I could do inside her studio. The walls were up and sheathed. I had wrapped the building with black building paper and set the fenestration—carefully flashing each window and door to keep the water out. I had framed the few interior walls to make way for the powder room and wide opening between the old shop and the new building. Now, my father's old comrades were hard at work pulling wire and pipe, packing the stud bays with insulation, and skimming the wallboard with joint compound. I could advance no further inside until these trades had finished their work. As the building neared completion, it must be protected from the weather; time for shingles.

Ironically, my father loved roofing. One could argue that roofing was even harder than the sheathing work he so detested, but there was something about it that appealed to him, anyway. He could drive a roofing nail in two whacks—one set the nail firmly, the second one sent it home. Fortunately for me, his air compressor was back from the repair shop, so I used the old roofing nailer, a tool punished by blasting out hundreds of nails an hour while being dropped and dragged across shingles so rough they made sandpaper feel like tissue. The anodized metallic looking finish had worn off the body of the tool, exposing the bare aluminum housing at all the wear points, showing just how hard these tools get pushed on site. The gun looked like it could barely fire one nail, yet when I pressed the short flat nose of the tool to the shingle and pulled the trigger, nail after nail popped relentlessly out of a tool born to do the roughest work on site. With my black paper rolled out, white metal drip edge tacked to the roof's perimeter, and red chalk lines snapped like thin red ladder rungs ascending the pitch, I nailed on the starter course and my first set.

The first set is slow, because you have to work facing downhill—toward the eaves, or off a ladder. After that, you're working uphill and you can get up to pace. Upon reaching speed, I saw immediately why my father liked this work, then saw through the lens of fond memory how he moved through his life—definitively, ever forward, always to the peak. Always toward the highest part of himself.

Like some of the tools my father used to practice his craft, he too, was relentless. He saw his life as a mission, a journey with important destinations along the way—destinations for which he wanted to be ready when he arrived. He also sometimes viewed the journey as a race. In other words, time mattered.

If you waste time on the roof, you waste time protecting the very thing you've built. Roofing is about speed, about making the most of the time you have up there by spending the least possible amount of it. Roofing is about moving in a lightning rhythm across black paper and up laddered lines to a crescendo that says, "I got here. I made it. I am capable." My father gained satisfaction from moving across the furlongs of that journey with purpose and direction. While he enjoyed stillness, calm, and peace, I could see now that he loved the energy of travel, although in all the years I admired him, I never knew him to leave the confines of the county line.

I, however, had left. I had traveled in my youth because, unlike my parents, I lacked something that I think fueled them on their every day journey through life. Despite the fact that I was too soon on my mother's hip, despite the fact they were poor, despite the fact that my father lost dreams of travel, adventure, and being a different man than he grew to be, they made it—and did so better than I have done—without the very thing I got in spades from each of them. They had struggle, conflict, and the sheet-soaking terror of midnight sweats as each of them bolted upright and wondered into the dark, "What are we going to do?" They had struggle and I think this is what gave them their great energy, gave them their unstoppable will to overcome. I got help.

And with that help came a life that was easier than theirs. I traveled in my youth while my father only dreamed of taking an adventure to Montana, a place relegated to books and TV shows. He stayed home and worked, so I could go. They had struggles, they gave me choice.

I also had time to make those choices. I had time to choose, yet my marriage had failed. His marriage was forced upon him by life and somehow he made it—in love—until the end.

The day's light sank and turned orange behind the leafy skyline of late summer hardwoods lining my mom's yard. I completed half of the roof, tanning my back in a forgiving summer sun that breezed over the roof peak, rippling over the materials laid out for my work. The hot water from the shower in my mom's bathroom, a doily-ed room very much inhabited by a grandmother, felt searing against the slightest first degree burn covering my back. The dirt of the day washed down the drain, and my new skin and shave was ready for Jesse and dinner.

* * *

"Madison," Jesse said, and curled a naked finger around mine at the bar as we downed drinks after a pleasant meal. "Madison is my middle name, after my grandmother."

At once, I felt myself falling for Jesse. The peace I felt when we touched each other left me wanting more of it every time I left her apartment. But, at the same time, I didn't like how all of this was going and I felt nonplussed. Since our first date, she hadn't asked me another question about me or my life. Instead, she talked (almost endlessly) about her own. If I could get a word in edgewise, she waited until something I said reminded her of some other story about herself and she was off to the races again. I couldn't escape the feeling that this looked better than it was, that something was missing there in the dark, behind everything.

At another moment in my life, I would've loved to know details like middle names and where grandmothers are from about a woman I felt myself caring for. Part of the problem was that I had already had that other moment. With Rachael. Instead of moving another step down a new path with Jesse, the memory of what Rachael and I had gushed into my consciousness like a great flood. She, too, had once curled her finger around mine in some conversation of intimacy and closeness where the topic is lost to history but the feeling is chiseled in the emotional bedrock of my heart. In that flood filling my heart, two vessels rose above the waves: guilt and hope.

A little more blank than I had been before Jesse reached out to me, I heard myself saying words to her, replying. Meanwhile, I was thinking that all I wanted was to maintain eye contact so that I would not appear as I truly felt. My face was a featureless stone while I mustered the energy for feigned emotion at yet one more of her self-absorbed stories. I got the sense that she was indulgent and lived for the moment. While that would've been fine for my youth, it didn't reconcile with the tenderness we shared just the night before or with what I wanted from someone I was to share my precious life with. I could see the glitter wearing off those peaceful moments shared by two isolated people who had tried and saved each other from loneliness. I knew that the hope I had felt with her before was fleeting, and that I wanted more, even from a casual relationship.

Her eyes shot past me in that moment during a brief pause in a long story, noticing something behind me and the growing phalanx of empty glasses in front of us in the cloudy pub. Her right hand instinctively reached for her purse. "Do you mind if I smoke?" she asked, and while I said, "No, of course not," I felt quite the opposite.

The hours and beers spilled into each other before Jesse and I spilled into her bed. The stale taste of ash and toothpaste on her tender, open mouth left me wanting something else. Despite this, I rolled under her sheets just the same, and our bodies came alive in the darkness, each searching in the other for something that wasn't there, each knowing that this was a quick fix on the road to some-where else.

Morning came quickly and I slipped out the door before she stirred. God, she was beautiful, her hair falling just so across her face as she slept peacefully under white sheets while beginnings of light collected on the half-pulled blinds. Once in my father's truck, I had to rest my throbbing skull on the hard plastic wheel for a second before sliding the key into the scratched steel ignition switch on the steel console. The lights came on, and as I drove through the open streets of my town, my energy began to return.

* * *

I placed bundles of shingles ahead of me and spread them across the roof so that I could reach, place, and nail each one. The movement became rhythmic, the progress narcotic, and I at once felt suddenly capable, like I had grown some, like there was something there inside me that hadn't previously existed. My hope for a brighter future turned into a belief that would quickly turn into the blueprint of a destiny I could build. It became clear to me as I straightened up my now lean body to move and look at my progress, that I had been building all summer. I looked up and saw the red layout lines stretching eave to eave before me; I could see a sensible course. The roof's peak was now not far away.

Moving through my own journey, with Rachael perhaps in my past and who-knows about Jesse in my future, I saw part of what undertaking an important mission requires: focus, purpose, move-ment—and, sometimes, unforgiving toughness. And because the work takes place in a dangerous land—way up and in the weath-er—it requires courage to see the mission through.

CHAPTER 12

DEAD END LEFT, COPE RIGHT

Do what's right, not what's easy.

JOB NAME:
  PELLETIER
PROJECT:
  CROWN MOLDING

FOR ME, CROWN MOLDING IS THE PIECE
DE RESISTANCE IN ANY ROOM I TRIM.
SPRINGING OFF THE WALL, CONNECTING
IT TO THE CEILING, CROWN MOLDING IS
THE DIFFERENCE BETWEEN A ROOM
THAT WORKS AND ONE THAT IS BEAUTIFUL.
TO TRANSITION BETWEEN PIECES OF
MOLDING IN AN INSIDE CORNER, I "COPE"
THE INSIDE CORNER. COPING WORKS
PERFECTLY ON OTHER MOLDINGS LIKE
SHOE, 1/4 ROUND, AND CHAIR RAIL—BUT
CROWN IS WHERE IT IS KING.

HOW-TO:

1. CUT AN INSIDE RIGHT MITER ON THE
MOLDING. DO THIS BY PLACING THE CROWN
IN THE MITER SAW UPSIDE DOWN AND
BACKWARDS. I USE A JIG TO HOLD THE
MOLDING IN THE CORRECT POSITION WITH
BOTH "FLATS" ON THE BACK OF THE

MOLDING AGAINST THE SAW DECK AND SAW FENCE.

2. DELINEATE THE PROFILE BY SCRIBING THE PROFILE EDGE WITH A PENCIL.

3. USE A COPING SAW TO CUT TO THE LINE. YOU'LL HAVE TO MAKE CUTS FROM VARIOUS ANGLES TO GET THE SAW INTO THE NOOKS AND CRANNIES OF THE MOLDING PROFILE. "BACK CUT" THE PROFILE. IN OTHER WORDS, DON'T JUST CUT THE COPE FLAT, ANGLE THE SAW SO IT REMOVES MATERIAL BEHIND THE PROFILE, CREATING A SHARP LEADING EDGE ALONG YOUR PENCIL LINE.

4. MATE THE COPE TO A TEST PIECE.

5. IF NOT PERFECT (YOU CAN PRETTY MUCH COUNT ON THEM NOT BEING PERFECT), MARK PLACES WHERE MOLDINGS DON'T MATE.

6. FINE TUNE THE COPE USING FILES (A CHAIN SAW SHARPENING FILE AND A

TRIANGULAR METAL CUTTING FILE WORK FOR ME).

COMMENTS:

IN CARPENTRY, I'VE LEARNED THERE IS RIGHT AND WRONG. I'VE ALSO LEARNED THAT, OFTEN, THERE IS NO GRAY AREA IN BETWEEN: EITHER THE WORK IS RIGHT OR IT ISN'T. THIS IS A SIMPLE BUT EXACTING RULE THAT MATTERS TO THE CARPENTER WHO CARES. DOING THE WORK RIGHT—AND TRULY LOVING THE CRAFT—TAKES EFFORT, THOUGHT, AND TIME.

I LEARNED THIS HANGING CROWN MOLDING IN ARTHUR PELLETIER'S HOUSE THE AUTUMN JUST AFTER WE DROPPED BRENDAN OFF ON HIS COLLEGE CAMPUS. (I REMEMBER THE THREE OF US SITTING ACROSS THE BENCH SEAT OF MY TRUCK AS WE DROVE OUT OF TOWN WITH ALL HIS STUFF LOADED IN BACK UNDER AN OIL SKIN TARP. I REMEMBER IT LIKE IT HAPPENED YESTERDAY.)

CROWN MOLDING IS THE BEST OF MOST
ROOMS FOR ME. A JOB DONE PROPERLY
DRAWS EYES TO IT. THE BEST WAY TO
TURN AN INSIDE CORNER WITH CROWN IS
TO COPE IT. COPING TAKES SKILL AND
PATIENCE, BUT IT IS CRUCIAL TO TAKE
THE TIME AND DO THE WORK PROPERLY.
FOR A CARELESS CARPENTER, MITERING
BOTH CORNERS IS EASIER BUT LEAVES
A LOWER-END JOB. AS MY BOSS RICK
ALWAYS TOLD ME: DO WHAT'S RIGHT, NOT
WHAT'S EASY.

A COPED JOINT IS TIGHTER AND LASTS
BETTER THAN A MITER JOINT. WHAT I
TRULY APPRECIATE ABOUT IT IS THAT A
COPED JOINT IS ADAPTABLE. IT
COMPENSATES FOR IMPERFECTIONS IN
THE WALL AND CEILING. IT
COMPENSATES FOR THE FLAWED
MATERIAL WE USE TO BUILD. MUCH LIKE
LIFE, THE CONDITIONS WE BUILD IN ARE
USUALLY IMPERFECT AND REQUIRE US TO
BE FLEXIBLE—WITHOUT ABANDONING OUR
PRINCIPLES OR OUR MISSION. I CAN SEE
IN A PERFECTLY COPED JOINT THE

CULMINATION OF ALL WE DO ON A
JOBSITE. ONLY TRIM WORK IS COPED AND
IT IS OFTEN THE LAST THING WE INSTALL
IN A HOUSE. TRIM WORK IS THE DETAIL
THAT MY CUSTOMERS SEE. IT'S THE VOICE
THAT SPEAKS TO THEM FOR THE REST OF
THE HOUSE'S LIFE, WHILE THE FRAMING
AND FOUNDATION REMAIN SILENT HIDDEN
BEHIND DRYWALL AND EARTH.

THERE MIGHT BE 16 FEET OF BEAUTIFUL
MOLDING RUNNING DEAD STRAIGHT ALONG
THE WALL AND CEILING WITH GLOSSY
PAINT AND SUBTLE SHADOW LINES
DRAWING EYES TOWARD IT, BUT IT IS THE
CORNER—A SINGLE, RAZOR THIN LINE
WHERE TWO PIECES MEET AND
TRANSITION FROM ONE TO ANOTHER
WHERE IT ALL MATTERS. THIS IS WHERE
IMPERFECTIONS CROP UP AND SPOIL GOOD
WORK.

IT IS HERE THAT I TRY TO BE AT MY MOST
WATCHFUL. IT'S HERE THAT I REALLY FIND
MYSELF LOVING THIS WORK.

Thoughts of Jesse, of her body, of the physical relief being with her provided faded from my consciousness as the morning faded into afternoon and the five-count pop-pop-pop-pop-pop of my roofing nailer filled the air like an audible heart murmur. I had roofed to the top, mechanically laying shingle after shingle until they were all in place and cut. I crouched at the ridge, dispensing roofing tar from a goop-covered caulk gun on the last and only exposed nail heads in the final shingle cap. I wasn't even thinking that my time here away from my business and my real life was coming quickly to an end. Instead, I felt the sun's warmth radiating off the black shingles. I put the tar-oozing caulk gun down and took a moment to appreciate how far I'd come. Just as I was about to enjoy an old memory of my father, his hand landing gently on my shoulder, silently turning me to appreciate some framing we had done in Arthur Pelletier's house, the sleek, silver mobile phone clipped to my toolbelt vibrated.

I looked at the caller ID and saw my own name and phone number. My heart jumped because I thought it might be Rachael calling from the house; she might want to talk. I felt that despite the fact that I had been trying to convince myself I could no longer feel anything for her, and no longer hope anything for us.

It wasn't Rachael. Laura's voice was on the other end of the phone. Neither of my girls ever initiated phone calls—it was always me who called them. And it was up to me to keep the fib going that I was away on business. "What's wrong?" came out of my mouth as I suddenly became aware of the sinkhole forming in my stomach. "Is everyone alright?"

"We're alright, but I have a question."

"What is it sweet pea?" I asked totally off guard. The innocence in her voice made me think she wanted to inquire about her bicycle or a book she was reading.

"When are you coming home, Pop?"

The pit in my stomach suddenly became the least of my worries as this question smashed me like an emotional fist, pushing the air from my body and desire to stand out of my legs. The reality of my dying marriage had just become more real, and it had now reached the girls.

"I'm coming home as soon as I'm done my work here," I hopelessly lied to my daughter in a voice I could hardly find believable, much less a nine-year-old.

"I went to Jenny's next door the other day to get my roller blades," she said, "and when I got back, I saw Mommy on the couch crying, Pop. Just sitting and crying. She was on the phone and I could hear her talking in a low voice about you, Pop, like you weren't ever coming home. She said that you were gone and that everything was different now." The pain in Laura's voice came across the telephone wire, across the miles between us like she was here in my arms and I could protect her.

"Are ever you coming back, Pop?" Laura asked in a voice old enough to know, but young enough to have no idea, a voice speaking from the precipice of a child's tears and an adult's pain. I sat down on the peak of the roof, and it occurred to me in a split second that I was totally comfortable up here and that it was only eight weeks ago that I had been riddled with fear and indecision in this very spot. Between a long summer camp and a fib that I was on an extended business trip, mixed with the general busyness of summertime for children, Rachael and I hoped we could keep the wool over our kids' eyes until she and I knew how to answer these questions.

"Your mom and I are having problems, sweet pea," I said, wishing I could reappear on her end of the telephone and hold her, just hold her. I felt the energy drain from my soul when the words, "I don't know when I'll be back," met the air. And with those words, the specters rattling chains in my heart at night became goblins that haunted the day. I felt myself sinking, as if the building atop which I sat in a gleaming late afternoon sun had been built in quicksand. I could envision my biggest little girl's wavy brown hair that had grown darker over the last couple of years. I could see her green eyes searching the air for the right words, and I felt the massive responsibility of being there for her while a little bit of her innocence faded away and became part of her past. I could feel her reaching out into the world to make sense of this, her first big mystery, and more than anything, I wanted her to be OK.

She asked another question, and in my grasp for an answer—for thoughts and words that meant something to her, that could move her from questioning toward understanding—a memory of my father as an old man coalesced in my mind as if it had been waiting there in the plasma for one last, vital ingredient to give it life. As if he were watching me from the ether of elsewhere and asking, "Don't you remember?"

* * *

Rachael and I had been married eight years when we paid a surprise visit to my folks' house on the way back from a half-business, half-pleasure trip near the beach my family had visited for as long as I could remember. We took the kids since the business I had to do—representing some affluent, repeat clients in the purchase of a second home—was near the beach I loved as a boy. I worked half the week, and then met up with my family for half a week of play and fun. Since we arrived at my parents on short notice, my father was unable to change his plans; he was doing a small weekend job hanging crown molding in a customer's dining room just on the other side of town. I hadn't worked with him in almost 20 years by that point, but found myself really wanting to see him in his element—on a jobsite, putting the finishing touches on a house addition—rather than in the known and easy surroundings of a house already built, so I went to be his helper for the day. My wife and mother spent the day talking while the girls played in the yard and explored the house.

Before I set out in my car, I tracked the girls down to say good-bye. I found them under the pull-down attic stairs in the hallway, looking for a way to reach the string. "Pop…," Laura said, and I reached up to the ceiling and pulled-down the heavy stairs. Laura, the big five-year-old sister didn't wait for me to say good-bye but instead lead the way up the pull-down stairs into the attic. Her blonde, three-year old sister, who was growing up fast caught up right behind her. "Bye," I smiled up the stairs to Laura, who stopped halfway to acknowledge me. "I'm going to see Grampa." Laura was very much a leader and loved to show off to her little sister that she knew things. Kelly, the blonde waves of her long, fine hair falling away from her neck as she looked up the stairway into the brown attic, was just beginning to like proving that she could keep up. I rubbed her head and waited as she started up the stairs and recalled that it wasn't long ago when she and I pretended this was the drawbridge to the princess's castle. She climbed them in her pink ballerina dress to go up and play, pretend, and dream. Now, she fancied herself some combination of ballerina and princess, but she was becoming more interested in keeping pace with her bigger sister.

I knew the street my father was working on, but had to crane my neck to look up the long driveway to make sure I didn't drive by the house. I came around a gentle curve in the road and saw my father's truck backed into a half-moon shaped driveway with his plywood cut station and blue and gray miter saw out front.

My father could trim a house by himself nearly as fast as a two-man crew. He was incredibly efficient and there was no wasted energy or extra moves. His cut station was perfectly set up with a miter saw, workbench, and clamps. He knew how to wrap his way around a room, and every lap he took, nailing up perfectly fitted pieces of trim at every door and window as he went, was better for his being there. His job today was only to hang the crown molding. He had trimmed the rest of the room during the week and wanted to finish this last bit off so the painters could get there the following Monday. Older now, wiser, and semi-retired, I could tell he still liked it when he had to push himself. I asked what in the hell he was doing working on the weekend.

"It keeps me young," he said as he released me from a hug. The genuineness of the surprise and warmth he felt backlit his fiery eyes. He locked eyes with me for a long moment, asked a few how-ya-doin' type questions, then got back to what he was doing.

"You'll see when we go inside, Boy, it's a 14x16-foot dining room, with four inside corners. I already cased the windows and doors and set the base molding and chair rail. Now all that's left is this crown. What I do is cut and cope all my pieces out here at one time before I go in and measure for length."

He had started calling me Boy again, sometime over the course of the last two years, as he swung himself into the semi-retired portion of his career. He always called me Boy when I was very young—a tough-guy term of endearment that made us both feel special, even though I had no idea how special I felt at the time, singled out with such a simple, affectionate nickname. He stopped calling me Boy sometime in the eighth grade when I was trying so hard to be a grown up, know-it-all kid. He sensed it made me feel my age, which I was so desperately trying not to be. I liked it again—and it made me feel young.

My father chatted about how business was good and that he only accepted the jobs he wanted these days, politely declining jobs too large or physical. He told me that the heavy framing work, roof tear-offs, or deeply involved remodels that he did as a younger man were getting to be too much for him. With my mother's teacher's pension and their savings, he really didn't need to work all that much. As we talked, he positioned the crown molding in the jig screwed to his work table. The jig perfectly positioned the crown at its proper spring angle so he could cut the inside right miter on the crown before coping it.

It was a leaden day, the sky heavy, close, and foreboding of rain, but that didn't seem to bother the man at the wheel of Herlihy Improvements. "So what I do here, Bren, is I miter all the inside rights first, stack the pieces here on the saw horses, then move each one back up to the work table. There, I clamp it and cope it."

The crispness in the summer air spoke more of the coming autumn than the summer we neared the end of, and I saw my father approaching the winter of his life. His hands looked old for the first time; but I could still feel the imprint of his bear hug on my back and knew there was no lack of power, strength, or capacity in them, and that the fire of exuberance still burned brightly in the furnace of his soul. Yet he appeared almost old to me and I admired the journey he had taken.

"You know, I really like doing trim work," my father continued, unaware of my silence. "Especially crown. I just love walking into a room with a properly proportioned crown detail. It gives a room mass and refinement. It says, 'I care,' somehow, without actually using words. And the only way to turn an inside corner with crown is to cope it." With that he, and his coping saw went to work back-cutting the profile of the piece. It was a detailed crown profile, so his saw had to enter the work from several directions to cut out the tiny beads and sweeping contours.

He worked carefully on the piece, and I could tell from the way the saw's teeth removed wood in smooth, gentle strokes that he kept them razor sharp. The man revered sharp tools and this little saw was no exception. As he cut and worked, he blew the tiny flakes of sawdust off his cut line so he could see, clearly straining to keep the saw as close as he could to the gleaming razor's edge between close enough and too far. I could see the finished profile materializing with each judicious stroke and before I knew it, he was done with the piece.

My father kept a scrap of the crown on his saw bench so he could do a test fit before taking the final piece inside the room for installation. He mated them and took a careful look at how they fit together, how the coped right-lapped over and melted into the dead-ended left. He checked it for a second, made a mark with his pencil, then turned the coped piece back over on the bench.

"There's a right way and a wrong way to do things, Boy," he told me as if I was in eighth grade, and pulled a metal file off the table to shave a fine hair off part of the cope that to me made a whisker look thick. "There," he said, "right on the money."

* * *

I had everything right there in that moment to divine the rationale philosophers spent their lives trying to prove. I had everything except one thing—my daughter's question. There, in that moment where flecks of sawdust hardly the size of a grain of beach sand fell from the teeth of my father's saw revealing a perfectly tuned sweep of crown molding, I could see the proof that there is right and wrong in my life, that there are answers—real, specific, comprehensible answers—to some of life's hardest questions. Like Michelangelo finding the David in a block of marble, careful, concerned, loving work can reveal those answers. As the crown goes around the room, transitions from one direction to another can be made; the context of those transitions—at its worst—can fail, but at its best, be beautiful. And the union between pieces can last.

"I love you, Laura. And I love your sister," I said to my little girl who was trying to understand something new in a world where she thought she had all the answers. "I love you and I will never, ever leave you."

CHAPTER 13

MAKER'S MARK

It's in working on something—
expending physical energy and precious
time, and not necessarily buying that
thing—that truly makes it yours.
And, truly makes it a treasure.

JOB NAME:
HERLIHY
PROJECT:
BASKETBALL HOOP

ONE OF MY FAVORITE PARTS ABOUT
BEING A CARPENTER IS KNOWING HOW TO
DO THINGS. I'VE GROWN TO UNDERSTAND
THAT IT'S IN WORKING ON SOMETHING,
SOMETHING YOU SPEND PHYSICAL ENERGY
AND PRECIOUS TIME ON, THAT TRULY
MAKES IT YOURS. AND TRULY MAKES IT A
TREASURE.

DURING BRENDAN'S FRESHMAN YEAR IN
HIGH SCHOOL—RIGHT BEFORE HE STARTED
WORKING ON MY JOBSITES—HE CAME
HOME FROM A FRIEND'S HOUSE AND
WANTED A BASKETBALL HOOP. BACK
THEN, THEY DIDN'T HAVE THE FOLD-DOWN
HOOPS WITH PLEXI-GLASS BACKBOARDS
YOU CAN BUY NOWADAYS. SO,
PRACTICALLY BEFORE HE WAS DONE
ASKING THE QUESTION, I HAD A HOOP
DESIGNED IN MY HEAD.

BRENDAN HAD ALSO BEEN ASKING ME
WHEN HE COULD START WORK ON MY
SITES. HE NAGGED ME THE WAY A
TEENAGER NAGS WHEN HE WANTS TO
BE OLDER THAN HE REALLY IS. I THOUGHT
THAT WORKING TOGETHER ON THIS HOOP
WOULD BE A GOOD WAY TO GET HIM
STARTED. HE COULD USE TOOLS AND
START SEEING HOW THINGS REALLY GO
TOGETHER.

I KNEW THAT MY BOY'S CHILDHOOD WOULD
SOON COME TO AN END. KAY AND I
TALKED ABOUT BRENDAN HELPING ME IN
THE SHOP BEFORE BED ONE NIGHT. SHE
REACHED OUT AND GENTLY MASSAGED
THE BACK OF MY NECK. SHE LOOKED INTO
MY EYES AND TOLD ME HOW PROUD I
WOULD BE OF HIM. SHE TALKED ABOUT
HOW HIGH SCHOOL BRIDGED THE TIME
BETWEEN BOYHOOD AND MANHOOD AND
BETWEEN HIS NEED FOR US AND HIS
NEED FOR HIS OWN FREEDOM. SHE TOLD
ME I WAS A GOOD DAD.

THAT WEEKEND OUT IN THE SHOP
BRENDAN MOVED AWKWARDLY, LUGGING

LONG MATERIAL. I SHOWED HIM HOW TO
MAKE CUTS WITH THE CIRCULAR SAW AND
CHOP SAW, AND HOW TO READ THE TAPE
MEASURE. THEN, I DISCOVERED ANOTHER
THING I LIKED ABOUT BEING ABLE TO DO
THINGS. I DISCOVERED THAT AS HE GREW
AND ENTERED A "LEAVE ME ALONE, POP"
PART OF HIS LIFE, THERE WERE THINGS
WE COULD DO TOGETHER. THESE WERE
THINGS THAT I HOPED WOULD BECOME
PART OF HIM. I LEARNED THAT AS
INDEPENDENT AS HE WANTED TO BE, WE
COULD STILL BUILD TOGETHER.

KAY AND I LEFT BRENDAN'S HOOP UP LONG
AFTER HE WENT OFF TO COLLEGE AND
THE HAIR ON OUR HEADS TURNED GRAYER.
MONTHS WOULD GO BY WHERE I'D SEE IT
AND NOT NOTICE IT. BUT THEN, SOMETIMES,
COMING IN LATE AFTER PLOWING, OR
BACKING OUT EARLY IN THE MORNING, I
WOULD NOTICE IT AND REMEMBER
BRENDAN AS HE WAS BACK THEN. HE
WAS GANGLY BUT HE TRIED SO HARD TO
BE GROWN UP. I'D THINK OF HIM HOLDING
THAT POWERFUL CIRCULAR SAW WHILE

LOOKING TO ME FOR REASSURANCE (EVEN THOUGH I KNEW HE DIDN'T WANT TO).

I REMEMBER THE NAILS HE BENT WHILE PUTTING THE HOOP TOGETHER AS HE MISSED THEM WITH THE HAMMER. I REMEMBER WORKING TOGETHER—FOR THE FIRST TIME—AND BEING AS ONE AT MOMENTS ON THE MISSION TO CREATE SOMETHING FROM JUST AN IDEA.

IT WAS NOT JUST THE THOUSANDS OF SHOTS WE PRACTICED. IT WASN'T THE TWO THOUSAND DAYS THAT HOOP STOOD OVER OUR STREET THAT MADE IT THE TREASURE I KEPT AS A REMINDER OF HIM LONG AFTER HE LEFT. IT WAS THAT WE DID IT TOGETHER. THAT HOOP IS PART OF HIM, IT'S PART OF ME BECAUSE WE TOUCHED THE WOOD. WE WORKED IT, FORMED IT, FASTENED IT. I HOPE THAT I AM PART OF MY BOY'S LIFE BECAUSE OF IT.

ANOTHER ONE OF MY FAVORITE THINGS ABOUT BEING A CARPENTER IS BEING ABLE TO MAKE ONE-OF-A-KIND THINGS

FOR THE PEOPLE I LOVE, THEY MAY NOT
ALWAYS BE THE BEST (ASK MY WIFE
ABOUT THE WOODEN SAILBOAT I MADE
HER FROM CEDAR DECK SCRAPS, I
SUPPOSE IT LOOKS OK SITTING ON A
SHELF, BUT IN WATER, WELL, IT FLOATS—
ON ITS SIDE), BUT I LIKE TO THINK THEY
ARE SOMEHOW SPECIAL, LIKE THE VISION
OF THIS BASKETBALL HOOP WHEN IT
FORMED IN MY MIND.

THE MAIN DESIGN STRATEGY IS TO BUILD
A POST THAT WON'T TWIST, WHICH OF
COURSE WILL MOVE THE HOOP OUT OF
LINE FROM THE COURT, THE TRICK IS TO
BUILD A BOX-BEAM INSTEAD OF USING A
SOLID POST.

HOW-TO:

1. MAKE THE BOX BEAM POST, ALL
MEASUREMENTS IN DRAWING ASSUME THE
POST BOTTOM IS BURIED TO A DEPTH OF 3
FEET.

2. CUT AND ASSEMBLE THE BACKBOARD
SUPPORT.

3. ERECT POST AND SUPPORTS;
STABILIZE IN HOLE.

4. FASTEN BACKBOARD/RIM ASSEMBLY
TO SUPPORTS.

BOX BEAM

1. NAIL OR SCREW 16' LONG 2X6s TO 16
FOOT-LONG 2X4s. THE 2X6 FACES ARE
THE FRONT AND BACK OF THE POST.

2. CUT NOTCHES FOR BACKBOARD
SUPPORTS ON THE 2X4 FACE OF THE POST
(SEE DRAWING FOR LOCATIONS, DEPTH).

3. TRIM THE TOP END BY CUTTING AROUND
IT WITH A CIRC SAW SO ALL BOARD ENDS
ARE FLUSH.

BACKBOARD SUPPORTS

1. CUT, ASSEMBLE, AND INSTALL
BACKBOARD SUPPORTS (SEE DRAWING).
SCREWS DRIVEN WITH A CORDLESS
DRILL/ DRIVER ARE BEST. WORK ON A
FLAT SURFACE, LIKE A CONCRETE FLOOR
OR LARGE WORKTABLE.

2. CUT AND INSTALL 2X8 POST CAP. DRILL 1" VENT HOLES IN POST TOP.

POST

ERECT POST. PLUMB IT ON TWO FACES. SQUARE IT TO COURT AREA. SECURE IN HOLE. I BRIDGE THE HOLE WITH 4'-LONG 2X4s AND FASTEN THEM TO THE POST. THEN, IN AN OPPOSING DIRECTION, I INSTALL 6'-LONG KICKER BRACES. POUR 80 LBS OF CONCRETE IN HOLE AND LET CURE.

BACKBOARD

1. CUT BACKBOARD.

2. WITH THE POST UP AND STABLE, MARK OUT RIM LOCATION ON BACKBOARD.

3. WORKING FROM A SAFE STEPLADDER, INSTALL BACKBOARD TO BACKBOARD SUPPORTS ABOVE COURT SURFACE. MAKE SURE IT IS LEVEL AND ITS BOTTOM EDGE IS ABOUT 9'6" TO 9'8" ABOVE COURT SURFACE.

4. INSTALL RIM EXACTLY 10' ABOVE COURT SURFACE ONTO BACKBOARD. THREAD ON THE NET.

5. TEACH CHILD TO SHOOT AND REBOUND
AS MUCH AS YOU CAN. THERE ARE NOT
ENOUGH SUNNY SATURDAYS IN THE WORLD
WHERE YOU CAN DO SOMETHING THAT
MATTERS AND IS FUN. THERE JUST
AREN'T ENOUGH.

"I miss your dad," Jake Capalien said to me as he raised a beefy hand to shake mine. His hands black from soldering copper tubing and kneading pipe dope around plumbing fittings, the 64-year-old pipe jockey had a calm confidence about him. "I've worked with every contractor in this town and I never knew a more honest man."

"Thank you, Jake," I told my father's old friend, both thrilled to be Gideon Herlihy's boy and trapped by the loneliness of having him no longer by my side.

"It's different without him, but this place looks great," Jake said with a calm, knowing grin. He picked up the white, five gallon plastic bucket of fittings, parts, and wrenches from next to the powder room he had just completed, then walked out to his truck.

"Jake! wait," I called after him, as I followed him toward the van. He didn't look back nor did he stop walking. He loaded the bucket into a compartment on the side of the rust-red, work-body truck.

"Don't even think about giving me a check," he hollered and glanced up at me approvingly before stepping into the cab and starting the engine. "Friends like Gideon Herlihy are rare. He'd do the same for me."

My frenzied week of subcontractors and my father's old friends stepping on each other to pull wire, pipe, finish drywall, and set fixtures was over. Again, it was just me with the project. Just me, my memories, my mission. And my questions. No longer could I avoid facing the mounting tomorrows in my life.

I had been working seven days a week since arriving here. Now, late August with the summer corn on the farm at the edge of town growing taller than me, I no longer knew if it was a weekend or mid-week without checking the newspaper. I suddenly felt gripped by a reality I had only scratched the surface of since receiving the sheaf of divorce papers from Rachael. Using the urgency of finishing the project as an excuse to not give it my full attention, I had half-heartedly retained a lawyer of my own. Checks had been written, phone calls made, and a strategy put in place. Now, I had to start the mechanical work of filling out my financial affidavit and addressing a parenting plan. I also had to find somewhere else to live, somewhere I could afford that was close to my girls.

Shoulder deep in credit card receipts and bank statements, I sat at the empty kitchen table letting a perfectly nice summer day pass me by for the dim light of an old fixture and the cold, gray calculator. My goal was to quantify both how much I made and how much I spent each week. I plowed through the electric, water, and phone bills; then cable, internet, and trash collection invoices. I estimated food costs, haircuts, vacations, and clothes. I looked into every detail of my life, my savings and my investments, before ascribing numbers to it all. I found this to be an enlightening exercise and enjoyed knowing where all my dollars went every week. But despite how much I believed that Rachael and I had grown apart—how much I knew that—I wished that this were not an exercise in ending something. Rather, I wished it were an exercise in improving it.

I crunched numbers for six hours, roughly the equivalent of a pot of coffee if measured by beverage consumption. I checked and double-checked everything on scrap paper before filling out the form provided by my attorney. I stood up from the paper-covered table and walked to the black coffee maker in the corner of the linoleum countertop to refill the green ceramic coffee mug before a final proofread, only to find a layer of coffee about as thick as a quarter sizzling against the Pyrex pot. I looked around the kitchen only to find it bare. Just to be sure, I listened, too: Nobody.

My mom was in Florida, my family was in our home without me, and the emptiness made me realize that Jesse and I were just a filling station for each other on separate roads to somewhere else. I would call her again, to fill the void of being alone, to feel the touch of somebody who liked me, to see into the eyes of another person, but the energy that pumped our blood in the beginning was something that was falling away from us as quickly as it began. The more I got to know Jesse, the more I realized we had less and less in common. She didn't mind that I had kids, for example, but she looked courteously bored if I ever talked about them for more than a few minutes, and that made me realize I needed a deeper connection. As I leaned on the counter, with my back to the kitchen window and the project that had consumed me just outside, it occurred to me that I was alone.

My daughters would not be in my life every day anymore, and I would not sit at a dinner table full of people who had a day's events to share. It occurred to me that I needed a place to live and I wondered how quiet it would be in there, how small it would feel, or if I would even put furniture in all the rooms. I thought of wherever I might move as a sterile, empty place. Then, I thought of the hospital, a snowstorm, and the day two years ago when Dad died.

* * *

My wife and daughters were out of town and I was a bachelor for the weekend. Snow was in the forecast, and I found myself leaving work early that Friday, heading to my parents' house for a quick hello before the snow was supposed to really hit. I do not recall having an odd feeling or any compulsion to be there as if I were needed—I just went. I called ahead to my mom to let her know I'd be there in an hour. She told me that she was running to the store and that Dad was working on the lawn. By the time I left the city's surface streets and curled the ascending ramp onto the highway, an early snow was sticking to the cold ground.

My father was in his backyard planting grass seed.

My father's pastime—and perennial frustration—was his lawn. He could transform a plain, wooden board into a shelf, box, deck, or home, but the man couldn't grow a blade of grass in his own yard to save his life—and not for lack of effort. His latest strategy, it appeared, was that if you put grass seeds down before it snowed, they'd be absorbed into the soil as the ground thawed and softened in the spring. Because they were covered by snow before they were drawn into the soil, the birds couldn't get at them and eat them, and the new seeds would sprout vigorously. He liked this trick because it was old, because it required intimate knowledge of the earth, seasons, and weather, because it was natural, and because (at least on the surface) it made perfect sense. That, and it was cheaper than hiring a lawn service. I loved my father, but I could hear the neighbors: dead of winter and there he is working on the lawn. I could see them smile and shake their heads at him and his distant drummer. I miss my father.

The snow fell quite heavily as I slowed the car and parked carefully on the flat street before my parents' short driveway. As I braked, I saw my basketball hoop—still there from when I was a teenager—and I saw it almost as if for the first time. While I never measured it myself, I am certain that the top of that red iron rim was exactly 10 feet above the asphalt that paved our lane. I recalled shooting foul shots through a frozen net one day after a heavy midnight snow had cancelled school, and my father had spent 48 hours plowing driveways and parking lots around town.

On the first day of that storm, the snow fell so fast you'd swear you could hear it hit the ground. My father was out before midnight. He began with commercial accounts like stores and shops so that they could open. Next, he started the driveways and walks of his residential customers so that they could get out.

I met up with friends on the first day, and we alternated whose house we hung around in and watched TV until it was time to come home for dinner. As I walked through the snow down my street, I could see that the town plows had been by, piling a snow bank like a long, white three-foot-thick electrical cable along each side of the street. My father had not been back, and despite the fact that he was driving all over town in a plow truck that could clear our driveway in about 120 seconds, I grabbed his coal shovel—he hated snow shovels—and spent the next half hour clearing the walk and making a path behind my mom's car.

When I woke the next morning, it was clear that Dad had come home for some food and a catnap after a 20-hour run. There was a can of something on the counter and a fork on the edge of the sink. While a glance out of the window showed that the storm had almost ended, school was still closed while the roads were cleared and deiced. As I walked out the door after a breakfast my mom had prepared, she called me back, indicating that the sweatshirt I had chosen as defense against the freezing temperatures wasn't quite enough. She handed me a blue knit cap and wrapped my neck in a scratchy, black woolen scarf.

She asked me to clear another path for her car so she could get out, as it had snowed all night. My real shoveling goal, however, was to clear the snow bank from my basketball court so I could shoot around while waiting for my friends to emerge from their houses. I dribbled down the edge of the driveway with my right hand; the old leather ball collected snow. I carried the shovel in my left only to find that my father had been there before me. Before leaving for his second blast, he had pushed the snow bank out of the way, cleared the court, and lowered his plow to open the road for our neighbors.

I shot around for a while, practicing jump shots from a three-point arc I had scraped into the last of the newly fallen snow on the street. However, the new snow made it impossible to dribble so I practiced foul shots instead, pacing off a line from the post out until I thought it looked far enough. I heard my father's truck turn the corner at the end of the street. His plow was up, but I could see him through the windshield waving his hand to clear out. He lowered the yellow blade, made two passes, and pushed away any snow that I hadn't already stamped down before swinging into the driveway next to my street-side basketball court.

I've pulled an all-nighter or two studying in college, but I really have no idea what it's like to need money so badly to know what working two, twenty-hour shifts in a row is like; driving and shoveling through a nighttime blizzard. He more spilled than hopped out of the cab and walked down to the court where I was 6-for-8 on foul shots. He squeezed his blue knit cap above his ears and over matted hair before extending his hands for the ball, indicating with his bloodshot eyes that I should get into the proper position for a rebound, something we had practiced so many times before we didn't need to say the words. I moved as slowly as he shot. We played around in silence for a few minutes before I walked over to him to ask him how he was.

Before I could speak, he put an exhausted arm around me and pulled me to him. He raised the rim of my cap over my forehead and pressed his whiskers to my face for a prickly kiss before walking up the driveway to go inside and pass out. At that moment, for five minutes in the snow of a cancelled school day, there was nothing else in the world but him and me. Without saying a single word, I knew my father loved me. And he loved me on a level beneath words, beyond the ability of language to capture it. He loved me like a father loves his child.

He walked up the driveway in silence. The forecast called for another day of snow.

This memory was part of me as I drove to my parents' house that fateful day two years ago. Snow peppered the air as I drove through a gathering storm to spend time with them for a reason I couldn't identify. I was grown up, married, and a father, myself, now. I sat in my car on what was once my old basketball court at the edge of the long, single car-width driveway that shot straight past the house and into the garage door of my dad's shop with my memory, seeing into the past.

I remember the Old Man never got that way. He was younger looking than his years, and he worked until just a few months before he died. He was active, engaged, and fast thinking. He went out and lived while other people his age just passively talked about resting. I recall seeing him as younger and more vibrant than my other friends' fathers—even Rachael's father, who was 10 years younger than my dad.

When I walked up the driveway, my shoes left prints in the powdery snow. My mother was still out at the store but my father's truck was wearing a cap of white. The house was empty, yet I noticed the shop lights were on as I glanced out the kitchen window.

I guess I should have known something was wrong, but I didn't. He hadn't been inside the house for hours, as mine were the lone footprints in the snow. I guess I should have known something was wrong when it was not a pile of scrap lumber that blocked the door, but a bucket of grass seed. I guess I should have known something was wrong when he looked slowly up at me from the concrete floor, his powerful shoulders propped on the leg of a worktable, his body listing to the right. His old eyes looked up at me, the fire now a fading ember. I guess I should have known something was wrong when I knelt, grabbed him with an incredible, powerful calm and searched his eyes. The glow came back to him and he reached up. His time was coming, but he wasn't done yet: there were still a few things to take care of.

I rushed him into his truck—there was no time for an ambulance. I put him in the passenger's side and carefully shut the door. I raced around the tailgate, slipping on the snow in my office shoes, then climbed in the driver's side. Slamming the heavy steel door knocked the snow from the glass, but the layer on the windshield remained. The trucks wipers brushed away the snow in a few labored strokes as I shifted the transmission into gear before speeding to the Emergency Room with snow blowing off the hood and roof and out of the bed like white smoke. The man of action he'd always been would have liked the adventure under other circumstances, and my adrenaline blocked the panic and the gravity of the situation from me. I was losing my father on the streets of our old town, but somehow, after all these years, even on the last day, we were still on a mission.

My father's once invincible frame draped over me at the Emergency Room, where I kicked the door open and pleaded, "Help!" The docs came and wheeled him away on a gurney. I guess I was still in shock as, I searched for a payphone to call my family, I imagined what his last seconds at his shop must have been like:

I imagined that he was at his bench, peering down the newly rounded edge of a pine plank through a puff of steamy breath before sweeping the sawdust off. I could see the blonde dust float into the air like fairy dust. I knew what the wood felt like. I could see his sinewy, old, powerful hands caress the pine before he moved across the room to his nailing bench for this board to be locked to its mate. Hammer out, he tapped the dovetail joint smooth, and it was then that his body stopped. I could see the hammer falling through the air with the speed of a single snowflake through a light, chilling breeze. As it hit, it bounced silently from the floor. I could hear the tuning fork ting of steel hitting concrete linger in the air long after the hammer came to rest. His body, exhausted, sailed calmly down behind it, luffing through an updraft like a silken sail sliding down a mast in light wind. He had lain there quietly, sawdust sticking to his back. The cold of the floor sought equilibrium with the heat of his body and stole its warmth as he looked at the grass seed still in the doorway, wishing beyond the limits of hope to see the spears of light-green seeds piercing the brown earth on a day yet to come, when the sun is warm, gentle, and bright.

I was grateful for that glimpse of a dream, which was forever clench-nailed in my consciousness. I found I had already dialed numbers while I stood lost in the dream. I heard my voice, as if I were a stranger across the room.

"It's Dad."

Forty-five minutes later, my mom entered the ER. She walked

briskly, as if she were still 25 and pouring a hundred coffees an hour at Lavallee's for tip money. She saw no need to hide her panic, yet her eyes were clear and she had the gall to ask if I was all right.

"He wants you," I said.

And it ended there in a room full of white walls, chrome bed rails, vinyl-jacketed copper wire, glass vials, plastic machines, metal doors, and not a length of wood. It ended there with the three of us. It ended how it began.

They stared at each other, into each other, and their lives ran across a synapse of love and shared memories between each other. His soul reached out from his body at that moment and I can't recall if it stopped snowing and the sun came out or if it kept falling feverishly and made blanket forts over all our cars.

I can remember, though, that it did happen and it happened the right way—the way he wanted it. We held him in our world during his last moments here by the hands, and we held him as long and as hard as we could, knowing full well that it is not by the hands one holds a man's soul.

My mom and I were there for the natural and necessary progression of life. All that lives dies. All that begins ends. The treasure is the journey, the mission, the points in between: all the "now" we forget to pay attention to because we're busy doing something else, too preoccupied, looking ahead, or reaching back. All the Now between Beginning and End, that's when life really happens.

I guess I should have known something was wrong when I was sad for me and not him. But, what ultimately sought my terror in the face of Death was not my father's passing, but my mother's retreat within herself. She leaned on me as we walked down the hall, fully aware that we were going home for the first times in our lives without him. He wasn't out working, drinking, or pushing snow. He was dead. We had to become new people, and she was so heavy with the weight of it, that she did not ask me how I was.

We went to the house. She sat at a kitchen table she had spent more time hovering over than sitting at. It was still old, and small, and the finish was worn from where hands and plates had rubbed it a billion times. I made her tea for the first time in my life while we waited in helpless silence and heart-crushing grief for the family to arrive, for my wife and kids to race from their weekend away to us, to hear them say they were sorry for us, and then sit helpless, hoping the gift of their presence and some food could somehow help what cannot be helped by anything except time.

I opened one of my father's beers, and then walked out to the shop. I reached in and shut off the lights before locking the door. I returned to the house, kicked the snow off my shoes, finally loosened my tie, and still, my mom did not ask how I was.

Our world had forever changed.

* * *

Back in the kitchen, back in the all too painful present, a pile of papers and figures before me, there were still no people. There were still only separation agreements, burnt coffee, and the signals of change everywhere. Despite the fact that many times over this summer I felt that I could find my way through this crisis, despite the fact that I had decided to undertake the mission of doing the right thing, despite the fact that I knew I was doing the right thing, nothing could eclipse how alone I felt, not even knowing that my father was up there somewhere, reaching through the ether, through the clouds behind the snow, to be with me on the deck of this ship.

Not even that could scare away my emptiness.

CHAPTER 14

T & G

*If you have to say any other words—
like "except"—after you've said done,
then you're not finished.*

You're almost finished, and that's different.

JOB NAME:
  PELLETIER
PROJECT:
  HARDWOOD FLOORS

HOW-TO:
NOTE: HARDWOOD OR "STRIP" FLOORS
SHOULD BE INSTALLED ACROSS THE
FLOOR JOISTS—NOT PARALLEL TO THEM.

1. SWEEP THE SUBFLOOR, THEN LAY AND
TAPE #15 TAR PAPER OVER IT. THIS
CREATES A BREAK, ELIMINATING A
WOOD-ON-WOOD CONNECTION THAT CAN
SQUEAK AND TO CREATE A VAPOR
BARRIER THAT KEEPS THE WOOD FROM
MOVING OR BUCKLING IF THERE IS TOO
MUCH MOISTURE BELOW IT.

2. MEASURE THE DISTANCE FROM THE
BASEBOARD OF THE FAR WALL TO THE
BASEBOARD OF THE WALL FROM WHICH
YOU PLAN TO START LAYING THE BOARDS.
IF THEY ARE THE SAME MEASUREMENT,
YOU CAN LAY YOUR FLOOR BOARDS RIGHT
AGAINST THE TRIM AND GO TO TOWN.

3. IF THEY ARE NOT THE SAME OR THERE IS A LARGE GAP UNDER YOUR TRIM BOARDS, YOU MUST MAKE A CONTROL POINT FROM WHICH TO WORK. I DO THIS BY MEASURING FROM THE FAR WALL TO WHERE THE FRONT—OR TONGUE—OF THE FIRST BOARD SHOULD BE ON THE STARTER WALL. USE A LONG, STRAIGHT STRIP OF FLOORING MATERIAL AS A GAUGE TO SHOW WHERE THE FRONT OF IT SHOULD LAY. ADJUST ITS POSITION RELATIVE TO THE NEAR WALL UNTIL THE MEASUREMENTS IN EACH CORNER OF THE ROOM ARE THE SAME.

REMEMBER THAT IF THERE IS A GAP, YOU CAN COVER IT WITH SHOE MOLDING. THE KEY IS NOT TO MAKE THE GAP LARGER THAN THE MOLDING IS WIDE. ONCE YOU GET THE MEASUREMENTS IN EACH CORNER TO MATCH (WITHIN 1/8"), REMOVE THE BOARDS AND SNAP A LINE.

THE GOAL IS TO GET THE FIRST COURSE OF FLOORING PARALLEL WITH THE FAR WALL SO THAT WHEN YOU FINALLY GET TO THE FAR WALL WITH FLOORING, THERE WON'T BE A GAP THAT REQUIRES BOARDS TO BE RIPPED AT PECULIAR ANGLES SO THEY FIT.

4. NAIL THE FIRST RUN OF BOARDS IN PLACE. WITH THIS DONE, RUN THE REST OF YOUR FLOORING.

5. WRAP THE BASEBOARD WITH SHOE MOLDING (AND COPE THE INSIDE CORNERS).

TONGUE   GROOVE

THERE'S ONE THING YOU NEED TO KNOW BEFORE TAKING THE NEXT STEP. THERE'S NO JOKE, QUIP, OR ONE-LINER YOU CAN THINK OF THAT HASN'T ALREADY BEEN TOLD ABOUT THE SEXUAL INNUENDO OF THE TONGUE-AND-GROOVE JOINT. ON ANY JOBSITE WITH A SHRED OF DIGNITY OR EXPERIENCE, THEY'RE JUST NOT THAT FUNNY. THE SAME IS TRUE ABOUT TUBES OF "CAULK," INNUENDO ABOUT USING KNEEPADS, AND VACUUMS THAT "SUCK." TYPICALLY MEATHEADS,

ROOKIES, AND PEOPLE NOT PAYING
ATTENTION THINK THESE JOKES ARE
FUNNY. IT'S JUST THE NAME OF A JOINT
THAT WORKS—AND HAS WORKED LONGER
THAN ANYONE ON THIS PLANET HAS
BEEN ALIVE. THE POINT IS TO SEE THE
FUNCTION BEHIND THE WORDS.

AWKWARD TO SAY? MAYBE.
INDISPENSABLE FOR A FLOOR THAT WILL
LAST? CERTAINLY.

COMMENTS:

AT ARTHUR PELLETIER'S HOUSE,
BRENDAN HAD BEEN AWAY AT SCHOOL
FOR A FEW MONTHS ALREADY BY THE
TIME THE HARDWOODS WERE TO BE
INSTALLED, AND I WAS ON A MISSION TO
CHANGE SOMETHING I DIDN'T LIKE ABOUT
MYSELF. FOR TOO MUCH OF MY CAREER, I
WAS ONE OF THOSE GUYS WHO, WHEN
THE CLIENT ASKED HOW THE PROJECT
WAS PROGRESSING, WOULD SAY, "DONE.
EXCEPT...." THEN, I'D RATTLE OFF A
LIST OF LITTLE THINGS THAT NEEDED TO

BE FINISHED. PELLETIER'S HOUSE WAS
TOO BIG A PROJECT FOR ME TO GET
BEHIND ON LITTLE THINGS THAT ALWAYS
DOGGED ME ON MY OTHER JOBS. I
THOUGHT HARD ABOUT WHAT I MEANT
WHEN I SAID "DONE" FOR THIS PROJECT. I
CHANGED MY SCHEDULE TO MATCH WHAT
I CAME UP WITH. TAKING THIS HARD LOOK
IS THE WAY I GOT A GOOD SENSE OF
HOW LONG THINGS ACTUALLY TAKE TO
COMPLETE—AND IT WAS A WHOLE HELL
OF A LOT LONGER THAN I ORIGINALLY
THOUGHT.

HERE'S WHAT "DONE" MEANS TO ME: IF
THERE ARE NO OTHER STEPS TO TAKE,
NOTHING ELSE TO DO TO SOMETHING, NO
ADJUSTMENTS, REFINEMENTS, OR
TWEAKS TO MAKE, THEN I'M DONE. UNTIL I
TURN THE KEY IN MY TRUCK AND DRIVE
OUT OF MY CUSTOMER'S DRIVEWAY WITH A
CHECK IN MY HAND, I'M NOT DONE. RATHER,
I'M "ALMOST DONE" AND THAT'S A BIG
DIFFERENCE.

I HAD PRACTICALLY KILLED MYSELF CHECKING FOR EVERY LAST DETAIL BEFORE INSTALLING THE WOOD FLOORS HERE. I MADE SURE EVERY CLOSET WAS PAINTED, EVERY SWITCH COVER WAS ON EVERY RECEPTACLE, THAT EVERY WINDOW OPENED AND DOOR CLOSED. I MADE SURE THAT ARTHUR WAS HAPPY. THEN, AND ONLY THEN, WOULD I INSTALL THE FLOORS AND SIGN OVER HIS NEW HOUSE TO HIM AND HIS WIFE.

WHILE INSTALLING A WOOD FLOOR PROPERLY REQUIRES SOME SKILL, THE BASIC PRINCIPLES ARE NOT HARD. IT TAKES CARE AND ATTENTION TO DO THE LAYOUT. THEN IT TAKES CHECKING IN FREQUENTLY—AND MAKING SURE THAT YOU'RE NOT LINING UP ANY JOINTS FROM COURSE TO COURSE. THEY SHOULD ALL BE STAGGERED. YOU HAVE TO MAKE SURE THINGS ARE MOVING FORWARD ACCURATELY AND THE PROJECT WILL FINISH AS YOU HAD HOPED.

This was the end. My mom would soon be back from Florida and I wanted her new studio to be completely finished. I planned to put a vase overflowing with flowers in there to welcome her when she got back.

I had just one more problem to solve before my promise to my mom was fulfilled. Her studio would be built, and I would have to leave her protection. So, while cranking through the financial affidavit for my impending divorce, I also caught up on the project budget and realized that we were nearly at the limit. When my father had done the materials list and specifications before his death, prices were a bit lower. OK, a lot lower, and it's something that I didn't check because I was so focused on relearning carpentry.

My father had spec'd solid maple floors to be installed, sanded, and finished with a clear urethane to give the floor a high wear quality and the bright, airy look my mom wanted. I called around to several suppliers and found that I would go over budget by about two grand. I suppose I could have written a check myself, and paid my way out of the problem. But I sensed that might not be exactly the right way to go, so I went down to Man Lushee's for some beer instead. Perhaps the frenzy of the day and my diet of caffeine and potato chips was clouding my head too much. I hoped the short drive from my mom's to Man Lushee's would clear my head some; then, over a cold beer and a napkin, I could figure out what to do about this floor problem.

At first, the only thing I could do was watch the sports report on TV and see—but not hear—which teams won and lost. My mind was too tired to pore over memories or look ahead into tomorrow. A few feet away, two friends sat and talked, laughed like hell at each other's jokes, and got another round of beers before they headed home. "I gotta get back," the one guy said. "Jan made dinner and the kids…." His words countersunk the image of how far I had come, how different my life was, and how many people were in it.

Before I knew it, another beer was in my belly, making it feel round and full, and I ordered some food. The sports report ended and another show began while the bartender stood at the tap filling another shiny glass with amber fluid as a muted desire to call Rachael turned in my mind.

"But she doesn't want to hear it," I said almost out loud and turned from the TV toward the table Jesse and I had often sat at before returning to her apartment. It was empty, and I tried point-lessly to make peace with the fact that I would never be in love again—not the way I was with Rachael—but that I must also leave this marriage and move forward. As another beer glass sweated in front of me, it occurred to me that although I was lonely, I had made the right choice to leave. Perhaps tomorrow I could command more happiness and my life would be incrementally more my own. I realized that I needed to live my life a new way. Were I to stay with Rachael and the person she had become, my future would be love-less, empty, cold, and dutiful. I believed this to be true, and resolved to live my life with the possibility that love could once again exist than with the guarantee that it would not.

Another beer—another pint of anesthetic—appeared before me on the bar.

* * *

Morning came. Unfortunately, the night had just ended and the cloud from the bar and beers was still in my head. I dressed and walked down the stairs before the sun rose. I headed right past the coffee pot, through the dimness of the backyard barely lit by morn-ing, and into my mom's—almost—new studio. Even though the lights worked, I flicked on a halogen work light. Its 1,000 watts of brilliance fractured the darkness. It shone directly at the bright, white east wall, which cast the light back up into every cranny of the space. Jake Capalien was right: this did look good and I heard my voice coming out of my mouth before I even had the thought. "God, it wasn't that long ago that I was ripping pine boards off of the garage frame and…Holy Shit! That's it!"

I grabbed the tape measure from my tool pouch and ran outside to those old, workmanlike, pine sheathing planks that had spent 80 years drying and hardening behind the cedar clapboards of the old garage—the same boards I had stickered and saved under my father's oilskin tarps. I measured how much square footage each 1x6 and 1x8 board covered, then added up all the boards. I then measured the square footage of floor space I had to cover. If I was careful, I could mill each of the sheathing planks on my father's router table into tongue-and-groove floorboards and have just enough to surface the new studio.

It took me half the morning to curb my excitement and get calm and collected enough to carefully calibrate my father's router so that each plank came out the same. First, I set the router up as a jointer so it could straighten the edges of each ancient plank. Then, I set it up to mill the tongue on each board. Finally, I switched bits and milled the groove on each board. I checked in after every few planks to make sure the router setting hadn't vibrated loose, and that each board was coming out the same. The aroma of the old pine smelled fresh and new as I processed and stacked each plank. My forearms were covered with sawdust shavings. When the hunger pang in my belly told me the lunch hour had arrived, I had no interest in stopping, so I went in and laid out the floor.

For the first time since I had been there, I felt like I had enough of my own experience to draw on and solve this problem by myself—truly like the carpenter I felt myself becoming. I had read my father's journal entry on laying out wood floors several times and had done that work with him at Arthur Pelletier's house on a weekend break from college. But today, this project was mine.

These resurrected floors were far from perfect and I hoped that the subcontractor I hired to sand and finish them could help hide some of their imperfections. Finally, by three in the afternoon, I could no longer ignore my hunger and decided to hop in the truck and grab some fast food. Sweaty, dirty, and proud, I took a last look at my work. I was at a perfect break point, having just set the entire floor in the original structure; I was ready to move into the new work. This was going to work. I could see that I was tight on material, so I would have to slow down a little, being careful not to waste any of this treasure.

My moment of pride was giving way to thoughts of a high-calorie lunch and the final phase of production when I heard my mom's yellow phone ringing inside the house. Nobody called me there, so I just planned to let it go when I realized that it might be my mom calling me with the itinerary for her flight home.

"Hello!" I gasped into the receiver, catching it on the last ring before the old micro cassette answering machine picked up.

"It's me, Bren," the voice said, barely finding its way between my breaths.

"Mom?" I wondered into the mouthpiece, certain it was not her.

"Brendan, it's me, Rachael."

I replied with stunned silence, my breath coming back to me, and my mind focusing on the newness of the old voice.

"Do you remember Craigville?" she asked, knowing full well I knew what Craigville was. "I'll be there in three hours." Rachael put down the phone in her car and dug a CD out of the console beneath her right arm as she turned a corner and shifted lanes, headed for the highway. Van Morrison's "Into the Mystic" poured quietly from her speakers, and her mind found the lines she was looking for between the notes and above the rhythm.

* * *

Craigville is the beach where Rachael and I met quite by accident after college. We bumped into each other—literally—in line at the snack bar they called the Barnacle, while overpaying for deliciously greasy beach food. I was so shocked by how good she looked in the black one-piece that I could barely utter the words "excuse me," much less ask her out. We both paid for our food and left the snack bar separately. I went back to the spot my friends and I had staked out and told them about her and what a goddam loser I was for being so tongue-tied. I'd never see her again—or so I thought—until she walked down the beach right in front of us.

"Go!" they said. "What's she going to do? Say no? So what? Do it!"

Challenged, I walked down the sand, my heels and toes sinking into the hot, dry granules before reaching the wave line where the water-soaked sand was firmer and changed color to deeper beige. I was so nervous walking up behind her—certain she'd think I was stalking her—that I couldn't say anything while I shadowed her between lifeguard towers. Finally, afraid she'd run out of beach and head up to her blanket, I blurted out, "Excuse me," much louder than I needed to.

I was so nervous as she turned her beautiful face to me that I crossed my big toes over the second toes—then made fists with my feet and buried them in the sand so she couldn't see. Her suntan was perfect and I could see how white the skin on her shoulder was until she unconsciously slipped a finger under the shoulder strap and adjusted it, ever so slightly moving her breast at the same time. I had caught up to her at the last lifeguard tower on the beach before a massive stone jetty poured itself into the sea.

I know she said something pleasant, which sort of calmed my nerves, even though I thought I would break my own toes because I was squeezing them so hard. We talked for a minute before I asked if I might join her on her walk.

"Sure," she said. "That would be nice. I'm heading out to the end of the jetty."

* * *

Barreling down the highway in my father's truck, watching the gas needle toggle every time I jumped on the gas pedal to pass a car, I realized that this would be the second time a challenge brought Rachael and I together at Craigville, a place that is special to me.

My father brought my mom and me there once a year. He loved the sand, the sun, and the breeze off the water. And Rachael and I had brought Laura and Kelly there since they were babies.

The wide, flat parking lot was nearly empty. There were a few people walking the water's edge wearing thin sweaters, shorts, but no shoes as the sun dipped in the sky. I sped the length of the parking lot, the motor roaring as I parked the truck as close to the jetty as I could, straddling yellow lines painted on the rough, fissured asphalt. Rachael's car was parked more carefully a row away.

I trudged through the soft sand, this time in worn work boots, not bare feet. I scrambled up the rocks with a cautious urgency, as if I was approaching a situation where something major was wrong, even though I was hopeful that something good was about to happen. Rachael sat facing the setting sun, her back to me, and to the jetty, looking outward toward the sea. She wore a sundress woven brightly with flowers and had a sweater wrapped around her neck. I approached, hopping the gaps in the massive granite jetty boulders, the rubber of my shoes silent against the immoveable stone.

"Rache?"

She turned calmly, her face pink, light, reflecting the changing colors of the sun reaching toward the horizon.

"I woke up today, Bren, and something was missing," she said, her eyes pleading with herself to hold back tears for just a few more minutes. "I woke up and we weren't there." Then tears flooded her eyes, and she reached out to me in a way I never thought possible.

"I don't want us to end, Brendan."

I don't want to wake up alone even just one more day. I thought you didn't love me anymore. I thought that you were keeping another baby from me because you stopped loving me, that you had stopped wanting.... I just lost sight of us. I know that I need more than just the girls. I don't want to live my life without love. What you said at the girls' camp.... I saw that fire that I fell in love with. That man that made me feel safe, he came back to me that day. You

272

looked at me with those eyes just filled with fire and passion and confidence. I haven't seen that in so long. I missed you. And I just. I want to love you until there's no more of you to love, Bren. I want you. I want us.

"And then, when I thought that I hadn't seen you—really seen you—in so long, that I had no idea what you were building this summer, I wanted to know, to see, to be there with you even for just a moment, so I thought maybe there was a sketch of it in your bedside drawer. I opened it and looked at the things you kept in there— pictures of you and me, of the girls, old notes, and a picture of me from the summer we met—all tucked in an old envelope. I remember walking into our room once, a long time ago, and watching you flip through those pictures as if you were reminding yourself of what was important to you, as if you were taking inventory. I looked around at my piles of scrapbooks and house full of picture frames and thought about how you could keep it all in an envelope, close to you all the time. You looked at them, admired them, sitting on the edge of the bed, then stuck them back in that old envelope and slid them into the drawer. I found the envelope and looked through it, searching for something. I also found this."

She reached out, handing me a manila file folder with papers inside.

"Read it," she said.

I sat down next to her and accepted the offer. With no idea what Rachael had just handed me, I froze my desire to say something and risk ruining the poetry of this moment that she had worked so hard to set up.

I looked into her eyes for a long moment and saw feeling in them, feeling that I hadn't seen in so many tides, before looking down at what she had just handed me. I saw that the folder now in my hand was old and that the paper peeking out from the inside was a page from my father's notebook.

"How did you get this?"

"I found it in your side table drawer," Rachael replied, "where you keep all our special pictures and notes."

A wave slipped up on the rocks and I could hear it filtering through the jetty boulders below us. Another came quickly behind it and I remembered how the folder got in there—I put it there.

My father had sorted each of his plan appendices—sketches of the gang boxes, special connection details, and a list of the subcontractors I should call—in separate manila folders, which he paper-clipped to the rolled-up plans. While trying to read the plans in bed under the halo of my side table lamp, I had tucked the separate manila folders into the drawer, prepared to read them later. The plans were too large to keep in the side table drawer, so I kept them in sight on top of the table. I remembered that on nights when sleeping was impossible. I'd grab the plans and the folders in the dark (so I wouldn't wake Rachael) and took them down to my office. Of course, it was the middle of the night and I couldn't think, so I ended up watching TV instead. After a few nights of this, I kept the project materials with the plans in my office. Obviously, this last folder never made it out of the drawer.

I looked again at the folder, as if for the first time, and I noticed an old photograph of my mother, father, and I, here, on this very beach. It was a photo he had kept tucked in the visor of his truck for as long as I could recall.

It was battered, faded, and weathered, like a flag left too many years to brave the sea's salty air. It had a quality new glossy photos can't have—history. In the photo, we were all young, and it was just the three of us, as it had always been. The history of three lifetimes jumped from the paper with palpable vibrancy, and I felt him up there, out there, all around us somehow, watching.

In the photo, he stood just taller than my mother, his mighty left arm wrapped so far around her shoulder that he could not pull her closer while she rested gently, like a column of light, in the crook of his arm. I stood in front and he clasped my rising hand. His smile was proud, intense, and conscious that loving his family was his purpose. My mother's smile was calm and her eyes joyful. I had what is now gone in this image, that I could only reclaim in memory, and what I saw in my little girls today. I was innocent, and behind us was my parent's beloved ocean.

I don't know if my father ever believed in God or an afterlife— or cared much if there was one—but I do know he believed that living well and deeply today counts for everything, and this photo was the proof. I know he was spiritual and believed that there was something other than what we can see. He believed in Faith, Courage, Greatness, and Beauty. They are the real and tangible components in the enlightening zeniths, in the coldest, darkest canyons, and in the average days in the valley of our lives.

In his mind, greatness eluded him because he believed that he could have done better. Yet, he also believed that being the best husband and father he could be was immensely valuable, and he knew that he did this well. Sitting there on a man-made mountain of granite, I more than knew he believed in me, I felt it without a conscious thought. I felt his faith in me in a new way. His words and thoughts were alive, and would stay with our family.

The world has truckloads of rich, real experience to offer, but there is the matter of bartering with Life to get it, for it has a cost. The price paid for a rich life is risk of failure—and risk is what Rachael had taken in coming here today.

My father used to say that nobody is entitled to anything. As a self-employed man, if he didn't work he didn't get paid—work and survival were the same thing to him. The quality of his life and of his family's life was based on how good a survivor he was. It was a simple code. What was true for his business and his life was true for me today, but on a different level. There was so much to live for, to survive for; goodness was there for the taking. But it doesn't happen without effort, without risks like the ones my father took every day, like Rachael took there before my eyes. Sometimes the hardest things are the best: achievement requires risk; happiness demands chance; and love pleads for trust.

Although my father never spoke of them to me (maybe because

275

it was me who interrupted them), I know he had dreams and saw himself as something other than a carpenter who rarely traveled past the county line. And I know those dreams—that passion and zeal for a good life and the will to see them through—are alive in me. I realized that this picture, more than any other I have seen, is a monument to my father's soul. In it, his proud will is visible, my mother's calm joy is tenable, and in it there is no harm that can pierce that armor. Not even death.

It would serve as an inspiration and would remind me forever that he was there watching, that the quest for greatness must be undertaken, and that my role in the world was to love my family and live deeply.

I looked up from the image of my history and I tried to look through the tears forming in my eyes into the future. As I began to think it was time to appreciate more, love more, and live more, I felt Rachael's fingertip touch the back of my hand and her head fell gently on my shoulder, spanning the widest chasm with the simplest kindness, and I felt myself drown in the tide of her touch.

"I cried this morning," she said. "I cried as much as I think I've ever cried. I looked around the house at the photos and frames, the colors and patterns, the things we worked so hard to put in there and I realized that without an "us" there to share it, they were just tokens. I miss us Brendan, and realize that our life is a voyage, our voyage together."

I looked at Rachael and saw her as I had never seen her before and as I'd always hoped I'd see her. She was stunning; her eyes shone out to me, lit a beacon that made me believe there was a safe harbor. I felt my fingers holding the folder between them while the corners of Rachael's mouth turned up.

I looked inside the folder and found something I had wondered about. I had read and reread my father's diary, and each time I got through it, there was something missing: the end. Clipped to the back of the photo, was a note to me—words that will stay with me forever.

TO MY SON,

IT IS LATE, THE DAY IS REFRESHINGLY COLD. I WANT TO PASS A FEW THINGS ON TO YOU. IT HAS JUST BEGUN TO SNOW AND THE AIR FEELS SO CRISP ON MY FACE. I'M HAPPY TO BE ALIVE TO SENSE THIS SIMPLE BEAUTY.

IN CASE YOU WERE WONDERING, LIFE REMAINS A MYSTERY UNTIL THE DAY WE PACK UP OUR TOOLS AND THERE'S NO OTHER JOB TO GO TO. AS WE PASS OUR DAYS ON EARTH, OUR LIFE HAPPENS TO US AS MUCH AS WE MAKE IT HAPPEN. WE DO HAVE CONTROL, BUT ONLY SO MUCH. IN THIS EBB AND FLOW I HAVE NOT BECOME THE MAN I THOUGHT I'D BE WHEN I WAS YOUNG. HOWEVER, I HAVE BECOME THE MAN I DREAMED I'D BE: A HUSBAND AND FATHER WITH A LOVING FAMILY, A WARM HEARTH, AND A LOVING HOME. YOUR DREAMS COME TRUE IN THE END, BRENDAN, IF YOU NURTURE AND WORK THEM, SO IT PAYS TO REMEMBER WHAT THEY ARE AND RUN TOWARDS THEM WITH

ALL YOUR BREATH AND BRAVERY.

I HOPE, MORE THAN ANYTHING, THAT YOU
HAVE DREAMS YOU WANT TO REALIZE.
WITHOUT DREAMS, I BELIEVE LIFE IS JUST
DUTY, JUST WORK, AND THEN IT'S OVER.
WHEN THE DAY IS DONE, ALL WE ARE IS
WHAT WE CAN FEEL IN THE STILLNESS
OF THE DARK. OUR DREAMS ARE WHO WE
ARE. THEY DRIVE US, MOVE US, MAKE US
LAUGH AND MAKE US CRY—IN AGONY AND
JOY—AND WE MUST NURTURE THEM OR
THEY WILL DIE.

I LOVE YOUR MOTHER FROM A PLACE TOO
DEEP IN MY SOUL FOR WORDS, BUT I'VE
SEEN YOU WITH YOUR WIFE, BOY, AND I
KNOW YOU'VE VISITED THAT PLACE, TOO.

YOUR MOTHER HAS MADE THE WORLD
INSPIRING TO LIVE IN AND HER LOVE IS MY
GREATEST TREASURE AND ENERGY. I
HAVE FAITH THAT YOU ARE THE SAME
WAY WITH YOUR WIFE, MY SON. THERE
ARE ALWAYS QUESTIONS AND CONFLICTS
IN A RELATIONSHIP, BUT LOVE IS THE

MOST PROFOUND FEELING WE HAVE.
NURTURE IT, CARE FOR IT; EXPRESS IT,
EXAMINE IT, GROW IT.

BE STRONG ENOUGH TO BELIEVE IN YOUR
WIFE—TO BE AS HONEST ABOUT EVERY
FEELING EACH OF YOU HAS—AND BE
BRAVE ENOUGH TO HAVE FAITH IN HER,
AND I PROMISE YOU WILL FIND TRUE
HAPPINESS AND JOY.

I HAVE TOWED A HARD LINE FOR LOTS OF
YEARS IN MY LIFE AND MADE MISTAKES
TOO GRAVE AND MANY TO MENTION;
HAPPINESS HAS ALWAYS BEEN A FIGHT
FOR ME. I NEVER THOUGHT WHEN I WAS A
BOY THAT I'D ONE DAY BE AN OLD MAN
SITTING HERE, ALONE, WRITING, USING A
SCRAP OF WOOD AS MY DESK.
NEVERTHELESS, HERE I SIT, A LIFE
BEHIND ME, MY HEART FULL OF
HAPPINESS. THERE IS SORROW, TOO.

WE SPEND MOST OF OUR DAYS PEERING
AT OUR LIVES AS IF WE WOULD LOOK
THROUGH A TELESCOPE. IN YOUTH WE,

LOOK FORWARD, AND THE IMAGES SEEM
BIG, BUT DISTANT, AND WITHOUT MUCH
DETAIL. WHEN WE GROW OLD, SOMEHOW
WHEN WE'RE NOT READY, THE
TELESCOPE GETS TURNED AROUND AND
WE PEER BACK AT OUR LIVES IN THE
OTHER DIRECTION, AND THEN WALK
BACKWARDS TO OUR NEXT DESTINATION.
THE IMAGE IN THE LENS IS SMALL AND
THERE IS ONLY ROOM THERE FOR THE
BRIGHTEST THINGS.

THESE THINGS ARE YOUR MOMENTS.
MOMENTS ARE WHAT YOU HAVE LIVED FOR
WHEN YOU'VE LIVED FOR SOMETHING—AND
YOU MUST LIVE FOR SOMETHING! OR YOU'LL
WANDER, WONDERING IF THE NEXT
CORNER HAS YOUR HAPPINESS, SUCCESS,
OR DESTINY BEHIND IT. WORSE YET, YOU'LL
NEVER WANDER OR WONDER AT ALL.

I'LL ALWAYS REMEMBER YOU IN YOUR CAP
AND GOWN, AND I'LL ALWAYS REMEMBER
THE HUG YOU GAVE ME WHEN LAURA WAS
BORN—AND THAT SAME HUG YOU GAVE
WHEN KELLY CAME TO US.

I'LL ALWAYS REMEMBER YOUR MOTHER'S DEEP AND GLEAMING EYES WHEN SHE SAID, "I LOVE YOU" FOR THE FIRST TIME TO ME. HER MIRACULOUS TOUCH IS LIKE AN EASING BREEZE ON A PERFECT SUMMER DAY. HER GENTLE HEART, IMMENSE STRENGTH, AND UNQUENCHABLE PASSION MADE MY LIFE A HAPPY AND SUCCESSFUL ONE.

I'LL ALWAYS REMEMBER SHOOTING BASKETS WITH YOU AND WATCHING YOUR GAMES, AND AS MUCH AS ANYTHING, WATCHING YOU PASS FROM BOYHOOD TO MANHOOD THAT LONG-AGO SUMMER IN ARTHUR PELLETIER'S HOUSE. I'M SO PROUD OF THE MAN YOU'VE BECOME.

ALL THAT JOY IS IN THE SMALL END OF MY TELESCOPE, BOY: A SHORT LIST OF ACHIEVEMENTS AND PEOPLE THAT ARE MY WORLD. THEY ARE WHAT I BOTH LEAVE BEHIND AND TAKE WITH ME. THEY ARE MY MOMENTS.

YOUR MOTHER GAVE ME THE MOMENTS

THAT MADE MY LIFE A TREASURE AND I
GAVE HER MOMENTS TO CHERISH, TOO. I
LOVE TO SEE IT WHEN YOU DO SOMETHING
THAT REMINDS ME OF HER. SHE IS ALIVE
IN YOU, BOY, AND YOU ARE LUCKIER FOR
HER THAN YOU ARE FOR ME.

WORK IS SLOW NOW, AND AS I GET READY
TO PUT MY PENCIL DOWN AND PACK UP THE
TOOLS, I WANT TO MAKE IT CLEAR TO YOU
THAT IF YOU EVER WALK IN THE DARK AS
YOUR MOTHER AND I HAVE, AND YOU FEEL
DESPERATELY ALONE, THERE IS A
MEANING TO WHAT WE DO—AND TO HELL
WITH THOSE WHO CAN'T OR WON'T SEE IT!
THERE IS MEANING AND IT COMES FROM
YOUR HEART, WILL, AND COURAGE. IF YOU
HAVE THOSE THINGS, YOU CAN HAVE THE
LIFE YOU'VE DREAMED OF—AS LONG AS
YOU DREAM OF IT. HAVING THE DREAM AND
BELIEVING YOU WANT IT IS THE HARD PART.

THE GREATEST SECRETS IN LIFE, THE
ANSWERS TO ALL THE "WHY'S?" WE'VE
EVER ASKED, ARE RIGHT UNDER OUR
NOSES WHEN WE HAVE PEOPLE AROUND

US WHO LOVE US, THE ANSWERS ARE IN
THEIR EYES AND HEARTS AND IN OUR
LOVE FOR THEM. THOSE ARE THE PEOPLE
AND RELATIONSHIPS WHO MATTER, AND
THAT IS OUR REASON FOR BEING.

IS THERE A GOD AND SO FORTH? I DON'T
KNOW, I'M NO CLOSER TO KNOWING TODAY
THAN THE DAY I WAS BORN. IF THERE IS
ONE, THOUGH, I'VE LIVED THE LIFE THAT
GOD GAVE ME AND IT'LL BE WAITING FOR
ME ON THE OTHER SIDE. I'LL LOOK HIM OR
HER IN THE EYE THEN. IS THERE A
WOMAN WHO SHARED A LIFETIME WITH
ME, LOVING ME, LOVING YOU, AND
BRINGING DEEP JOY TO OUR FAMILY?
YES. SHE'S RIGHT HERE, HOLDING THE
SECRETS OF EXISTENCE DEEP IN HER
GENTLE, FAITHFUL HEART.

AS I CLOSE UP THE LAST BOX HERE, AND
WRITE MYSELF ONE FINAL NOTE SO I
DON'T FORGET, THE MEANING TO MY LIFE
HAS BEEN IN ACHIEVING MY MOMENTS
AND BEING LOVED EVERY DAY BY YOU
AND YOUR MOTHER. I HAVE QUESTIONS

THAT NAG ME, AND I CAN WONDER EVERY
DAY IF I'VE DONE THE RIGHT THINGS IN
LIFE, OR I CAN HAVE FAITH THAT I'VE
LIVED THE LIFE THAT I WAS HANDED AND
CONTROLLED THE TIDES THE BEST I
COULD, AND THAT I HAVE GIVEN THE
WORLD SOMEONE IT CAN BE PROUD OF.
AS I PEER BACK THROUGH THE
TELESCOPE, I SEE YOU, MY SON, AND I
REALIZE WITH EVERY CELL IN MY BODY
THAT THERE IS A REASON FOR BEING
ALIVE, AND THERE ARE SOME THINGS I
WANT YOU TO DO FOR YOUR OLD POP....

I WANT YOU TO LIVE TO BE A HAPPY MAN. I
WANT YOU TO HOLD YOUR WIFE CLOSE TO
YOU AND BELIEVE SHE HAS THE ANSWERS
FOR WHICH YOU SEARCH, AND BE READY TO
GENTLY GIVE HER ANSWERS WHEN SHE
NEEDS YOU. I ALSO WANT YOU TO SEE THE
OCEAN EVERY YEAR, BECAUSE IT IS THE
BIGGEST, MOST BEAUTIFUL, MOST VIBRANT
THING IN THIS WORLD. I WANT YOU TO KNOW
ONE LAST THING:

YOU ARE MY MOMENT, BOY.

EPILOGUE

HOME

DATE: CHRISTMAS
PROJECT: THE (NOT SO
LITTLE) RED WAGON

HOW-TO:

I CHOSE FRAMING LUMBER AND
#2 SPRUCE FOR MY LITTLE
GIRLS` WAGON, AND BIG
RUBBER TIRES FOR TOWING
ACROSS BEACH SAND. IT`S
WORKMANLIKE, I THINK. I
RUBBED THE BARE WOOD WITH
LUSTROUS BOILED LINSEED OIL
TO HIGHLIGHT THE LUMBER`S
NATURAL GRAIN.

THERE`S SOMETHING HONEST
ABOUT TURNING ROUGH STOCK
INTO SOMETHING BEAUTIFUL,
SOMETHING THAT WILL LAST,
SOMETHING TRULY PART OF ME.
AND MY FUTURE.

COMMENTS:

ONE YEAR AGO, RACHAEL AND I
HAD LOST OUR WAY. ONE YEAR
AGO, I STOOD IN THIS VERY
GARAGE LOOKING FOR A TOOL
POUCH MY FATHER HAD GIVEN ME
TO BUILD ARTHUR PELLETIER'S
HOUSE WITH HIM, A TOOL POUCH
HE SPENT HIS LIFE TRYING TO
FILL WITH A CARPENTER'S

KNOWLEDGE AND WISDOM. I
LOOKED FOR IT AS AN ADULT TO
GO BACK HOME AND FULFILL A
PROMISE HE MADE TO MY
MOTHER, TO BUILD HER STUDIO,
BUT FULFILLING THAT PROMISE
WAS AS MUCH AN EXCUSE TO GET
AWAY FROM MY MARRIAGE AS IT
WAS TO BUILD SOMETHING NEW.
ONE YEAR AGO, I WAS BLIND.

MY FATHER IS GONE, BUT THEY
ARE STILL HERE—THE WOMEN IN
MY LIFE. MY TIRELESS MOTHER,
MY BEAUTIFUL DAUGHTERS, AND
MY WIFE, RACHAEL, WHO RISKED
SOMETHING TO BRING US BACK
TOGETHER. THEY REMAIN. AS
MUCH AS I LOVED MY FATHER, IT
WAS MY MOTHER WHO HELD
THINGS TOGETHER AND TOOK
CARE OF BOTH OF US WHEN THE

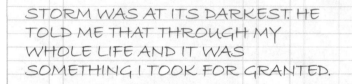

STORM WAS AT ITS DARKEST. HE
TOLD ME THAT THROUGH MY
WHOLE LIFE AND IT WAS
SOMETHING I TOOK FOR GRANTED.

TODAY, I WEAR THAT SAME OLD
POUCH, BUT IT IS PART OF THIS
HOUSE NOW, PART OF OUR
HOUSE. I`VE MOVED MY
FATHER`S TOOLS BACK HERE,
AND INSTEAD OF FILLING THE
GARAGE BAY WITH OUR CARS, IT
IS NOW A WOOD SHOP. I`M
PLEASED WITH THE WAGON I`M
BUILDING FOR THE FAMILY SO WE
CAN TOW OUR THINGS ACROSS
THE LUMPY BEACH SAND TO THE
WATER`S EDGE.

I put down the pencil and picked up a sheet of sandpaper to smooth out a wagon plank. I was pleased with the wagon, but I was even more pleased when Laura came out of the house, bringing me a steaming thermos of hot cocoa.

"Here's some cocoa, Pop," she said, pretending to be too cool to be interested, trying hard not to let me see she was checking out my progress.

"Almost finished," I said as I made the last few 120-grit passes of the evening. Warm, gray air passed over my lips to meet the frigid winter temperature.

Inside, I found Rachael sitting with Kelly, helping her fill out Christmas cards. The light above the table garlanded her hair. She was beautiful. She looked up into my eyes. We each paused for a moment, connected without saying a word—like a kiss in a snowstorm—and in that moment, nothing was more important. After a year of questions and pain and progress, I at last felt whole.

We're home.

ABOUT THE AUTHOR

Mark Clement is a carpenter, writer, and father. As the Executive Editor of *Tools of the Trade* magazine, he is a recognized leader in tool and how-to information for building pros. In his spare time, he enjoys competing in adventure races and triathlons. Mark lives in Ambler, Penn.